Death of an Editor

A Cabin by the Lake Mystery

DEATH OF AN EDITOR

A Cabin by the Lake Mystery

by Linda Norlander

LEVEL
BEST BOOKS

First published by Level Best Books 19 May 2020

Copyright © 19 May 2020 by Linda Norlander

This novel is entirely a work of fiction. The names, characters and incidents portrayed in it are the work of the author's imagination. Any resemblance to actual persons, living or dead, events or localities is entirely coincidental.

First edition

ISBN: 978-1-947915-54-1

This book was professionally typeset on Reedsy.
Find out more at reedsy.com

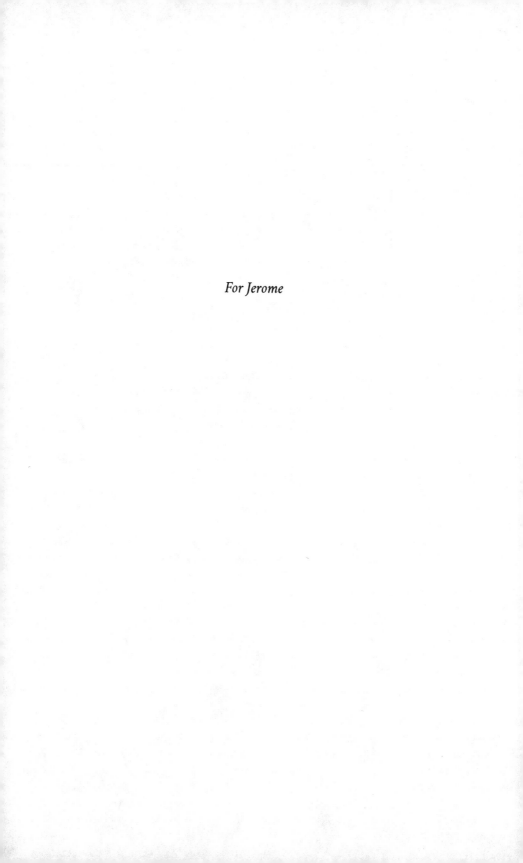

For Jerome

Contents

Chapter One: Death of an Editor

About the time poor Ed, the janitor, found Nancy Bywater's strangled body in the office of our small Northwoods newspaper, the *Killdeer Times*, I was immersed in editing a manuscript for Florice Annabelle LeMay. The manuscript was an endless romance called *Knight of Lust* set during the time of King Arthur. I swore if I read another paragraph with the words "manhood," "codpiece," or "surging steed," I would throw it in the fireplace.

However, my blue pencil scribblings on *Knight of Lust* were a poor alibi for what I was doing at the time of Nancy Bywater's murder. In fact, I knew nothing about her death until LeRoy Pruitt, Jackpine County sheriff's deputy, knocked on my door the next morning.

I lived in an isolated log cabin down a rutted gravel road from the Lake Larissa Lodge. Other than an occasional lost tourist and a few friends, I had no traffic on the road, so I was surprised when I heard the patrol car's wheels crunching in my driveway.

My great watch dog Bronte, asleep on her cushion in the living room, didn't bark at Deputy LeRoy until the car door slammed. Her first noise was tentative—more an "urf" then a "woof." Then, as I stood up to look, she tore past me and threw herself against the screen door, barking and growling in a near frenzy.

"Bronte!" I grabbed her collar and pulled her back. She bared her teeth as the deputy peered in through the screen.

"You'd better put her away or I'll shoot her." Though his voice was low and threatening, I heard the fear in it.

I tugged Bronte into the bedroom and closed the door. "Sorry, old girl." I'd never seen her so worked up.

I opened the door to him in a pair of pajama bottoms and a black long-sleeved T-shirt. These were my work clothes since I had fled New York City for rural Killdeer in northern Minnesota. The deputy looked me up and down as if he was appraising a horse. Already, I didn't like this man.

"Can I help you?" I stepped back, aware I wore nothing under the T-shirt.

"Are you Jamie Forest?"

"Yes."

He held out a business card. "Is that you?"

The card read *Jamie Forest, MFA, Editing, Manuscript Critiques, and Publishing Expertise.*

I looked at it, remembering my friend Willow had stopped me from adding the tagline "I know where the commas go."

"Not professional," she'd said.

Once he stepped inside the cabin, I read the name tag pinned to his shirt pocket. LeRoy Pruitt, Deputy. Even though it was early in the morning and the air was still cool, sweat stained the armpits of his white shirt.

"What do you want?" Normally, I tend to be polite and welcoming. However, I didn't like LeRoy, and I especially didn't like the police—not after what had happened in New York. I didn't offer him a chair, but he walked over to the kitchen table, which was covered with manuscript pages, and made himself at home.

He sat, leaning back with his arms folded over the beginning of a belly paunch. He had a thin face with a crooked nose and a haircut that looked like someone had styled it using a mixing bowl. A long-healed scar ran from the bottom of his lip to his chin. A bead of perspiration dribbled down the side of his face. If he hadn't been in uniform, I'd have pegged him as a local barfly.

My instincts told me to be careful with this man. I turned away from him and poured myself a mug of lukewarm coffee. I hoped he didn't see how my hands shook as I lifted the pot from the stove. I didn't offer him any.

Again, I said, "What do you want?" I stayed near the stove, leaning up against the counter with the table between us.

LeRoy gave me a creepy feeling. I understood why Bronte didn't like him. "Do you know Nancy Bywater?"

"Nancy Bywater?" I blinked in surprise. Why would he ask me about her?

As editor of the *Killdeer Times*, Nancy and I had gone head-to-head when she refused to publish my counterpoint to her editorial about the Racine Mining Company. They wanted to open up state and federal lands to mining. She thought it would be good for Killdeer's economic development. I thought it would be a disaster for the forest and wetlands. Our Lady Slipper Trail Group was working with the Friends of the Boundary Waters to make sure the mining company didn't spoil the pristine wilderness surrounding Lake Larissa.

"I really don't know her."

He leaned forward. "What do you mean by 'don't know her'? I heard you two had a fight the other day."

The sarcasm in his voice had such a theatrical nuance to it I almost laughed. Almost. But as I watched him, it occurred to me that LeRoy wasn't a man with a sense of humor.

I shrugged, still wondering why he was asking me about her. "It was a professional disagreement." I paused. "I'm not saying anything more until you tell me what's going on." I'd learned in New York that the less you said to law enforcement, the better.

My tone must have taken him aback. He sat up straighter, and his lips curled into a smirk. "Nancy Bywater is dead. She was found strangled this morning."

My jaw dropped. "Strangled, as in murdered?" It took me a moment to wrap my head around what he'd just said. I might not have liked how she ran the newspaper, but I certainly didn't want her dead. "What happened?"

LeRoy didn't take his gaze off me as I set my coffee mug down on the counter. His voice had an accusing tone. "Where were you last night?"

All of a sudden, the light went on in my head. The business card, the officiousness of the deputy. Somehow, I was implicated in her death. A chill ran through me, and I hugged myself.

"I was here." I pointed to the printed pages scattered over the table. "I'm under deadline to get this done."

LeRoy squinted at one of the marked-up pages. He silently formed the words as he read one of the most clichéd sex scenes in the manuscript. A look of suspicion crossed his face. "You write this stuff?"

I shook my head. "No. I'm a freelance editor."

"You should be ashamed." He continued to read.

"It's a living," I murmured and was instantly sorry I'd said it. Florice LeMay might have been a hack writer, but she'd put her heart and soul into this book, and she was paying me good money to make it marketable. Who knew how many hours she'd spent researching cod pieces.

I couldn't believe I was having this conversation on a beautiful Monday morning in the piney woods. "Listen, I'm not sure what you need from me, but I've been holed up here since Saturday morning, working. My dog and this worn-out blue pencil can attest to it."

Again, it was clear LeRoy didn't have a sense of humor. "So, no one saw you here last night?"

Damn. When would I learn to keep my mouth shut with these people?

He held up my business card and waved it. "We found this next to her. Can you explain why it was there?"

I stared at him, amazed. Did he think I killed Nancy and then left my calling card? The little voice in the back of my head chanted, *don't say anything. Don't say anything.* But the advice didn't make it to my mouth. "Do you think I'm an idiot? Would I harm someone and then leave my card? What kind of an investigation is this?"

LeRoy stood up, pushing the chair back with such force it nearly tipped over. "Are you calling me stupid?"

Oh boy.

In seconds, he'd moved around the table and had me backed up into the counter, his face so close to mine I smelled his stale coffee breath. In the bedroom, Bronte howled with fury. LeRoy pressed his body against mine, pushing me farther into the counter. The edge of the counter dug into my back, his hardness against my belly.

4

CHAPTER ONE: DEATH OF AN EDITOR

"Stop!" I pushed at him. "What are you doing?"

He continued to press, and anger and lust shone in his eyes. His breath came in pants like a dog in heat.

Bronte threw herself against the bedroom door as I struggled to get away from him. Was this really happening?

In a hoarse voice, he demanded, "Where were you last night?"

"Back off and I'll tell you!" I shrieked the words loud enough to rattle his eardrums.

A fury boiled over in me. I grabbed my mug and threw the coffee in his face. Startled, he let up, and I slipped to the side, making a run for the door. He roared after me. At that moment, the realization shot through me. I was alone, down an isolated road and the person hired by the citizens of Jackpine County to "protect and to serve" wanted to hurt me.

He was about to catch me, and God knows what would have happened, except that another car rolled into the driveway. I prayed it wouldn't be reinforcements for Deputy Leroy.

Chapter Two: Friends

I made it as far as the doorway when a female voice called from outside. "Jamie? Are you in there? Your dog's making a racket."

LeRoy snatched a kitchen towel off the counter and wiped his face. His skin was beet red and sweat poured down his forehead. His chest heaved as he worked to catch his breath. Grabbing my arm, he squeezed tight. "You'd better not say anything. We know where you live." He emphasized *we*.

Of course, he knew where I lived. Everyone in the Killdeer community knew where I lived. It was hard to be anonymous around here.

"Hey, Willow. Come on in." I shook off his hand and willed my pounding heart to slow down.

She burst through the doorway and stopped dead when she saw LeRoy. Several emotions crossed her face, starting with confusion and ending with hostility. She lowered her voice. "Hello, LeRoy. Stopping by for a chat? Looks like you spilled some coffee."

I could tell by her tone and by LeRoy's glower that something had passed between them. I hoped he wouldn't threaten to shoot her like he'd threatened my dog. Meanwhile, Bronte continued to howl from the bedroom.

The standoff between LeRoy and Willow lasted only long enough for my other friend Rob to come lumbering in. Rob had gray-white hair pulled back in a tight single braid and the chiseled face of his Ojibwe ancestors. On top of that, he was built like an aging Paul Bunyan, burly and muscular from years of physical labor. His frame filled the doorway.

"So," I said. "Should I make introductions?"

The deputy tapped his belt as if making sure we knew his gun was in place.

I think he expected us all to jump. No one moved.

"I'm just following up on some leads," he growled.

Really? I thought he was just working himself up to assault me.

"You mean on Nancy Bywater?" Willow's voice was flat. "Why would you come here?"

Perhaps it was the sense of relief that friends had arrived. Perhaps it was my disdain for law enforcement. Perhaps it was my need to ignore the voice in my head that said, *keep your mouth shut, Jamie.* I glared at LeRoy. "He wanted to know if I killed her."

LeRoy opened his mouth then closed it. The expression on his face said I'd gone too far once again.

"I'll be talking to you down at the station, Miss Forest." He stomped out, nearly knocking Rob over to get through the doorway.

After he left, the first thing I did was let Bronte out. The second was to collapse on my couch, hugging my grandmother's musty crocheted afghan. Willow brought me a mug of coffee and set it on the end table. I didn't say anything until I heard the sound of the sheriff's car receding down the road.

"What a despicable man. Thank God you came when you did. He had me backed into the counter." I shivered.

"You could report him." Willow pointed to her phone. "I'll make the call."

I shook my head. "My word against his. What are the odds anything would happen?"

Willow shrugged. "Around here? Not good. God knows why Rick Fowler hired him as a deputy. The man's a sleezeball."

"A sleezeball with a gun," Rob added.

We all sighed in unison, staring out the front window.

I took a gulp of my coffee, wishing it had something stronger in it. "What brings you two down the lane just in the nick of time?" I looked at Willow. "Shouldn't you be at work?"

Willow was the only veterinarian within sixty miles. She stood tall and strong, unlike her name. Her Ojibwe ancestry showed in the caramel color of her skin, the thick dark hair she kept tied in a ponytail and the roundness of her face. She had a striking kind of beauty, especially with her hazel eyes that sometimes appeared green and sometimes appeared brown.

Willow stirred her coffee. "We were having coffee this morning at the Loonfeather when we heard about Nancy. The place was abuzz."

"Your name came up," Rob added.

I shook my head. "I don't get it. I only met her a couple of times. Why would people talk about me?" In truth, I knew the answer. I was the foreigner in town, and I'd already made some waves working with the Lady Slipper Trail Group. People knew about my argument with Nancy.

"We wanted to let you know about it in case the sheriff showed up."

"Too late," I said.

"I called, but all I got was voicemail. It was a nice morning, no calls on sick animals, so we decided we should take a little drive to your cottage in the woods."

Rob added, "Willow is a maniac on these roads. Did you know that?"

I did know that. In fact, I'd once threatened to jump out of her car and call an Uber. She'd laughed and said, "Good luck with that." Uber wasn't much of a Northwoods enterprise.

Rob worked part-time as Willow's assistant. He called it a little extra money to supplement his social security, but everyone knew it was because of his love for the animals. Rob cared for the dogs and cats and the small animals at the clinic.

"So, what did LeRoy, the most despicable law enforcement officer in the state have to say?"

"They found my business card by...by the body, I guess. Wondered where I was last night." I shivered again.

"Oh." Willow's expression turned thoughtful. "I suppose that puts you on the short list of suspects."

"I'll admit I wasn't fond of Nancy. I thought she was too close to the mining company and their interests. But not liking her is a lot different than wanting her dead."

"Agreed." Rob nodded. "She didn't have any friends with the Lady Slippers, that's for sure."

The Lady Slippers was a group dedicated to preserving the Lady Slipper

Trail, a hiking and skiing trail between the town of Killdeer and Lake Larissa. The trail ended on my property, and I was the chief publicist for the group.

Bronte wagged her tail and tried to crawl into my lap. She was a 90-pound rescue dog who liked to think of herself as a lap poodle.

I shooed her away. "Go to your rug."

Still wagging her tail, she settled at my feet instead.

"Obedience school flunk-out, I'm afraid." I kept it light, even though my insides were still shaking.

Willow's phone lit up with the ringtone of a loon. She walked out to the porch as she answered it. I looked at Rob, wondering if I should tell him how much LeRoy scared me. Did I make too much of it? Had I brought it on with my smart-mouth comments?

"I can't imagine that someone would actually kill Nancy. My God." I grimaced, trying not to picture what she must have looked like when she was found.

Rob grunted. He was a great listener and a man of few words.

Willow walked back in. "Sorry, Jamie. We have to go. Horse emergency up at the Copper Lake Casino."

"New mode of transportation?"

She sighed. "They offer carriage rides in the summer to attract more tourists who come with kids. One of the horses is sick." She motioned to Rob. "I'll drop you back at the clinic."

At the door, she stopped. "Say, why aren't you answering your phone?"

I pointed at the mess of papers on my kitchen table. "I'm under deadline and didn't want to be disturbed. I've been getting solicitation calls from a realty company. They're eager to buy my humble shack in the woods. I turned the ringer off."

"Well, turn it back on."

"Yes, ma'am."

I stood on the back steps with Bronte at my side and waved as they drove away. The air was alive with the smell of pine and tamarack and the buzz of insects. I loved the rhythm of nature here in northern Minnesota. I loved the whisper of the wind through the tall pines and aspens and the rustle of the squirrels as they ran up the trees. But I still missed the sounds of the big city, the beeping of trucks as they backed up, the bonk of the tennis balls against the concrete courts across from my Queens apartment.

"Oh well." I patted Bronte on the head. "You wouldn't have liked being a city dog."

She licked my hand and then bounded off the porch in pursuit of a chipmunk.

I sorted through the manuscript and stacked it in chapter order. My phone was under the final chapter where Constance, the heroine with her flaming red hair, rode bareback behind Sir Eddard, her knight. Together they galloped down the beach to a new life.

Outside, Bronte happily made woofing sounds as the chipmunks teased her.

I switched the phone's ringer back on and listened to the messages. The first was a crank call, a whisper that simply said, "Get out of this county. We know where you live."

Where had I just heard that? I sighed and deleted it. Ever since I'd joined the Lady Slipper Trail project, I'd gotten at least one of those calls a day.

I tapped the next message and caught my breath, "Oh my God."

Last night, while I was in a sea of blue pencil markings, Nancy Bywater had called. She left a voice mail at 10:36 p.m.

"Jamie?" The sound was staticky and hard to decipher. "Something..." More static. "Need to tell you..." A pause. "Important...may be in danger." The message ended.

Despite the midsummer warmth of the cabin and the chirping of the birds outside, a chill ran up my spine. Not only the message, but something in her voice. Something that sounded like fear and desperation.

Chapter Three: New York

I stood stock still, staring at the phone. I had to report this message. If I didn't, LeRoy would want to know why she called. I had to move from this spot by the kitchen table.

This spot of comfort and safety, the old wooden planks beneath my feet newly sanded and varnished. But I couldn't get my muscles to work. People talk about being paralyzed by fear and trauma. For a few moments, I felt that paralysis. Like everything was transporting me back to that night in my Queens apartment—the night six armed men wearing SWAT gear broke through the door.

***

It was four in the morning in mid-July. My third-floor apartment held the heat and humidity of the day, despite the window fan. I was in a restless sleep, awake and then dozing. In the morning I would be meeting for the last time with the lawyers to sign off on the divorce. I hoped Andrew wouldn't bring the new love of his life with him to the meeting, but he was arrogant enough that he might.

While I cogitated about this, the SWAT team gathered outside the building, waiting for the super to let them in. While I pictured the tall, exotic Venezuelan model turned makeup artist who had captured Andrew's immature heart, the six men crept silently up the staircase. As I dozed off, they slammed through the door, shattering the doorframe and screaming at me to put my hands up.

Funny thoughts can fly through your head during moments like that. It was so unreal that, for an instant, I thought I was still asleep as I opened my eyes to automatic weapons pointing at me. For another instant, I thought this was a joke set up by Andrew, as his last bitter farewell.

This was no joke.

"What?" I choked out. "Who are you? I have no money."

"Shut up." One of them grabbed me by the arm and yanked me off the bed. Before I knew it, they had me cuffed in a plastic zip tie and were hauling me out of my apartment.

I screamed, but a gloved hand covered my mouth and the only thing that came out was a muffled cry. Behind me, I heard the sounds of things being thrown around, books ripped off the shelves, and dishes breaking.

Until they deposited me in the back of a squad car, I was still convinced this was a very bad practical joke. Later, much later, it would turn out to be a huge mistake on the part of a drug enforcement task force. Until then, though, I was locked up in a holding cell with fourteen other women. They called me Snow White because I had the lightest skin in the room as I shivered in my T-shirt night gown and tried to make myself as small as possible.

***

Bronte's barking pulled me out of my momentary stupor. She wanted to come in. I opened the screen door and she looked at me with a smile, a small creature held in her mouth. Yes, I believed that 90-pound part-lab could smile.

She dropped the little chipmunk at my feet, expecting a pat on the head.

"Oh, Bronte. Bad dog."

Puzzled, she backed away, pawing at the chipmunk. I knelt down to see it was only stunned. Quickly, I grabbed a kitchen towel and wrapped it around the chipmunk who was starting to come to. "Come on, Chip or Dale or whoever you are. It's back to your tree."

Outside, beneath a tall aspen, I let it go. Watching it scramble up the tree, I felt like a cloud had just lifted. The chipmunk had survived to see his freedom again, and I had survived both LeRoy and the New York drug task force. It was time to visit the sheriff and pray he was in and his deputy was not.

Once I was showered and Bronte was fed, I gathered *Knight of Lust* and packaged it up. Writers like Florice LeMay liked edits on paper, not online. Although I'd never met her in person, I pictured her to be a retired school teacher who had a distain for the internet. She always mailed her manuscripts to me, and I always returned them filled with blue pencil edits. As far as I knew, nothing she'd written had ever gotten published. This was her third manuscript. Who knew? Her big break might come with *Lust*. Besides, she was one of my best customers.

The drive to Killdeer took me a half mile down my private rutted tract to the Lake Larissa Lodge. My Subaru with 100,000 miles creaked as I jounced down the road. Someday, I hoped to get the driveway graded and graveled. But, one step at a time. At least I had running water in the cabin now, thanks to a new well, septic system, and drain field.

Once I reached the lodge, I had paved roads all the way into town. As I drove by, I saw the parking lot was full. This was high season for them, the summer months when families came to spend time enjoying the clear waters of the lake, the manicured mini-golf course, and the lodge's fine food.

A family sat at a picnic table behind the lodge, their children playing in a wood-chip-covered playground. When I was little and my parents brought me here to the cabin, I used to walk down our road and blend in with the kids who stayed at the lodge. That was how I met Willow. Her father was the lodge's maintenance man.

I'd like to say those were the days of childhood bliss, but they weren't. My mother, by then, was acting stranger and stranger. She'd fly into rages for no apparent reason and then five minutes later act like nothing had happened. Dad would shrug and say, "Oh, she's having one of her moods."

But it wasn't a "mood." It was a rare brain disorder slowly robbing her of her reason. By the time I was twelve, she was being cared for in a nursing home in upstate New York, two hours from our apartment in Manhattan.

Until last spring, my only visit to the family cabin after age ten was when I was sixteen and we came up in the early fall to scatter her ashes. By the time I returned at age thirty-four, the cabin had gone significantly downhill and my life was in disarray.

The midday sun streamed through the pines as I drove to town. I passed a couple leisurely bicycling down the road. I honked and waved at them with a smile. I loved this time of the year with the fresh air and the strobe lighting as I passed in and out of the shade of the giant evergreen trees. This was so different from the mid-summer heat of the city and the smells of exhaust and garbage.

Did I miss New York? Absolutely. Would I move back there? The jury was out on that one.

At the intersection onto the main highway, I waited for a logging truck to pass. It was followed by an empty dump truck. I watched them disappear down the road and thought about the Racine Mining Company and their slick public relations people.

With the new push on the government to deregulate the forest lands, Racine had swept into town with a plan to open copper and nickel mining on the southern border of the county. An open pit iron ore mine had been abandoned there. They claimed they'd studied the land, they'd consulted with environmentalists, and they had new technology that would allow the mining without harming the forests and the waters.

I pictured the dead open pit mines that had been left behind the last time mining was a big industry.

Rob, who knew the land better than anyone in the county, was convinced they were lying. "The only way to get that copper out of the earth is to cut into it. Waste from the operation would kill Lake Larissa and the land around the lake."

Back in May, I'd reviewed the fact sheet they presented to the county board. Few people, other than Willow, knew one of my jobs out of college had been as a freelance fact-checker for a couple of well-respected magazines. I knew how to ferret out misinformation.

The fact sheet was filled with misinformation and outright lies. It quoted studies that didn't exist and experts that someone had made up.

My recent confrontation with Nancy Bywater had ended with me saying, "You can't publish 'fake news.' This is fake!"

The Lady Slipper Trail Group stood firmly against the mining operation.

But we were small going up against a monster company with unlimited resources and people on the highest levels of the federal government with massive financial ties to the industry.

I pulled onto the highway and decided my second stop after seeing the sheriff would be a visit to our state senator, Blaine McConnell. His family owned Lake Larissa Lodge, and he was a long-time friend of the Lady Slipper Trail Group.

My head was so jammed with thoughts, including the message on my voicemail, I hardly noticed how the Subaru kept pulling to the right.

"Come on." I turned the steering wheel to keep the car on the road. "What is this?"

Suddenly the car veered off the road with a clunking, flapping sound. I braked and pulled onto the gravel shoulder, barely avoiding a plunge into the ditch.

When the car stopped, I sat for a moment, trying to catch my breath and calm my heart. This wasn't turning out to be a good day. The right front tire was flat, and I was in the wetlands area known as the "great marsh" by the locals. Not only was it a swamp teeming with mosquitos, but it was also a cell phone dead zone. I would either have to wait for a Good Samaritan to come by or hike for help.

Of course, I was wearing sandals. Not only sandals, but cute, little strappy sandals, great for ads in *Vogue* magazine and useless for walking.

I inspected the flat tire. I knew so little about car maintenance. Growing up in Manhattan, I'd had no reason to drive. I'd finally broken down and gotten a driver's license when I turned twenty-one, not for driving, but for identification. I didn't own a car until I bought this old Subaru last spring to move to Minnesota.

The first mosquito landed on my arm. By the time I'd swatted it off, several more were buzzing around my ears. Staring at the ruined tire would only get me eaten alive. I hurried back to the car, flapping my arms and diving head first onto the seat. In a sitcom, this would have been a funny scene. In real life, I was so desperate to get away from the insects I banged my head against the steering wheel and almost slammed the door on my foot.

With the door closed behind me, I rubbed my banged head and considered my options. I couldn't sit here long, with all the windows up. The car was already heating, and the air-conditioning was ready for hospice.

"So, I broil to death inside or die of massive mosquito bites?" Suddenly, Queens, New York, with its summer smell of garbage and oppressive heat, was looking good. No mosquitoes, no deer flies, and perfect cell reception.

I tried my phone and sure enough, it had no bars.

A logging truck roared by without stopping. It disappeared down the road, and I wished I'd been smart enough to have mosquito repellent stashed in the car. I was clearly a neophyte when it came to travel in this part of the country.

"Well," I sighed. "It looks like I walk."

The bog was about midway between the lodge and town. I needed to decide on my direction. When I stepped out of the car, a gust of humid, swamp-smelling air ruffled my short hair. It occurred to me that if I walked away from the breeze, it might save me some mosquito landings.

I headed for town and had made it about twenty yards when a piece of gravel lodged in my skinny, useless sandal. As I reached over to pick it out, another logging truck roared by, nearly knocking me into the ditch. For a moment, a spray of dust blinded me. As I blinked the grit out of my eyes, I heard the sound of a vehicle slowing behind me. Maybe the Good Samaritan had arrived.

When I turned, though, eyes blurred and watering, the first thing I saw was the front grill of the sheriff's cruiser. Damn, stranded and my help would turn out to be my good friend LeRoy.

My hands turned cold and damp in the heat as I thought about his scarred face and the look in his eyes as he pressed against me in my kitchen. Flight or fight?

Chapter Four: State Trooper

Could I disappear into the swamp? The blades of wet, reedy grass rose through the soft earth while cattails swayed in the breeze. The wetlands sounded alive with birds and frogs and the hum of insects. If I cut through to the north, I might make it far enough to get cell service. On the other hand, I was wearing those stupid sandals, capris, and a tank top that exposed my arms, neck, and back to the buzzing, biting insects. I imagined collapsing into the muck of the swamp and being eaten by the creatures that lived in the mire. Besides, who would I call? The sheriff?

Sighing, I turned to the cruiser.

To my relief, the person walking toward me wasn't Deputy LeRoy Pruitt but a state trooper with a broad-brimmed maroon-colored hat. His name tag neatly pinned above his badge read *James*.

"Trouble?" He was tall, maybe six foot three and lean. I couldn't tell with his dark glasses on, but I guessed him to be about my age. He looked at me with a slight upturn of his mouth.

"Flat tire." I pointed to my car. "And no cell reception."

"Well, let's take a look."

The tone of his voice was casual and reassuring. I walked beside him, noting he looked fit in his pressed shirt and dark pants. Unlike Leroy, his stomach was flat, with no hint of a growing gut. Still, he was a policeman, and I felt reluctant to say much to him.

Before we reached my car, he turned to me and held out his hand. "Jim Monroe. Pleased to meet you. And sorry, but I'm required to check your license and registration."

His grip was strong, maybe a little too strong. Once we were at the car, I pulled out my license and dug through the junk in the glove compartment to find the car registration.

"Ah," he smiled reading my license. "Another James."

"Jamie. I'm told I was named after a friend of my father's. I like to believe I was named after Jamie Lee Curtis for her role in *Halloween*."

"Hmm. Well, I was definitely not named after the president. And I prefer to be called Jim." He pointed to the cruiser. "I have to make sure you're not a criminal. Then we'll deal with the tire."

I stood in the heat, hugging myself, as he sat in his cruiser tapping things into a computer. What if my name popped up from the mess in New York? I couldn't go through that again. For a second, the image of that holding cell stuck in my head. I saw the drunken woman who had plopped down beside me and slurred, "Wanna know the secret?" She didn't wait for my answer. "The secret is to keep your mouth shut." Then she'd cackled. "Snow White, one of your dwarves will come and bail you out. You wait and see."

I was breathing hard as I watched the trooper. *Settle down, breathe normally.* Then I laughed a little. Who can breathe normally when they're told to?

Jim Monroe stepped out of his vehicle with a friendly expression. "I guess I don't have to arrest you."

I forced a small smile.

"Let's see what you've got here." He hunkered down by the tire and studied it for a long time.

Squatting next to him, I was aware of a hint of something like apple from his aftershave.

He pointed to the top of the tire. "That's your leak." He then squat-walked to the back tire. "Hmmm. You've got a problem here, too."

I squinted at the small puncture in the tire. "But that doesn't make sense. How could I get holes in both of my tires?"

He shrugged, pushing himself to a standing position. "Vandals do that sometimes." He looked at me and I couldn't read the expression behind his mirrored glasses. "Sometimes a lover's spat."

This time I laughed out loud. I should have stayed serious, but the thought of a lover's quarrel was so ridiculous. "I guarantee you that's not the problem." I thought about Andrew, my ex, and laughed again. "Right now, the only love in my life is my dog, and I don't think she's handy enough to do this."

"Vandals then?"

Since I'd moved into the cabin with Bronte as my guard, I'd had no problems with intruders, other than a skunk and her brood of skunkettes. Maybe it had happened while I was doing trail work. Maybe a summer person snuck down the road to punch the tire. Maybe LeRoy...

Another logging truck growled by. This time, the driver slowed, probably because of the flashing lights on the cruiser.

Jim watched it go by, shaking his head. "They go too fast on this road. One of these days someone is going to get killed."

I nodded in agreement.

"So," he turned to his cruiser, "how about if I radio Toby's Auto Repair and have him tow your car into Killdeer. You can either stay put and wait, or I'll give you a lift into town."

Staying put in this heat seemed like a bad idea. "I'll take that lift, as long as I don't have to ride in the back." I shivered involuntarily.

When I opened my car door to grab the manuscript, a blast of hot air almost took my breath away. Waiting for the tow truck was definitely not an option.

Once we were on the way, I turned to Jim. "Thank you. I'm not sure I would have survived the heat and the mosquitoes."

"Funny how the tourist ads don't mention Minnesota is the land of ten thousand lakes and ten million mosquitoes."

"And Lyme disease and giardia."

"That too."

For a few minutes, we rode in silence. I was sneaking looks at him as he drove. He had a hawk-like nose and a shadow on his face and chin, even though he was clean-shaven.

He broke the silence. "You're not from around here, are you?"

He wasn't the first person to make that comment, "I'm trying to work on my accent—get the New York out of it, but so far I haven't been successful."

"I think New York is a great place to visit—but I wouldn't want to live there."

I thought about all I missed from New York. "We used to come to our family cabin here when I was little. I always thought Killdeer was a great place to visit, but I wouldn't want to live here. Things change."

My phone beeped with a text. We were now out of the dead zone. I checked it. An unknown number with a message said, **like your tires???**

"What?"

"Problem?" Jim glanced at me.

"Prank texter." The anonymous texts unnerved me, but not enough to tell anyone.

He's a nice guy. Tell him. Again, I felt paralyzed. The same paralysis I'd felt when I heard Nancy's message.

"It's a whole new world out there with all the communication technology, the hacking, the robocalls, the fraudsters." He shook his head. "Keeps law enforcement busy."

So does murder. I hoped the sheriff would be in. I wasn't about to say anything to anybody else.

"I think you should report those tires. You'll need to for insurance. Can I drop you at the sheriff's office?"

I nodded and refrained from telling him that was my original destination. He didn't need to know about the voicemail and my interrogation by LeRoy Pruitt.

We pulled up in front of the Jackpine County sheriff's office. The parking lot of the one- story brick building was nearly full.

"Looks pretty busy here," I said.

"Murder in town. We don't have much of that around here."

"Oh?" I decided to play dumb to see if Jim knew anything. He didn't take the bait.

Jim walked around and opened the door for me. "I'll walk you in and point you in the direction of the person you need to file the report with. I'm thinking it will be pretty chaotic in there right now.

"Maybe I should come back later."

He shook his head. "Better to get it done. Maybe they'll catch whoever punctured your tires."

He didn't say what I thought—*fat chance.*

We reached the door at the same time Sheriff Rick Fowler did from up the street. His head was down, and his brow furrowed. He didn't notice us until Jim said, "Good afternoon."

When the sheriff looked up, he stared at me with a puzzled expression. "I was looking for you."

Now it was Jim's turn to be puzzled. I stood there willing my feet not to take off and run.

"Why don't you come inside so we can talk?" The sheriff's voice was neutral, but it clearly said, *this isn't a choice.*

Chapter Five: The Sheriff's Office

At least the sheriff didn't make me put my hands behind my back so he could bind them with a plastic tie. In fact, he was very polite as he walked me into the building. "Watch your step." He pointed to the threshold of the door. "People have tripped on this."

He lightly took my elbow like I was an eighty-year-old granny. I fought the urge to pull away as he guided me inside. I glanced back. Jim watched all this with a look of surprise but said nothing as he followed us inside.

The new building wasn't anything like the jail in Queens with its peeling paint and sewer smell. It had more the feel of a real estate office with gray cubicles and pieces of art on the wall. I recognized one of Rob's landscape paintings hanging behind the receptionist. In it, the reflection of pines on the glassy surface of a lake appeared to shimmer. Rob's artistry had a live quality to it that was hard to describe.

I hardly appreciated it, though, as my heart raced. What did the sheriff want?

The office was a beehive of activity. Several people gathered around a whiteboard as one of the other deputies from Jackpine County made notes.

"Sheriff?" he looked over at us. "We have some questions."

"Give me a few minutes." They stared at me as he ushered me past the reception desk. The receptionist frowned before turning to Jim. "Good to see you, Jimbo. It's been a while."

I didn't look back, but I could feel his eyes on me as the sheriff guided me through the room.

"We'll go to my office." At least it wasn't a dank little windowless interrogation room with cement floors and a chipped Formica table. In fact, the sun poured into the office, giving it an air of openness, despite the piles of paper on the desk and the messy bookcase against the wall.

He pointed to a chair in front of his desk. I sat down, noting how low the chair was. I was five-foot-three and I felt like a kindergartner in a high school desk. I recognized the management technique of putting a desk between the boss and the employee and making sure the employee's chair sat low. It was a power thing, and I immediately tensed up.

Except that, instead of sitting behind the desk, the sheriff pulled out his chair and brought it around so we were facing each other. I wasn't sure if this was better or worse than having him tower over me or having the desk as a barrier.

"I'm sorry." He leaned toward me. "I know we've met before, but I'm Rick Fowler and I prefer to be called Rick rather than Sheriff. Sheriff Fowler was my dad's name, you know."

I didn't know, nor did I care. He was shorter than Jim and heavier. He looked like someone who was on his way to obesity in a few years. He had a pasty color to his face and deep circles under his eyes. Nancy Bywater's death couldn't have been easy on him.

The air-conditioning blasted out cold air. I hugged myself to keep warm.

"Listen, I talked with LeRoy after he visited you. He said he asked you where you were last night."

I shuddered inwardly, thinking about the morning's conversation. "I was working all weekend editing a manuscript. I needed to get it done and in the mail today." I pointed to the package on my lap. "I don't have anyone who can vouch for me."

"You didn't go to the lodge or get groceries or anything?"

He studied my face, and heat rose from my neck. I was torn between the voice I so often ignored that said, *only answer the questions. Don't offer anything more.* And the need to ask, *do you think I had anything to do with this?*

Once again, the voice in my head lost. "Listen, Sheriff...uh...Rick. I don't know anything about Nancy Bywater's death. I haven't seen her since last week when we had our discussion about the propaganda put out by Racine

Mining. My dog and my blue pencil are the only ones who can vouch I was working on the manuscript all weekend. If you'd like, I'll show you all the edits."

I didn't realize how much my voice had risen as I talked until Rick put up his hand to stop me.

"Okay. Okay."

I clamped my mouth shut, realizing how defensive I must have sounded.

"So, let's back up. I'm just trying to understand Ms. Bywater and who might want to hurt her."

I frowned at him. Why would I want to hurt her? Did my business card make me the prime suspect?

"Tell me about your discussion with her. I'm told by her office assistant that it got quite heated."

I took a deep breath. The voice said, *keep it simple.* "You probably know I'm doing some publicity work for the Lady Slipper Trail. We're trying to get the word out on our work. But we're also trying to get the word out on the potential harm that could come if Racine Mining gets their permits to dig in Jackpine County."

He nodded, keeping his gaze on me. "Go on."

"Racine Mining put out a fact sheet on the economic and environmental impact their operation would have on the county, the wilderness, and even the Boundary Waters Canoe Area. I reviewed it and found significant errors."

"And?" he prompted me.

"I shared this with Nancy after she'd published a positive article about how Racine would be an economic boost and not harm the environment. I asked if I could write a rebuttal. She refused."

"Do you know why she refused?"

I remembered the look on Nancy's face when I'd asked. It seemed like she went from interest to doubt to fear. "She said it was now 'old news.' And I said, 'Then you're printing *fake news* without an explanation.'"

"I hear it got a little heated."

I shrugged.

"I also heard you threatened her."

Now I sat up straight again, the heat rising up my neck and into my cheeks. *Keep calm.* "I said something about a...about a possible lawsuit." Of course, I didn't mean it. I was already dealing with an endless lawsuit back in New York. I wasn't interested in being involved in another.

Before he could say anything more, his receptionist tapped at the door. "Can you step out for a moment?"

He sighed as if in pain as he walked out of the room. While I waited, I gazed at the papers on his desk. He had several printed spreadsheets with columns of numbers. One was marked up with notes in red pencil. I guessed that a lot of his job was budgeting and figuring out funding. That was why he'd been at the county board meeting when I first met him. He wanted to add another deputy and the board had grilled him about how this would be paid for.

I thought about my own spreadsheet back at the cabin that told me how much I needed to make in my fledgling editing business and how much additional remodeling of the cabin would cost. Curious about the complexity of running a sheriff's office, I leaned over to study the spreadsheet. One of the notations on the side jumped out at me. "Chk Racine offer."

Was Racine Mining offering money to his office? I squinted, looking for more notes when I saw something familiar sticking out from the bottom of one of his piles.

That awful feeling that a softball had just dropped from my chest to my gut ran through me. I recognized the magazine heading. It was a copy of last year's article in *The New York Times Magazine* that featured the headline, "What If Police Get the Name Wrong?" I knew every word of that article. I knew every edit, every comma, and every name featured in the article because I had written it.

The last thing I wanted was for it to follow me all the way to the remote wilderness of Minnesota. I sank back and pressed the palms of my hands against my temples.

"Are you okay?"

I turned to see Rick in the doorway. He had a concerned expression.

"Little headache, that's all."

He stayed in the doorway. "I think I have what I need from you. Perhaps in a day or two you could stop by and give us a formal statement."

This would have been the time to tell the sheriff about the message on my phone and how it might be a clue. This would have been the time to tell him how his deputy had threatened me. I could have pointed out that LeRoy Pruitt was the only person I knew who could have punched a hole in my tire. But I knew from past experience that law enforcement people, whether in the right or not, tended to stick together. And in another state, I had created a major headache for them. Did that protectionism reach this far?

As I walked out, a tinge of guilt about the message on my phone ran through me, but I assured myself it had nothing to do with the murder. And besides, they might confiscate my phone, which was my lifeline to my work and to the internet. It was amazing how we could so easily talk ourselves out of doing the right thing.

Jim met me at the reception desk. "I checked with Toby. He said he had your car in tow."

"Thank you for taking care of that."

"No problem."

The receptionist's gaze lasered through me before she turned back to her computer. In the area with the whiteboard, everyone had suddenly gone silent. As I walked out the doorway, I felt both cold and totally creeped out. Did they all think I was somehow responsible for Nancy Bywater's death?

Chapter Six: Blaine McConnell

The visit to the sheriff's office unnerved me enough that I decided to walk over to the little town park and sit quietly for a few minutes. The park, a square block with a sagging old bandstand in the middle, was empty. Often tourists stopped and picnicked on their way to Lake Larissa. Today, with the heat and humidity, I was alone.

The park reminded me of the little city park across the street from my apartment in Queens. It had a tattered and used look I found comforting. I sat on a wooden bench, noting the initials that had been carved into it—LN+JM, Ron+Sandy, EH+FM. I wondered if any of them were still together.

Back all those years ago when Andrew and I were dewy-eyed and in love, he said he'd carve our names on a bench in Central Park because then the world would know. I nixed his plan for practical reasons. "You'd probably get caught and have to pay a huge fine. Besides, who would ever know it was us?"

He was hurt, and the expression on his face reminded me of a dog who had just been scolded. Over the years, he'd used that expression a lot. But then, he was an actor. I wondered if he'd carved his initials yet with his makeup artist.

"Damn, Jamie, you're getting snarky," I said out loud.

I grabbed the package with the manuscript in it off the bench and walked to the post office. I loved the Killdeer post office. I loved its dusty smell, the wall of post office boxes set in the dark hardwood, and the floorboards that creaked when you walked across them to the window. It had an old-timey, peaceful feel to it.

The post office was a WPA project during the late 1930s. Like many of the WPA works, it was built out of local fieldstone, with hands-on crafting. From the outside, it appeared to be a simple, squarish building. Inside, though, was the real treasure, a Boratko mural depicting loggers at work in the forest. I think it was the warmth of the colors, muted reds and oranges, that attracted me.

One of my last memories of my mother before she slipped into that dark place and never came out was of the two of us standing in line at the post office. We were sending postcards of Northern Minnesota back to my school friends in Manhattan. She stooped down to me and pointed to the mural. "See that man bending over the giant log? He could have been your grandfather."

Several years later, Dad and I were doing our summer exploration of art in New York City. One day we found ourselves in the Richmond County Courthouse on Staten Island looking at a painting called *Indian Harvesting*. The style reminded me of the post office in Killdeer. Dad pointed to the Native women in the mural and told me that my mother's mother—my grandmother—was full-blooded Ojibwe and, like the women in the mural, she'd probably been involved with similar harvesting. It was one of the only times Dad ever referred to my Native American heritage.

Today, when I walked up to the window with my package, I wasn't at peace. The heavy cloud of Nancy Bywater's death hung over my head. Why would I feel guilty about it? Perhaps because of the unkind thoughts I'd had about her after the confrontation at the *Killdeer Times*. I'd walked out of that meeting secretly wishing she'd get fired for publishing false information. I even entertained the thought that, after the firing, I'd step forward to edit the little weekly. I would make the *Times* a premier small-town newspaper.

Or perhaps it was that my phone held a possible clue and I wasn't ready to let anyone know about it.

I set the package on the counter.

The clerk, an older man, fumbled through the new computerized system. "Used to be I could weigh the packages and send them off," he

28

grumbled. "Now I have to ask all these questions and give you all these choices—overnight, insurance, tracking—damned computers."

I decided to pay a little extra to have *Knight of Lust* tracked. Florice LeMay would be highly disappointed if it got lost in the mail. He stamped the package and shuffled back to a canvass cart. I stood for another moment, taking in the mural.

The door opened behind me and a hearty voice said, "Jamie Forest. Admiring the artwork? Good to see you."

Startled, I turned to see Blaine McConnell, former lifeguard at Larissa Lodge and now the district's state senator, grinning at me.

"Out pressing the flesh?" I smiled.

In the past couple of weeks, as I'd worked with the Lady Slipper Trail group, I'd spent enough time with Blaine to experience his easy manner. I thought of him as a good ally to have if we needed to get the legislature to intervene to protect the wilderness. Blaine's family owned the Larissa Lodge, and he was on the state land-use legislative committee.

He was shorter than Jim and stockier but still in good shape for a man in his early forties, who spent much of his time with his constituents at bean feeds and pancake breakfasts.

Looking at him now, his hair receding and no longer sun bleached, I remembered the summer as a ten-year-old swimming at the lodge. I'd had a crush on him. At sixteen, he seemed old and wise and mature as he sat in his high lifeguard chair twirling his silver whistle on a rope. Though he told me recently that he definitely remembered me, I was pretty sure that was the politician in him. I was hardly distinguishable from the mob of kids in the water back then.

"Office hours today?" I asked.

His face crinkled into a good-natured smile. "Bombarded with complaints—why didn't I get my social security disability? Who's going to pay for mother's nursing home—you know, the usual." He shrugged. "By the way, are you ready to sell that broken-down shack of yours to me? I promise to preserve the land."

Blaine and I bantered back and forth about my cabin every time I saw him.

I couldn't tell if he was serious about buying the place, but someone wanted it. I thought about my weekly "check-in call" from a local realtor.

I shook my head. "Sorry, now that I have a toilet that flushes, I'm good."

His hazel eyes crinkled with laughter. "The offer is always out there."

The postal clerk stood at the window with a sour expression. Blaine leaned to me and whispered, "He's worried about post office consolidation. Might lose this branch."

I looked at the mural. "Please save the mural if that happens," I whispered back.

He lightly squeezed my upper arm before he strode over to the window with his hand out. "How are you, Henry?"

Outside, I felt like I'd walked into a steam room. The heat and humidity held in the smells of downtown—the bakery, the bark mulch in the large flower pots on the street corners, the lingering rot of the garbage cans in the alley. In some ways, it was like walking to the subway in Queens and, in other ways, it was a different world.

When I passed two women on the sidewalk, one of them looked back at me.

She whispered loudly, "That's the one they're talking about. Not from around here."

I hurried along, pretending she was referring to someone else.

Behind me, Blaine's booming voice called to someone. People in New York tended to keep their heads down and mind their own space. As you walked down the street, you heard a rainbow of languages. Here, you heard, "Hi, how are ya?"

Ahead, a small group milled in front of the *Times* office. I wondered if I should cross the street to avoid them. However, some of the voices carried, and I succumbed to curiosity.

"Terrible thing."

"They say she was drunk."

"I heard she was having an affair."

I made my way through the crowd, feeling suddenly indignant. Whatever Nancy was in life, she didn't deserve strangers speculating about her like she was a cheap tabloid star.

Just as I passed the door, LeRoy stepped outside. He carried himself with an officiousness that might have drawn laughs in a sitcom but looked stupid here. I put my head down and tried to slip through the group before he saw me.

Too late.

"Miss Forest." He emphasized the "Miss."

I stopped and turned. He had his chest puffed up like a bandy rooster. I half expected him to crow.

"We need to talk."

The people milling around all stopped talking at once and stared at me. I recognized a few people, including one of the county board members.

For once, I obeyed that voice that said, *keep quiet.*

"Would you like to step inside?" It wasn't a question.

The last thing I wanted was to be inside the *Times* office alone with LeRoy. I stood stock still and said nothing.

The peacock grin on his face faded. "I said, would you like to step inside?"

Someone nudged me as if to shake me awake. I felt, more than saw, a growing distrust among the crowd.

A whispered voice said, "Isn't she the one who had the fight with that editor last week?"

"You mean that woman from out east? I hear she's in the Mafia."

I opened my mouth to tell him I'd already talked with the sheriff when a voice sounded from behind me.

"Hey, LeRoy Pruitt, is that you?" Blaine pushed his way through the crowd.

LeRoy stared, an uncertain expression crossing his face. I wasn't sure if he was intimidated by Blaine or simply confused.

Blaine walked up to LeRoy and grabbed his hand, pumping it like a true politician. "God, what a terrible tragedy. Is this your investigation?"

I took the opportunity to quickly slip away.

Norma, a large, brassy-looking woman with too much eye makeup and hair that had been bleached so badly it looked like dried straw, touched my arm as I left. "Don't you have to talk to him?"

31

"No. I've already talked to the sheriff." Norma was one of the Lady Slipper Trail volunteers.

"Good." She lowered her voice. "I don't like him."

Norma might have had poor taste when it came to personal grooming, but she was good at reading people.

"I agree."

"Not real fond of the other one, either."

"Blaine?"

She harrumphed. "Womanizer, they say. That's why the marriage broke up."

I saw Blaine as a glad-hander but not a womanizer. Then again, what did I know?

"Where are you headed? I'll walk with you."

Behind us, it sounded like the little crowd was breaking up.

I told her about my flat tire and that Toby had towed it to his shop. "Jim, the state trooper who helped me out, said it looked like it had been punctured, and I had a puncture in the other tire."

She took my arm in a protective gesture. "Watch your step. We have some people around here who aren't only stupid, they're dangerous."

The Racine Mining Company had set up a small office a block from the *Times*. As we walked by, I noted the office was dark. In the window was an artist's sketch of new housing on the edge of town that Racine promised to build for people who came to work for the mine. It included a square with a fountain and benches and people strolling.

I pointed to it. "Looks pretty enticing."

"Huh," Norma snorted. "Another way for them to rob the people. Own the housing and own the stores, and pretty soon everyone is 'another day older and deeper in debt' to the mining companies and their overpaid CEOs. We've been courted like this before. Usually by a bunch of money-grubbing crooks who don't give a damn about the environment."

Norma was a member of the local Ojibwe tribe. She and her family had probably lost a lot over the generations to the "money-grubbing crooks."

"Well, no one's in the office today. I hope that means they've given up and moved to another country to destroy the wilderness."

"Doubt it, though I heard they're putting pressure on the county board to approve their land use permits. If something doesn't come through in the next few weeks, they'll take their business elsewhere."

"Sounds good to me." I nodded.

She shook her head. "With people out of work around here, things are heating up. And now this murder? Who knows?"

A pickup truck slowed as we stood in front of the office. A man with a baseball hat and dark glasses rolled down his window and yelled, "Killer!" He hit the gas and was a half a block away before I could react.

Chapter Seven: The Warning

Norma gave him the finger. "Donald Pruitt, you're a jerk! Just because your cousin is a deputy doesn't give you any special rights!" She turned to me. "So, what was that all about?"

I guessed that LeRoy had blabbed to his cousin about his number one suspect. I shrugged. I didn't need to drag Norma into my little drama. "Maybe he thinks I'm one of *The Sopranos* from television. All people with a New York accent are mobsters, you know."

"Pah! He'd be stupid enough."

We parted before I reached the auto repair shop. "See you on Sunday?" We had a Lady Slipper meeting to talk about possible grant sources of funding for the trail upgrades.

"I'll see. I've been picking up extra shifts at the hospital since the night nurse is on maternity leave."

I doubted she'd come even if she wasn't working. Norma was a physical workhorse on the trail but thoroughly disliked meetings and decision-making. Her attitude was just "show me where to put the wood chips and I'll do my part."

She started to walk away and then turned back to me. "Jamie, keep your eyes open. This fight with the mining company could get nasty. I've seen it before."

Like slashed tires? Or an overzealous deputy? Overhead the sun faded for a moment as a white, fluffy cloud obscured it.

Toby greeted me with a sour grunt. Even though an air conditioner rattled in the office of his auto repair shop, beads of sweat dripped down the sides of his face. His gray coveralls barely zipped over his stomach, and he sighed heavily as he moved. If he'd been a woman, I would have guessed him at eight months pregnant.

He showed me the new tires he'd put on my car. "I checked to make sure your other tires are in good shape. They're worn but good enough until winter comes."

Great, I'd have to replace those tires, too. Another expense. I handed him my credit card. After I'd signed, he gave me the paperwork. "Show this to your insurance guy. They'll probably pay for the tow at least. Bad thing when someone slashes a tire."

As I walked out the door, I wondered if his last words were meant as a warning, too.

The car was oppressively hot when I slipped into the driver's seat. I rolled down the windows, feeling I couldn't quite catch my breath. I needed to get back to the tranquility of my cabin.

People were still gathered in front of the *Times* office as I drove by, but I saw no sign of LeRoy. I shivered as the air conditioner spit out tepid, dank-smelling air.

Once home, Bronte greeted me like I'd been away on a month-long vacation. I had to admit it was nice to have someone who actually missed me. My ex-husband barely noticed when I hauled myself in at three in the morning after a grueling fact-checking session. He was too busy learning lines for his next commercial tryout or next play callback.

I remembered Dad's gentle words when I'd told him I was in love with Andrew. "You sure you want to marry an actor?"

"He's good, Dad. I know he'll do well." And he did, eventually landing a plumb role as Mr. Right Digestion for an antacid product.

When he told me about the successful audition, I'd laughed about it. "Not exactly Shakespeare."

Andrew had assumed a hurt expression. "It still requires talent."

I never expected Mr. Right Digestion to fall in love with his makeup artist while I was preoccupied with Dad's failing health. It would have been a great script for a soap opera except it was real life for me. Dad died before I found out Andrew's long absences for on-location shoots were really spent on location in the makeup artist's apartment a subway stop from our place.

"Never marry an actor," I said to Bronte as she happily licked my arm.

I checked my phone for messages, hoping someone wanted to contract with me for editing. Instead, I had a text from Willow.

You home? Like to stop by.

It had come in while I was dealing with Toby and the tire. I texted back.

Home now. Beer in the fridge.

I grabbed an IPA from the refrigerator and walked out to my screened porch. It faced the lake, and I could see the water shimmering beyond the open lawn to the water.

Bronte settled at my feet.

"This is the life, my dog friend."

Outside, a pair of squirrels scampered up a tree. Bronte didn't even raise her ears. I rocked in the old wicker chair, remembering the excitement of coming here as a child. We flew to Minneapolis, rented a car and drove for hours to get here. The cabin always looked so welcoming after the long trip from New York.

Before Dad unlocked the door, Mom stood under the tall pine to the side of the porch with her arms spread as if she was in prayer. She took a deep breath and smiled with such a look of wonder. I ran barefoot down to the rocky shore of the lake. We had a small sandy beach, but what I truly loved was a large smooth rock on the shore that I could sit on and watch the loons swimming in the lake.

For a few moments, I forgot about Nancy Bywater, Deputy LeRoy, the sheriff, and the magazine on his desk. Instead, I relished the cold beer, the slight breeze that cooled the air, and the smell of pine needles. My eyelids became heavy as I relaxed to the chatter of the chipmunks and the call of the red-winged blackbirds.

I dreamed I was back in my Queens apartment with the windows open and a slight breeze on my face. My eyes opened to a man wearing all black, including a black ski mask. He barked at me, and I couldn't understand what he was saying. I opened my mouth to ask and nothing came out except an "ah, ah." He came nearer, growing in size until I felt like I couldn't breathe. I tried to find my phone to call 911, but I couldn't see it in the dark.

I woke with a start to the sound of Willow's voice. "Hey, girl, settle down." It came from inside the cabin as Bronte yipped with delight.

I opened my eyes with a gasp. I'd hoped these nightmares would go away once I moved to the seclusion of the cabin. In fact, they'd gotten worse. I even bought a dream catcher to hang over my bed, thinking it might help.

"You know," Rob had said when I brought it back to the cabin, "the Ojibwe made dreamcatchers to protect the children. Adults were supposed to study their dreams and learn from them."

I wasn't learning much from my nightmares, so I hung it up over the bed. All it caught was dust.

Willow walked out to the porch, holding a bottle of beer in one hand and a pizza box in the other. "Sausage and mushroom. You better not tell me you've suddenly gone vegan."

I stretched, hiding the cold fright that had overtaken me. Someday, I would tell Willow the whole story about that night that turned my life upside down. I would give her details that weren't included in the *New York Times*. I would tell her that, even after "the special taskforce" discovered they'd arrested the wrong person, they'd closed ranks and insisted they'd done nothing wrong. I would tell her about the ongoing fear I had of people in law enforcement. Maybe I'd even share with her my nightmares. But right now, I was content to simply have her as a friend.

"Thanks." I took a slice and savored the sausage as grease dripped down my chin.

Willow smelled of antiseptic and shampoo. Her hair, pulled back into a long ponytail, was still damp from the shower.

"Did you cure the horse?"

She shrugged, grabbing another slice of pizza. "They have some pretty green people running that stable. I suggested they get old Conroy to help them out. He's cranky and arthritic, but he knows horses."

Willow knew everyone in this community and, even though she could be outspoken and sometimes abrasive, people admired her. She was one of "their own," while I was the "tree hugger from out east."

"So, I hear you got arrested by Jim Monroe and hauled into the sheriff's office."

"Word does travel fast." I shrugged. "Anyway, it wasn't an arrest."

"Really?" Willow's eyes narrowed.

I told her about the tires and the ride from Jim. "He seems like a decent guy. For a law officer, that is."

"He's homegrown, like me. A bit of Ojibwe blood coursing through his veins." She took another slice of pizza. Willow, despite her name, could put away food for three or four. "I think he has a live-in girlfriend. Or at least he did. You interested?"

"Naw. Too nice for me. I'm looking for a drugged-out ex-felon." I pointed to my biceps. "You know, one with lots of nasty tattoos."

She laughed. "I'm sure we can come up with somebody."

We ate in silence for a few minutes. Bronte spent her time looking at us with her big brown eyes, hoping for a treat. On Willow's advice, I was strict about feeding her only dog food. If she ate anything else, it was because she caught it herself outside.

I thought about the afternoon and the group by the *Times* office. "Leaving LeRoy at the crime scene seems like a poor choice." I shuddered inwardly, thinking again about how he had backed me up against the counter this morning. "There's something wrong with that man."

"Oh, he's just dumber than a three-dollar dog, that's all." Willow shrugged off my comment, but I noted a faint catch in her voice.

"But you have some history with him."

Willow continued to chew on her pizza but said nothing. I found this strange, considering her attitude toward him this morning. I decided to change the subject and tell her about my weekend of editing.

"So, my client tried to rewrite the Arthurian legend from the viewpoint of a poor servant girl in the castle. It reads like a soft-core porn *Cinderella*."

Willow groaned. "And your job is to make it publishable?"

"Walking on water might be easier." I frowned. "Maybe I'm not cut out for editing and ghostwriting. My Master of Fine Arts degree didn't prepare me for the likes of Florice LeMay." I thought about my diminished bank account and wondered how long I could luxuriate in the wilderness before the money from Dad's estate ran out.

Willow set the bottle of beer down by her feet and rocked slowly back and forth. I watched her and felt like something was off. She was usually talkative and outgoing to the point of irritation. She seemed contemplative tonight.

I thought about Dad's phrase when I was too quiet. "A penny for your thoughts."

"Huh?"

"You're so quiet."

She glanced at me. "Oh. I was just thinking about Nancy Bywater. Who would kill her?"

Bronte stood up and shook herself. She walked to the screen door, her nails clicking on the wooden boards.

"Out?"

She wagged her tail. When I stood to let her out, I noted an odd expression on Willow's face—almost as if she wasn't sure where she was. Maybe she was sleep deprived from her veterinarian work.

I thought about the cryptic message on my phone. "Do you think Nancy knew something that got her killed?" I was about to share the voicemail message with Willow when Bronte started barking furiously at the sound of a car approaching.

"Now who can that be?"

I ran out in time to see a rock smash against the side of the cabin as the car did a quick U-turn and sped away. Whoever threw it was aiming for a window but fortunately missed. Bronte continued to bark as she chased it.

The car disappeared down the driveway, dust and dirt spewing behind it. I walked over and picked up the rock that had fallen into the flower bed under the kitchen window. It had broken off one of the marigolds when it landed. The rock had a note wrapped around it secured with a rubber band. Willow came running up to me as I opened the note.

"Crap," I whispered. "What is this?"

The note read in childish block letters *YANKEE GO HOME*.

I handed it to Willow, expecting her to laugh. She surprised me. "It seems you're under siege."

It wasn't her words, though, but her expression—almost a look of satisfaction. When I took the note back, though, her expression had changed to one of concern. "Jamie, it would be a good idea if you locked your doors at night."

Oh hell. Had I escaped New York to be taunted by clichés?

Chapter Eight: The Article

Willow stared down the road where a small cloud of dust was still visible. "Did you see the car?"

I closed my eyes and visualized the car doing a quick turnaround. "Dark SUV. Tinted windows." I thought about *The Sopranos* and television's depiction of mobsters and almost started to laugh. This had to be a joke.

We settled back on the porch with another beer. Mosquitoes hummed outside the screen as they swarmed for their evening feeding. Bronte sat with her head on my lap. I looked at her and remembered I needed to check her for ticks tonight. The tick collar on her was only partially effective.

"I don't think Nancy Bywater's death would bring a dark SUV all the way out here. So, let's talk about Racine and why they might be after you." Willow leaned forward with her elbows on her knees. "What did you really find in that report they provided for the public?"

I pictured the fifteen-page document, expertly laid out with several graphs, pullouts of quotes from "experts" and language that would choke an academic. It came complete with a page in six-point type of references.

"It looks professional and legitimate. Let me show you." I beckoned Willow into the kitchen where my laptop was sitting on the table. "I got an electronic copy of it from Rob, who'd gotten it from one of his county board friends."

I pulled the file up on the laptop as Willow settled into a chair next to me. "See, when it's printed out on slick paper in full color, it will dazzle you."

"But?"

"Well, for one thing, these pullout quotes are fake. Dr. Emile Landreau, Ph.D., of McGill University who says, 'The environmental impact will be minimal' doesn't exist."

Willow looked surprised. "How do you know?"

I'm sure she expected I had a deep knowledge of the internet and that's how I found this out. However, the answer was much simpler. "I looked him up at McGill and couldn't find a listing for him. So, I called the department that he supposedly headed. They'd never heard of him."

"Wow, that's pretty blatant."

"I wondered what else might be fake here." I turned to the back page with all the references to studies quoted.

Willow moved in closer, squinting at the small type. I enlarged it for her and pointed out the third reference. "Do you see, *The Journal of Mining and Environmental Integrity*? It's an online journal where the authors actually pay to have their articles published."

"Really?"

"With the booming growth of the internet, these questionable journals have popped up in every field. You know the old academic adage 'publish or perish.' For five hundred dollars, you, too, can be published."

Willow looked at me with wonderment. "And here I thought your talent was in the comma placement, not scientific research."

I laughed. "God, no. I'm not a researcher, but I did work long and hard as a fact checker. I also worked with an excellent librarian at Columbia University who clued me in on these types of journals."

Bronte walked over and nuzzled my thigh. I scratched behind her ears, and she settled at my feet. Meanwhile, Willow took out two more beers. If I remembered my count right, this would be number three. I'd been known in the past as "three and out."

As she sat down next to me, I said, "Don't you dare spill on my laptop. I wrecked one with a glass of wine a couple of years ago."

She laughed. "I'll keep it on the floor." She set the beer down on the floor next to her. I did the same.

"Okay, I did a little deeper dive on the journal and found out the editor had the same name as one of the marketing VPs at Racine. I also found out the author of the article, unlike Dr. Emile from McGill, really does exist."

"It could be legitimate research."

I nodded. "Could be, except he's an adjunct professor at a for-profit online university and an employee of Stiller Corporation, which happens to be owned by Racine Mining." Closing my laptop, I sighed. "This is what I was trying to tell Nancy as she prattled on about the minimal effect the mine would have on the environment and on Lake Larissa. But she wouldn't budge."

I thought about that conversation. I usually wasn't what people would label as a pushy New Yorker. But she'd sat with her lips pressed together and a stony expression when I'd asked her to please run my counterpoint. I felt like I was up against one of those right-wing conspiracists who thought I was an Islamist radical. I finally lost it when she said, in a prim little voice, "How would you know, anyway?" It reminded me too much of a schoolyard spat.

I'd raised my voice and pointed at her. "Because Dr. Emile Landreau doesn't exist. They made this all up!" I wanted to leap across the table and strangle her.

Willow must have noticed the expression on my face as I thought about my burning desire to get my hands around her neck. "You okay?"

I took a deep breath and let it out slowly. "I wonder if Nancy had the same effect on other people that she did on me." My voice dropped off. "For a moment, in her office, I really did want to strangle her."

Willow reached over and punched me in the arm. "But you didn't. Did you?"

Startled, I stared at her but saw only amusement in her eyes.

Before she left, she warned again, "Lock your doors, okay?"

I pointed to Bronte. "My bruiser of a guard dog will keep me safe."

She reached down and scratched her behind the ears. "Take care of her, my furry friend."

I watched the taillights of her van disappear down the road. A slight mist rose from the lake in the dusk. I loved to sit on the rock by the water and watch the sun go down, but tonight I stayed in and made sure the front and back door were locked. The woods felt unfriendly, like something dark had invaded them.

Chapter Nine: The Cabin by the Lake

I woke with a start as Bronte yipped in her sleep. A shadowy glow filled the bedroom from the full moon. Bronte snored softly, curled up near my feet.

When I'd first gotten her this spring, Willow had advised that I keep her in a kennel at night. "She'll feel safer there, and you can train her to stay off your bed." Willow wasn't a fan of people sleeping with their pets. "Humans have too many germs. Makes the poor puppies and kitties sick."

Bronte had been abandoned near the Larissa Lodge with a broken leg. Rob nursed her back to health and then, without consulting me, brought her to the cabin.

"This dog will be good for you." Rob was a man of few words.

"I don't want a dog." I really didn't want anyone or anything to rely on me.

My vision of living in the wilderness was solitude. Rob didn't give me much choice—no negotiation, no "just try her for a couple of nights"—he simply left the dog, the kennel, and a leash and drove away.

The dog howled that first night until I let her out of the kennel. She looked at me with those dark eyes that said "I will love you unconditionally." *Oh shit.* After that she slept happily on my bed. It took me a month before I finally confessed to Willow that the dog was sleeping with me.

"Probably beats your ex-husband."

I thought about Andrew and his lovely makeup artist. "No kidding."

While Bronte slept on, I got up and padded to the kitchen. The moon beamed down on the forest, casting long shadows. I stood at the kitchen window and watched the quiet, remembering how spooked I'd been when I first moved up here. All my life, except for those few weeks in the summer as a child, I'd lived with the noise of the city. Even in the quietest hours of the night, the city was alive with cars and trucks and sirens. Here the only noise deep in the night came from the chirp of the crickets or the crescendo of the cicadas.

I made a cup of tea and sat down with my phone. I replayed Nancy's voicemail several times, noting that the message had come in at 10:36 p.m. When did they think she was killed? I closed my eyes and pictured the whiteboard in the sheriff's office with information about Nancy. Did it have a time of death? As I focused on the board, I saw the deputy's scrawling handwriting. Then I saw *TOD 12-4am*. I'd watched enough television crime shows to know they could pinpoint it pretty well by the temperature of the liver. So, she'd called me shortly before she died. I shuddered. I really should have told the sheriff. If they had her cell phone, they'd be able to trace a call to me fairly easily.

As best as I could, I transcribed the call onto my computer. "Jamie, something... Need to tell you... Important...may be in danger."

If the sheriff needed my phone, at least I would still have the message. Why? I wasn't sure, except my New York experience told me to write down everything and date stamp it.

I composed an email to myself with the transcribed text and a summary of everything I could think of that had happened regarding Nancy, including the rock with the note on it and LeRoy's menacing behavior. I pressed send.

I would call the sheriff tomorrow and, if necessary, surrender my phone. Hopefully, this would be the end of it, and I could go back to drumming up business from people who aspired to become bodice-ripping romance writers.

Exhausted, I crawled back in bed, expecting to toss and turn with full-moon fever. Instead, I sank into a deep sleep. When I woke up, the bedroom was drenched in sun and Bronte barked frantically as someone knocked at the door.

"Coming," I called, blinking hard. The bedside clock read 9:12 a.m.

Throwing on a robe, I scrambled to the kitchen door, where Bronte stood with her teeth bared. I hoped it wasn't LeRoy. Pulling my robe tight across my chest, I opened the door to the UPS driver in her brown shorts and shirt.

"Bronte, sit."

She sat, which surprised me.

The driver handed me a large manila envelope and had me sign for it. "Boy, you're not easy to find down the end of this road."

"How did you find me?"

She pointed back toward the lodge. "The receptionist told me."

"Oh." I remembered Leroy's words, "I know where you live." Apparently, Mavis, the receptionist did too.

After she'd driven away, I let Bronte out and put the pot on for coffee. The package, I assumed, was from another one of my clients, a retired engineer who wrote a memoir about his wife. When he first contacted me, I was reluctant to take on his project because memoir wasn't my strong suit. I decided, though, that if I could do a bodice-ripper, I could do a memoir. Writing was writing, and a paycheck was food on the table.

I set the package aside. When the coffee was ready, I toasted an English muffin and took my breakfast out to the porch. The porch was a small screened-in room to the right of the front door. Facing the lake, it provided a cool place on hot summer nights when the breeze from the west whispered through the screens. It also saved me from being eaten by the mosquitoes.

Through the trees, I noted a hint of red in the sky. Dad used to tell me, "Red sky in the morning, sailors take warning. Red sky at night, sailors delight." Living in the big city, sky color wasn't a big deal to me. Here in the woods, it probably meant a storm front moving in. The old thermometer nailed onto a tree in front of the porch already read 82 degrees. The air, like yesterday, was still and heavy, as if we sat in the middle of the tropics. Climate change? If so, it was even more crucial to protect the environment.

Bronte scratched at the porch door. When I let her in, she was wet from a dip in the lake. Instead of jumping into the part of the water that was clean, she liked to wade through the stagnant swampy area that bordered my little beach.

"Phew. You smell like green muck."

She happily shook herself off before I could grab her collar and tug her back outside. Now we both smelled like swamp. Considering everything, I hoped this would be the worst I'd have to deal with today.

The shower refreshed me. In the fogged bathroom mirror, I noted I had filled out a little since moving to the lake. The past year had been so fraught with drama, I'd lost my appetite and dropped below 100 pounds. At five foot three and almost 110 pounds, I looked far less like an anorexic waif than I had in the spring.

I toweled my short, dark hair as I stepped into the main room of the cabin. The cabin was a simple, basic structure and, in some ways, similar to the apartments I grew up in. It consisted of a large room with windows overlooking the lake. The kitchen along one wall opened to a living area. A hallway led to the only downstairs bedroom and the bathroom. A steep staircase—more like a ladder—on the other side of the fieldstone fireplace, led up to the loft. I'd spent my childhood summers sleeping in the loft under the A-line of the roof. Right now, the loft was the home to the meager possessions I'd brought from New York—most still packed in cardboard boxes.

When I arrived in the spring, the cabin needed significant repairs, including a new well and septic system. I'd spent the majority of my inheritance, including most of Dad's life insurance policy, to make the place habitable, especially for the winter.

Rob had done much of the work, and as I sat in the kitchen looking at the cabinets and the countertops, I appreciated his craftsmanship. I sipped my coffee and mused about my life here, isolated down a rough and rutted road, surrounded by trees and the quiet of the forest. Why had I chosen to come here?

The easiest answer was to get away from the New York Police Department and the special task force that mistook me, Jamie Forest, for a person named Jamie Forester. What a difference an "er" could make. I learned later that Jamie Forester was male and Hispanic. He brought in drugs, most recently tainted opioids that were killing people. A year and a half ago, the special task force wanted him and wanted him ASAP.

I, of course, knew none of this. In the midst of working through my divorce, I'd changed my name back from Jamie Nother to Forest. Again, unbeknownst to me, a clerical error put an "er" in my name and thus I became Jamie Forester.

Now, as I sat in my kitchen admiring Rob's cabinetry, I wondered if that was the only reason I'd fled. Yes, after my incarceration I was spooked every time I saw a police car and every time I saw a transit cop. Would they think I was the notorious Jamie Forester? Yes, I'd gotten nowhere in filing a complaint with the police department about my treatment. Yes, New York City had suddenly become a darker more dangerous place for me.

But maybe it was something else. Maybe a restlessness and a sense that my life was going nowhere. Maybe I was being pursued by more ghosts than those of the "special task force." Maybe, even as a child, when I closed my eyes and thought about home, the first image I had was the sitting rock by Lake Larissa.

"What do you think?" I looked at Bronte, who still smelled of swamp.

Bronte wasn't much of a conversationalist.

My phone rang. It was another unknown name. I debated and finally answered. "Hello?"

"Jamie Forest?" The male voice was raspy. A chill shot down my spine. Was this one of those callers who whispered and hung up?

"Yes?"

He hesitated. "Um…this is Phil Sessions. Um…the owner of the *Killdeer Times*."

Oh please. Don't ask me about Nancy. "Yes?"

"Would you be willing to come into town and talk?"

The heat and humidity closed in on me. Sweat dripped down my arm. He wanted to interview me about her death. What would I say? "I don't know what you need from me."

He hesitated a moment. "I've heard you do editing. I need a temporary editor until we can…uh fill the position."

I stared at the phone. Was he offering me a job?

Outside grew suddenly dark and a low rumble of thunder filled the air.

Chapter Ten: Phil Sessions and the *Times*

I hesitated long enough that Phil asked, "Are you still there? Did we get cut off?"

"Sorry." I cleared my throat. "You took me by surprise. How did you find out about me?"

Another pause. Meanwhile, another low rumble of thunder. "Well, I…uh…Jilly down at the paper suggested it."

"Jilly?"

"She's the office manager and bookkeeper. She said you'd written something she thought was quite good and she'd heard you did freelance editing." He paused. "That's what you do, right? Freelance editing?"

I pictured the *Times* office and remembered a short, stocky woman behind the desk. Probably the same person who told LeRoy about my discussion with Nancy.

"Yes, I do. You'll have to excuse me, but I wasn't expecting this call. You know that the sheriff is…ah looking at me?" How could I say I was a suspect in Nancy's murder?

"Hmm…yes. You didn't do it, did you? If so, I probably couldn't use you."

Damn, did he have a sense of humor? Another low rumble of thunder followed by the weak yellow of distant lightning.

I thought about my vanishing bank account and decided, what the heck. "Okay, I'll meet with you. But no commitment. I have a few errands in town, so I can stop by this afternoon. And, by the way, the answer is no, I didn't do it."

"That's a relief on both issues." He sounded like he was chuckling. "The paper needs to be ready by tomorrow to get to the printer. I'll be around all day and probably all night."

The paper came out on Thursday, which meant Phil was in a crunch to get it out. I had some sympathy for deadlines, having worked them most of my adult life.

Once I set the phone down, I looked at Bronte. "Do I really want to do this?"

Bronte lifted her head and yawned but had no words of wisdom for me.

While I tidied up the kitchen, a boom of thunder sent Bronte scrambling to hide under the bed. With a flash of lightning, the heavens opened up, and, for about ten minutes, the wind whipped through the trees and the rain pelted the roof, obscuring my view of the lake. As suddenly as it had started, it stopped, and the sun came out, glinting off the wet grass and leaves.

Bronte emerged from under the bed, wagging her tail.

"You're a coward, you know that?"

It felt cool and fresh as I slid behind the wheel of the Subaru. The brief storm had washed away the heavy air. As my tires splashed through puddles in the driveway, I rolled down my window and breathed in the scents of the wet pine needles. The only thing that marred my trip down the driveway was a cacophony of crows in front of an overgrown entrance to the driveway of an abandoned property between my cabin and the lodge. The crows were picking at something dead in front of the barbed wire fence with its faded *No Trespassing* sign. I don't know why, but I always felt a sense of evil when I went by the sign.

"Stop it, Jamie," I said aloud. "It's just some crows and something dead." My words didn't lessen my feeling that something bad had happened on that property.

After I'd passed the birds, my mood lightened until I thought about what I was up to in town. My first stop would be the sheriff's office. If he took my phone, I'd need to go to the drug store and see if they had a cheap phone with a calling card. Then I'd have to make sure my contact list was backed up and I could get internet access. The list seemed endless enough that I almost talked myself into keeping the voicemail to myself. Almost.

Steam rose off the pavement as the water evaporated in the sun. The drive into Killdeer felt like a contradiction, the mist rising from the road and the harsh sunlight bearing down from the clear blue skies. I also felt like a contradiction. Here I was volunteering to possibly lose my life-line phone and perhaps get arrested in the process. And if I didn't get arrested, I was going to take the place of the woman LeRoy Pruitt thought I'd strangled.

I parked on the street across from the *Times* office. No one was gathered at the door today. An old sedan, its fenders rusted and its muffler dragging on the pavement, clattered down the street as the driver accelerated. It reminded me of the constant noise in front of my Queens apartment.

When I opened the door to the sheriff's office, I expected to hear the hum of activity. However, the room was empty, except for the receptionist. Down the hallway, though, several voices rose, and I felt a buzz of excitement in the air. Something must have happened.

The receptionist looked at me. "Yes?"

If I was the prime suspect, I thought she would have at least reacted. For a very brief moment, I felt disappointed. "I'd like to see Sheriff Fowler. I have some information for him."

She frowned, pressing her lips together. "He's pretty busy right now."

My first inclination was to take this as my cue to flee. If he was too busy, then what I had must not be that important. Instead, I stood a little taller and forced myself to say in a louder voice. "I really need to see him."

She sighed and motioned to a plastic chair sitting against the wall. "I'll see if he has a few minutes."

I sat down and noted that the whiteboard had been turned around so I couldn't see what was on it. While I waited, I thought about what I would say about the voicemail. Would I lie and say I'd just discovered it? Would he take it as evidence that I hadn't been home when the call came through? Once he'd heard it, would I advise him to look at Racine Mining?

I was jolted out of my thoughts when LeRoy emerged from one of the rooms in the back. I didn't like the smirk on his face, and I steeled myself to tell him I would only talk with his boss. Except, after a leering look toward me, he settled into a chair at a desk and ignored me.

When the sheriff finally emerged almost thirty minutes later, he motioned for me to come to his office. As I walked by LeRoy, I could have sworn he put his foot out to trip me. I stumbled enough that he had to grab my arm. "Whoa. You been drinking?" He said it loud enough that the receptionist turned around to look.

I jerked away, wishing a swarm of deer flies would come in and take chunks of flesh out of his face.

Rick pointed to the same chair I'd sat in yesterday. This time he stood, leaning against the door with his arms folded. He appeared even more exhausted than yesterday, with a drawn expression and deeper circles under his eyes. "What can I do for you?"

I took my cell phone out of my bag. "I got a voicemail from Nancy Bywater on Sunday night. I had my phone off, so I didn't hear it until much later, but it might be evidence."

Rick gave me a tolerant look. I realized he'd probably been bombarded with "evidence" and tipsters. He nodded.

I played the message. He listened but didn't react.

"Do you want me to play it again?"

"No need. I heard it."

After all this, he didn't want it?

"Really?" I fought off a totally irrational urge to plead my case and say, *of course it's relevant. It's the clue that will solve the murder.*

"We have someone in custody, and we're pretty confident we have the right person."

"Oh." I was taken aback. "So soon?"

A deputy who wasn't LeRoy approached the door. "We have him in the interview room if you'd like to join us."

He stood up straight, put his hands together, and cracked his knuckles. "As you can see, I'm pretty busy here. If you would agree not to erase that voicemail in case, for some reason, we need it, I think we're done."

"I...I could give you a transcript if that would help." Why was I persisting on this?

He nodded. "Sounds good."

As he walked me out of the office, I glanced down the hallway to see a tall, thin young man with shoulder-length dark hair in handcuffs being led to one of the side rooms. For a moment, he turned to me, and I could see he was Native American like Rob. His large brown eyes were wide, and he looked both scared and haunted.

Why would a kid who couldn't be more than twenty strangle Nancy? I walked out into the fresh air that smelled like newly mown grass and wondered if they had the wrong person.

Chapter Eleven: The Press Conference

This felt all wrong, and I didn't know why.

"Hey," a voice called from the side parking lot.

I turned.

Jim Monroe closed the door to his cruiser. "How are the tires?"

"Doing as well as can be expected."

He wrinkled his brow before he broke out in a smile. "Glad to hear it."

When he reached the door to the sheriff's office, I took a step toward him. "I hear they caught someone." I figured he might know something about it.

"That's what I hear."

I guessed he wasn't going to gossip to me. "That's a relief."

We stood facing each other. I didn't know what else to say to him. "Well, I've got to go." I turned abruptly and walked quickly down the sidewalk.

The whole encounter reminded me of junior high school and how tongue-tied I'd get around boys. Heat rose up from my neck. What I didn't need right now was a boyfriend, especially one in law enforcement. What had Willow said about him? He had a live-in girlfriend. I was off the hook.

Phil from the *Times* turned out to be someone who didn't tie up my tongue. He looked to be in his mid-fifties and overweight, with silver gray hair and a sparkle to his eyes. As soon as I walked into the office and saw him standing at a giant desk laughing with Jilly, I felt at ease.

He beckoned me in. "You must be Jamie. Glad you could come." He turned to Jilly. "I assume you two have met?"

I immediately tensed up, expecting Jilly would throw me an icy look that said "you fought with Nancy." Instead, she too, smiled. "Not really. But heard you."

I cleared my throat. "I...you...must have been in the office when I came in to talk with Nancy."

"No disrespect for the dead, but Nancy was wrong not to listen to you." She turned back to her work.

Phil and I sat down at the desk that used to belong to Nancy. I noted a cardboard box shoved in the corner that had some of her personal effects, including a coffee mug, a photo, a cheap wood carving of a deer, and the fact sheet put out by Racine.

Phil cleared his throat. "In case you're wondering who I am, I own this paper and several others. I generally don't get involved in the day-to-day work." He folded his hands on the desk. "Been there, done that. Drank too much, had the required heart attack, and now I try to take it easy and let the money roll in."

Behind me, Jilly snickered. "That's why you have that condo on a private island in the Caribbean, right?"

He grinned at her. "I might could afford it if I didn't have to pay the help. You'd better watch it."

I realized as I watched the banter that this was something I missed once I went from a regular job to freelancing. Freelance gigs gave me independence but also isolation, which I thought I needed and which ended up being a problem when I was stuck behind bars in the Queens holding cell with no one to call.

Phil leaned forward. "Here's the deal. I need a temporary editor until I can find a replacement. Usually I get them pretty fresh out of college and turn them over to my regular staff to break in. But it's mid-summer, and I doubt I'll find someone, at least someone who knows how to put a sentence together, for at least a month."

I'd walked in with my guard up, ready to say no, but as he talked, I thought, well, maybe. Small town newspaper editor? What would Andrew Mr. Right Digestion think of that?

He named a salary that was paltry but more than I was making in my business. "And, a bonus if you increase circulation and revenues by ten percent." Again, the grin.

"Pah! Don't listen to him. No chance of that happening." Jilly shook her head.

"Let me think about it." Did I really want to commit to this?

"Offer's good until Friday. Then I'm turning the operation over to one of my other overtaxed, underpaid editors." He chuckled. "You wouldn't want that to happen, would you? Be responsible for burning out an aspiring young journalist?"

I put up my hand to stop him. "I don't have any experience running a newspaper. My job in New York was fact checking and copyediting. My degree is in nineteenth century female poets, not journalism." I hesitated. "And you know they questioned me about Nancy's death. People might think I was after her job."

Jilly laughed out loud. "Honestly, Nancy would have strangled herself to get out of this job."

Phil sent Jilly a genuine shocked expression before clearing his throat. "Seriously, I could use the help."

We were interrupted by the phone. He picked it up. *"Killdeer Times."* He listened for a few moments before hanging up. "Here's your chance to try it out. That was the sheriff's office. He's holding a press conference in ten minutes regarding an arrest in Nancy's death."

The room was suddenly quiet. I pictured the tall, terrified young man, and knew I had to find out more. "I'll go if you come with me. I'm not sure Killdeer is quite ready to see me running the town newspaper." I remembered the guy in the pickup truck yelling "Killer."

Phil grabbed a steno pad and pen. "Let's go find out what they know."

As he slipped the pen into his shirt pocket, I smiled to myself. I could easily record the conference with my phone—no need for paper and pen. What decade was he living in?

Unlike the White House press conferences, this one was held in a small conference room in the county courthouse. Only ten people, besides the sheriff, LeRoy, and two other deputies, were present. Rick wasn't interested in publicity and had called the briefing so hastily the local television station from Duluth couldn't get there in time. Besides the two of us, the mayor of Killdeer, several county board members, a reporter from the Killdeer radio station, and Jim Monroe were the only attendees.

Phil and I sat in the front row while Rick read a statement. He stood in front of us like a fifth grader who had to give a book report. Public speaking wasn't one of the sheriff's strong suits.

"I have a statement to read and then will briefly answer questions." He began, reading in a monotone, not looking at his audience. "In the matter of Nancy Bywater's death, we have detained a suspect pending formal charges. Thanks to a tip from a concerned citizen, we were able to apprehend him, along with some of Ms. Bywater's possessions. We are providing no further details at this time."

Phil immediately raised his hand. "Can you tell us more about the person you have in custody?"

Rick shook his head, but Phil persisted with an engaging smile. "Well, maybe some general information? Male or female? Age? Where he or she came from?"

Rick shifted uncomfortably before he cleared his throat. "I...uh can tell you the suspect is a male in his early twenties."

I didn't even raise my hand, just blurted out. "Is he connected to Ms. Bywater—friend, relative, employee?"

"I can't give out that information."

Rick put his hands up as people around me murmured. "You will get more complete information in due time. Thank you."

As we filed out of the courthouse, Phil said, "I'll give the sheriff credit. That was one of the least informative press conferences I've ever seen."

I'd never actually been to one, but I agreed. "Something isn't right here." I kept my voice low, noting LeRoy was lurking close by.

Jim Monroe joined us with a nod to Phil. "That was quick."

"You mean the press conference or the arrest?"

"Both."

I wanted to ask him if he knew more, but LeRoy jogged up to us.

"Good police work, huh?"

Phil glanced sideways at him. "Your arrest?"

LeRoy's lips twitched, but he said nothing.

Anger built in me, and my cheeks burned. "I guess that means I'm no longer your prime suspect?"

Before he could respond, Jim interrupted. "Hey, LeRoy, I have some questions for you." He stepped to the side and motioned LeRoy to follow him.

As they walked away, a shiver ran through me remembering how he pressed me up against the counter yesterday.

We were a half block away from the courthouse when Blaine greeted us. "I hear the sheriff had some news."

Phil's shoulders stiffened. He smiled at Blaine, but I saw no amusement in his eyes. "It would appear they have caught the killer."

"Very good." Blaine turned to me. "And you went to the news conference?"

"I'm considering helping out at the *Times* until Phil can get a new editor. I thought I'd tag along."

Phil cleared his throat. "Uh, yes. I'll be looking for an editor, of course."

I sensed tension between the two. Behind Blaine's friendly smile was something else. Anger? Confusion? Fear?

We stood in an uncomfortable silence for a few seconds until Blaine said, "Well, good. I have business to attend to. Never a dull moment."

As soon as he walked away, Phil relaxed.

"Do you two have a problem?"

"Oh, no. Nothing like that." Phil's voice dropped off as he picked up the pace. "We need to get back to work. Got a paper to get out."

Inwardly, I shrugged. It was none of my business.

Chapter Twelve: The Loonfeather

J ust before we reached the *Times* office, I noticed a Native American woman walking with her two children.

A little tow-haired boy of about six approached them and asked in a loud voice, "Are you Indians?"

The little boy's mother quickly pulled him away with a "Shush. That's not polite."

I watched the little scene and thought about New York and the array of skin colors and languages that were simply part of the landscape. Turning to Phil, I asked, "What's the scoop around here about how the community tolerates…uh…diversity?" I wasn't sure whether it was okay to use the term "Indian" anymore.

"If you're talking about African-Americans, we don't see many. If we do, they're usually tourists and it's no big deal."

"What about the Indians?"

"Why do you ask?" Phil seemed distracted. Apparently, he hadn't witnessed the little boy's question.

I told him about seeing the handcuffed young man in the sheriff's office. "He was clearly Native American."

"Oh?"

Before we reached the office, I asked the question that was nagging at me. "Do you think he will get a fair investigation and trial?"

Phil stopped, and his expression was serious. "I honestly don't know. We have some great people in this community, but we also have an old-guard base that are frankly some of the most intolerant people I've ever met."

"How about the sheriff? Will he be fair?"

Phil walked in without answering, and, for a moment, that cold, moldy holding cell in Queens flashed through my head. No one who hadn't committed a terrible crime should have to experience that kind of treatment.

For the next hour, Phil showed me what they did to get the paper ready to send to the print shop. I watched him, feeling totally out of my element. What did I know about creating headlines, page design, weekly newspaper content, or online versions of the paper? I knew about poems and wordsmithing and how to research whether a codpiece existed in King Arthur's time.

Phil finally looked at me after working on the paste up of the articles. "Need a break? Let's go get a beer." He motioned to Jilly. "Want to join us?"

She shook her head. "I've got teenagers. I need to get home and shoo them out of the house. I'm sure they've been on their phones playing games since they got up at noon." She made a tsking sound. "The smartphone must have been invented by Voldemort for an evil takeover of the world."

Considering the recent mess with our national election, I had to agree. Electronic media had certainly changed the landscape. I imagined it had changed things for small-town papers as well.

We walked down the block to the Loonfeather, a combination bar and grill. Inside, it was cool and dark. The bar had an old-timey feel to it, with oak woodwork and a genuine brass rail. There was even a dart board in the back room. We sat at a table near the window, where the blinds had been pulled tight against the glare of the sun. I ordered a tap IPA and Phil had a diet Coke with a lemon.

When it came, he held it up in a toast. "Here's hoping you take my offer."

We clinked glasses. "Not sure yet, unless I can devote a page or so every week to poetry."

Phil laughed. "That would definitely increase the circulation."

As we were toasting, the door opened, and LeRoy walked in. He was still in uniform and swaggered in a way that looked both menacing and dumb. He glanced at us with his perpetual smirk and sat down at the bar.

I leaned close to Phil. "I don't trust him."

"Neither does half the community. He's like Trump—his base loves him, some despise him, and the rest of us shrug him off as a dope."

I had to admit Phil was growing on me. "So, what's your story? Did you grow up around here?"

"Nope. I Actually grew up in Chicago. Used to come here with my dad and uncles to fish and camp when I was a teenager. Went to journalism school at Northwestern and did a summer internship at the *Killdeer Times*." He laughed. "The editor of the *Times* was in his sixties and spent most of his time here." He pointed to the bar. "I ended up running the paper that summer, and when I graduated, the editor retired, and I got the job. I've been around here ever since."

"But you don't edit the paper anymore?"

He finished his Diet Coke and signaled the bartender for another. "After a few years, I bought the paper, and then I bought several more. Small-town newspapers don't make a person wealthy, but they pay their own way. If nothing else, they're the only place for all the county legal business—a consistent source of revenue."

I'd read a recent article about how small newspapers were on the decline leaving many communities without a source of local news. I was about to ask Phil about it when the door to the bar opened.

The man who walked in sat next to LeRoy. I recognized him right away as Donald Pruitt, the pickup truck driver who'd called me a "killer" before roaring away. Without pointing to him, I said quietly, "That guy that sat next to LeRoy must be his base."

"Definitely good old boys." He leaned over the table toward me. "I think the Pruitts must have some kind of hold over Rick Fowler. No one in their right mind would have hired LeRoy as a deputy."

"If I take the job, I'll make sure my investigative reporter gets right on it."

Phil's expression turned serious. "Careful around them."

The bartender brought another Coke for Phil, while I nursed my beer. I wanted to know more about the ambience of the community regarding the Native Americans. For a community so close to the reservation, I'd seen very few of them in town, other than Norma, Rob, and Willow.

The young man in the sheriff's office had struck a nerve—that strange feeling I had every once in a while—like I knew something that I didn't. "I don't get the sense the Indians and the whites are comfortable together."

"It's a little complicated. The tribes have been here a lot longer than the whites. But, of course, we moved on in and made a mess out of their culture. Hauled their kids off to boarding schools and left them with the poorest land."

I finished my beer. "My mother was half Ojibwe. I think that's how I ended up with the cabin and the twenty acres it sits on. I don't know much else about my family."

"You're lucky to have such a prime piece of property. A lot of the Native Americans fell prey to developers and speculators, who swept in at a time when people were poor and hungry and bought up the land for a pittance. At least that's the rumor about how Larissa Lodge got started."

"Really?"

"I'm told that Blaine McConnell's grandfather Mitchell was a wheeler-dealer and a scoundrel. A number of families got burned by him. Old history, though. Larissa Lodge has been good for the community. At least the white community. Some of the Native people, though, say he built it on sacred ground."

"I wonder if that means my cabin is also on sacred ground."

Phil shrugged. "Back in the seventies, before my time, when the American Indian Movement was active, there were some demonstrations and some dust-ups. It wasn't reported well in the *Killdeer Times*, of course, because small-town newspapers were all about supporting local businesses. And the biggest local business around here was tourism after the mine closed."

"What happened?"

"Some talk at the time was that Mitchell dug up an old burial ground, dumped the remains in the lake, and built the lodge over it." He leaned back. "Of course, when this came out, Mitchell quickly denied it."

I shivered, thinking about what an insult that must have been. "Wow. Imagine if that had been turned around and someone dug up the Lutheran Cemetery and did the same to great-grandma and great-grandpa."

At the bar, LeRoy and his cousin snickered. I looked up to see him sneering at me. My dad used to tell me, "Ignore the ignorant. They aren't worth your time." But I had a bad feeling about both LeRoy and his cousin that I couldn't shake.

"The rumor about the unburying of the dead led to some legal action that went nowhere," Phil continued. "It hurt the lodge business for a couple of years and then a savvy PR person turned around and claimed the lodge was haunted."

"And people came back?"

"In droves until we had a recession. The lodge has had its ups and downs, but it looks like Blaine is keeping it afloat. His father, Mickey, nearly lost the property some years back. He was more interested in young women than running a resort, they say."

I thought about the main lodge, constructed of local timber, with its large stone fireplace and intricate hanging quilts. I hated to think that all those souls resting in the ground had been dug up and dumped to make that building.

Phil looked at his watch. "Oops. Sorry. I still have work to do. When do you think you'll have an answer for me?"

"You really want to hire me sight unseen?"

He laughed. "You're looking at a desperate man. Besides, I read that article you wrote for the *New York Times*. You have talent."

Something inside me sank. Clearly, I was known to the community. I wanted to get away from that chapter in my life.

As we walked out, I made sure to keep Phil between LeRoy and me. I didn't want to be grabbed, and I didn't want a scene. Before we could get by them, I was overwhelmed by the scent of Drakkar Noir. I knew it well because it had been Andrew's favorite cologne. I cringed and wondered if LeRoy's cousin had dumped a bottle of it in his lap. The cologne didn't fit with the Neanderthal look of the Pruitts.

Jim walked through the doorway wearing his trooper's uniform about the time I sneezed from the cologne.

His face crinkled into a smile. "Bless you. We meet once again."

"Seems to be the case." I sniffled.

LeRoy and his cousin turned around to look at Jim. "Hey, buddy, you're late." LeRoy patted the empty stool next to him.

Quickly, I said, "Nice seeing you. Gotta dash." When had I ever said "dash" in my entire life? I was flustered, not only because Jim flustered me but because it looked like he was meeting LeRoy.

Once outside, Phil asked. "Is Jim a friend of yours?"

"Not really. I had a flat tire yesterday and he helped me."

"Oh?" he raised his eyebrows.

I didn't say anything more as we walked toward the *Times* office.

Outside the office, Phil shook my hand and said, "Call me tomorrow."

Once I'd climbed into my hot car, I sat for a moment, knowing I'd say yes to Phil and not knowing exactly why. I also knew this would turn my life upside down once again.

Chapter Thirteen: Willow

I sat on the screened porch that evening and watched the sun go down. The water rippled in a slight breeze, and two loons called out. Normally, I would bask in their sound, but Phil's story about the burial ground had upset me. It was as if someone had disturbed the sanctity of the lake. Were some of my ancestors unburied by Blaine's grandfather?

Bronte flopped down by my feet and sighed. I looked at her and wondered why I couldn't relax like a dog and let the cares of the day go. My brain was on hyperdrive, moving from Nancy to the young man arrested to the newspaper offer to the men who tore me from my bed in Queens to the rock thrown at my cabin. But something else, too, was hanging over me. I sipped on iced tea and tried to empty my head.

Sometimes, when I had the "head race," I could calm down by doing a Jamie version of meditation. In it, I closed my eyes and envisioned a white wall. The wall surrounded me and held out all the raging thoughts. I took in several deep breaths and concentrated on relaxing my shoulders, my arms, my fingers, and, remarkably, my tongue. Slowly, I allowed one subject in. This time, to my surprise, the subject that inched its way through the white wall wasn't Nancy, the burial ground, or the paper. It was Willow.

Since my evening with Willow, something so small, like a pebble in a shoe, had bothered me. As I sat with my head bowed and the evening call of the crickets in the background, it came to me.

Yesterday, when I'd talked about LeRoy, she'd changed the subject. Not only had she changed the subject, but her expression had been closed, like this wasn't a topic to bring up. Had she been hurt in some way by him?

She'd said she had history with him. Was there a connection? What did I really know about Willow?

We bonded the last summer I'd come with Mom and Dad when I was ten. She was a scrappy kid who was always in the water. I noticed her from the first time I waded into Lake Larissa under the watchful eye of Blaine, the lifeguard. While I struggled to learn to dog paddle, she swam like she'd been born into the water. The summer kids ignored me like they knew from the beginning I wasn't one of them. But they gathered around Willow, especially the boys, splashing and yelling and showing off.

It wasn't as if I was afraid of the water. I wasn't. But I wasn't a good swimmer. Even though our apartment complex in Manhattan had a gym and a pool, Dad was too busy to take me, and Mom was sinking into her own dark world. I watched the summer kids play and wished I could be part of it.

One day, Willow looked back and noticed me for the first time. She had long, shining dark hair and, at ten, a body that looked both slender and powerful. Her skin had turned a deep tan and glistened from the water. She swam back to me. "Why don't you come out any farther?"

I shrugged and mumbled, "Not a good swimmer."

She assessed me in the same way I'd later seen her assess a horse. "I'll teach you."

We became fast friends after that, even though I never went to her house and she never came to mine. She told me her mother was sick, too, when I finally confided that my mother didn't act like other mothers. I felt a kinship with her that I never felt again with any other friends. Over the years, though, Willow and I lost touch.

I reached down and patted Bronte on the head. "What is it about Willow that bothers me?"

Bronte sat up and put her head on my lap.

In one of those odd coincidences, after the nightmare arrest and after I'd published the article about it, Willow had found me. The article, with my email address at the end, garnered a surprising response, both positive and negative. The negative ones accused me of being a "cop-hating liberal" and were often filled with obscene and violent threats. One even said that if he saw me on the street, he would shoot me because he knew I was guilty. After a couple of days of reading through the emails, I quit because I found them both threatening and upsetting.

Willow's email arrived several weeks after the onrush had died down. She simply said, "Are you the Jamie Forest I used to swim with in Lake Larissa? If so, I miss your dog paddle."

I emailed her right back and, after a couple of weeks of correspondence, we talked on the phone. She filled me in on the state of the cabin. "Old Sadie from the realty company is about to retire. I think she's let things go. You might want to consider selling it before it's not worth anything."

For me, the cabin was that place that would always be there. When I was locked in the cell in Queens, scared and as alone as I'd ever felt, I'd closed my eyes and thought of the cabin by the lake. It calmed me enough to get me through those wretched hours.

"I don't think I'm ready to sell."

After a long pause, Willow said, "Well then, why don't you come out here and see for yourself?"

That was about the time the condo board where I sublet my apartment decided I was too notorious and wanted me out. With their eviction letter in hand, I thought, hell, why not move permanently?

When I arrived with the U-Haul and all my possessions, I found the cabin needed work but was habitable. More importantly, I found the rock by the water, where I used to sit as a kid, was still there and still a place of peace.

"Willow rescued me from that nasty crowded city I was living in," I told Bronte. Then I laughed. Perhaps, instead of worrying about Willow, I needed to worry a little more about myself. Here I was sitting in the dark, trying to explain things to a dog who loved nothing more than to roll in dead fish.

My thoughts were abruptly interrupted when Bronte lifted her head and growled. "What is it?" I thought immediately about the rock and the threat. As quietly as possible, I tugged her collar and pulled her into the cabin. Both the front door and the side door were open.

I closed and locked them, noting the cheap locks would have made me a laughing stock in New York.

Bronte continued to growl. I listened for sounds of a car coming down my road but heard nothing. In fact, I heard nothing but Bronte's growling, not even the chorus of crickets or the gentle shimmer of the pines in the night breeze. It was an eerie, dead quiet, as if the wilderness knew something dark lurked in the woods.

A chill overtook me. Anyone or anything who visited at this hour was bad news.

Chapter Fourteen: Something in the Woods

T hey came quietly and stealthily, not through the woods but in a canoe. I didn't see them because I concentrated on peering through the side window at the darkened road. I didn't hear them because they were good, and I wasn't looking in the right direction.

But Bronte did, bless her heart. Bronte ran to the front door that faced the lake and began to bark. In the midst of her wild barking, a BB gun blast pierced the air. followed by another and another. At least two shooters were outside. The front window next to the little porch shattered.

I took a dive to the floor. Bronte continued to bark and leap at the front door. The shooting stopped for a moment. Were they reloading? Keeping low, I squat-walked to the front door and grabbed Bronte by the collar. "It's okay, girl," I whispered, double checking the door was locked.

In the quiet, I stayed low and ran for the back door. Just as I checked the lock, the guns started again. This time they shot out the kitchen window. One of the BBs caught the light above the sink, and the cabin was thrown into darkness. The only light that remained came from the green digital clock on the microwave.

Bronte suddenly quieted as if the darkness spooked her. Instead of barking, she whimpered. For a moment, I feared she'd been hit by glass or a BB.

"Come on, girl," I whispered to her.

She found her way to me still whimpering.

"Are you hurt?"

She was shivering.

My heart pounded as I pulled her close to me. "We have to get out of here, okay?"

For a few moments, it was deadly quiet. Phone. I needed to find my phone to call for help, and then we would make a sprint for my car. I heard low voices and a tittering noise followed by, "Got 'em." Would they shoot again? How long would it take for them to circle around to the back? My car was parked about ten feet from the side door. Maybe I could make it with a serious dash.

I patted Bronte and told her to stay as I crawled to the kitchen table. I was sure I'd left my phone in my bag when I'd come home. The bag was hanging over one of the chairs. As my eyes adjusted, I made out the outline of the bag.

"Please, please, be there." I reached the bag, noting again how quiet it had become. "Come on! Come on!" My hand dug through the contents of the bag. I felt my wallet, my keys, a glasses case, and several pens but no phone.

"Dammit! Where is it?" Then I remembered. I'd had it with me on the porch as I watched the sunset.

The kitchen felt like it was closing in on me. They would get me, whoever they were. I couldn't outrun them. They were probably at the door right now, waiting for me, hoping I would panic and try to get to my car. If they were trying to scare me, they had succeeded.

I had a quick image of the holding cell in Queens and how, after several hours of sitting on the hard bench breathing in the foul air of cheap perfume, unwashed bodies, and mold, I'd suddenly been engulfed with a sense of panic. I couldn't breathe. I stood up, hoping the air was fresher and cleaner. My feet in the paper booties they'd given me were wet from something I'd stepped in. As I gasped for air, the woman with the wine breath and the stiff straw hair had patted me on the back and said, "Take a deep breath, dearie. You'll be okay. But next time watch where you step." At that point, in that miserable cell with fourteen other miserable women, I simply started to laugh. What else could I do?

I took a deep breath, noting how clear and pure the air was in my cabin. I squat-walked into the living room. "Come on, let's set ourselves down on the couch and wait. You can even sit in my lap." It would do me no good to panic.

We settled onto the couch and I counted the minutes. What was taking them so long? I expected they would go for more windows or try to break in. Bronte stretched out with her paws and head on my lap. I scratched behind her ears and listened as she made almost silent sighing noises. We must have sat like that for about five minutes before something occurred to me.

Bronte wasn't barking or whining or making anything but contented noises. If the shooters were still out there, she would still be excited—barking, growling, whining, or something.

"They're gone, aren't they?"

Gently, I pushed her off and stood up. The only sound I heard was a slight breeze whispering through the broken windows. Stepping gingerly over the shattered glass on the floor, I opened the front door. Again, only the breeze and the resurging rise of the crickets. Bronte padded after me. In the distance, it sounded like a canoe glided through the water. Whoever they were, they'd come by the lake, not the dark SUV of the other day.

"Careful, girl. Watch for the glass."

An almost full moon shed soft light onto the porch. My phone sat next to the rocking chair. I grabbed it and hurried back into the cabin, thankful I had shoes on.

With shaking hands, I pressed the phone and it lit up. The 911 operator answered immediately. "Nine-one-one, what's your emergency?"

"Someone shot at my windows." My voice shook as I tried to explain the gun blasts and the broken windows.

"Ma'am, are they still shooting?"

"No. I think they're gone."

"Stay locked inside. I'm dispatching help now."

I debated whether to wait or to make a run for the car and drive away.

Meanwhile, the 911 dispatcher kept talking to me, kept asking me questions. "Please stay on the line."

People talked about how long it seemed to be after an emergency call before help arrived. Even if it was only seconds, it seemed like hours. In my case, I heard a vehicle crunching down the gravel driveway within minutes. Was it help or was it the shooter?

Bronte started to growl, a low, quiet rumble as the vehicle neared.

I peered out the window, only to see headlights shining on my car. "Oh shit!" In the light I saw they had shot out the front tires. God, my insurance was about to go up.

Bronte's growl rose from a rumble to a bark and a growl. I grabbed her by the collar as her barking grew. She went nuts when someone banged on the door.

"Jamie, are you all right?"

It was a male voice.

"Are you in there?"

Blaine, the lifeguard, the state senator, was at my door.

"Wait." I tugged Bronte back into the bedroom and closed the door. The last thing I needed was her attacking Blaine.

When I opened the door, I must have looked shell-shocked because he put his arms around me and held me tight, slowly walking me back into the cabin.

In that irrational moment, I noticed he smelled minty, like he'd just rinsed with mouthwash. In that irrational moment, minty was the best thing I'd smelled all day.

"Are you all right?"

"I don't know." Reluctantly, I pulled away from him, and suddenly I was shivering with the same fear I'd had in that cell. "Someone shot at my windows."

In the bedroom, Bronte barked with fury as she scratched at the door.

Chapter Fifteen: Invitation to Stay at the Lodge

With Blaine next to me, I felt stronger and safer. I turned on the overhead kitchen light and saw the shards of shattered glass. "Christ," he surveyed it. "What a mess."

"They got my car, too." I pointed outside.

"Geez, what were they after?"

I took a deep, shuddering breath, and his arms were around me again. "I don't know." My words came out as a whisper.

I might have stayed enfolded in his warmth, but the 911 operator was nearly shouting into my phone. I'd forgotten about her. "Ma'am, are you all right?"

Blaine took the phone from me. He had an officious tone as he spoke. "I'm with her now. She'll be fine."

"Who is this?"

"Blaine McConnell from the lodge down the road. I'll wait with her until the sheriff arrives. Thank you." I thought it strange that he then clicked "end" on the call. He must have read my expression. "No need to keep the dispatcher tied up."

As I looked at him, it occurred to me he wasn't connected with the 911 system. How did he know to come? A momentary cold crept up the back of my neck as my shoulders stiffened.

He smiled at me. "Ah, you are wondering why I am here."

"It's been a strange night."

"I heard the rifle shots. We've had some problems with vandalism at the lodge, and they sounded like they came from your direction. I heard about the rock incident and worried about you."

Bronte had settled to periodic woofs by this time. I guess she thought I was safe. "Can I let my poor dog out? It's been a hard night for her."

His eyes sparkled with amusement. I remembered, as a ten-year-old, watching him up in his lifeguard chair with that same kind of expression. But this wasn't a night to be amused.

As I turned to the bedroom to let Bronte out, she started barking once again. Behind me, I thought I heard a little disgusted sigh from Blaine, but when I turned, he was looking at the door. The sheriff had arrived. God, I hoped it wouldn't be LeRoy, but if it was, at least Blaine was here. I hoped LeRoy was dead drunk at the Loonfeather with his cousin and Jim Monroe.

To my relief, Rick Fowler stepped out of the cruiser. I met him at the door. He looked a little confused when Blaine walked up behind me. "Ms. Forest, I heard you had some trouble here."

I opened the door and pointed to the mess of glass. "It hasn't been a quiet night."

I told him how the shots came from the lakeside of the cabin. And, no, I hadn't heard anyone approach but I thought I heard the sound of a canoe on the water when the shooting was over.

Blaine added, "I heard the shots and thought I should check them out. I've had windows in my cabins shot out before." A look passed between the two of them that I could not read.

Rick used his flashlight to inspect the outside of the cabin. I stayed inside with Blaine. "I don't understand why anyone would shoot at my cabin."

Bronte stood by me, watching Blaine. When he leaned over to give her a pat on the head, she growled and bared her teeth.

"Bronte, be nice."

She continued to growl.

Blaine pulled his hand back. "I haven't met too many dogs who don't like me. You know, dog bites are a political hazard."

I glared at Bronte, who backed up a little. "She's probably just spooked by everything that's happened." I grabbed her collar and hauled her back into the bedroom.

The sheriff came back, holding a couple of spent BBs. "Looks like an old-fashioned BB gun. Half the kids in this county own one. Any idea why someone would want to shoot at your cabin?"

Barring LeRoy, I couldn't think of a soul. I decided it wouldn't be a good idea to name his deputy. "I know a few people thought I...um...might have something to do with Nancy's death. Perhaps they were out to scare me."

From Rick's expression, I could see he was skeptical. Not only skeptical, but completely exhausted. Vandalism at a lake cabin was probably a low priority for him right now.

Blaine spoke in a way that sounded like he was talking to himself. "The concern about Racine and the environment has brought up some old wounds, things that happened before my time."

"Could this have anything to do with the Lady Slipper Trail and our opposition to the mine?"

Rick shrugged. "Could just be kids."

I felt dismissed, as if someone shattering my windows and shooting out my tires was no big deal. It hardly helped restore any faith I had in law enforcement.

Blaine rested his hand lightly on my shoulder, as if to reassure me. "Rick, this worries me. I know you're up to your eyeballs in this murder investigation, but I want to make sure your office follows up."

I said "thanks" under my breath. At least someone was trying to help.

Rick took a few photos of the damage and asked me to come in the next day to file a report. He pointed at the two broken windows. "Better get someone to board those up for the time being. Otherwise, you might end up with a raccoon in your cabin."

Boarding up broken windows wasn't in my skillset, but I thought a few garbage bags tacked over them would suffice for the night. And hopefully, it wouldn't rain.

"Listen, Jamie. Why don't you stay at the lodge tonight? We've got a few open rooms. I'll get one of my staff to patch up the windows until you can have them replaced."

I was grateful for his offer and his presence, and I was tempted. Plus, I remembered I'd heard he was newly divorced. For a second, I let my imagination get away with me.

The sheriff looked at me as if he was waiting for an answer. I might have wanted Blaine to be glued to my hip right now, but I needed to gut this one out. I tried not to show how scared I really was.

"Thanks, I appreciate the offer, but I need to stay here with my poor dog." I pointed to the broken windows. "I'll cover them with plastic tonight and get them fixed tomorrow."

Along with my car—damn it.

"Are you sure?" Blaine glanced at the couch. "I could stay."

I was seriously thinking I would say yes when Willow's van came roaring up the drive.

She marched in. "What the hell?"

Bronte howled from the bedroom, and I suddenly felt like my cabin, my retreat from society, had become Grand Central Station.

Chapter Sixteen: The Abandoned Baby

"How?" I looked at her in confusion. "How did you know?"

She glanced at Blaine. "The desk clerk at the lodge told me. Blaine and I were planning to meet tonight about the trail."

"Oh." Why, I wondered, would they meet without the rest of the group? Before I could ask, Blaine's cell phone rang, and he excused himself.

Willow bent down and picked up a shard of glass. She held it up to me. "Been shooting out your windows?"

"I guess I got a little bored. Too quiet here."

She walked over to where I kept my broom and dustpan and began sweeping up the mess. After one panful, she set the broom down and studied me with a concerned expression. "Jamie, this isn't good. Someone doesn't like you. I don't think you should stay here tonight."

I glanced out the door, where Blaine stood talking on his cell. "Blaine has already offered a room at the inn. I'm going to stay. Bronte will protect me."

I didn't add, *Bronte will growl and keep me up all night.* But whoever was trying to scare me, I didn't want to give in to them.

"Then, I'll stay." The set to Willow's mouth said don't argue.

I shrugged. "My couch is your couch."

Blaine and Sheriff Rick came back in at the same time.

Rick massaged the small of his back. "I don't think whoever did this will be back."

How could he be sure?

"If he comes back…" Willow made a fist. "We'll be ready."

The sheriff nodded and left, still massaging his back.

"He looks like he's in pain," I said.

"Old football injury from high school." Blaine nodded at the door. "I remember the game. He got tackled by one of the reservation boys. It did some real damage."

I wondered for a moment if I detected a hint of disparagement when he said the word "reservation." But when I looked at Blaine, he had a benign smile.

After a brief discussion of what I would have to do to get my windows repaired, Blaine left. As soon as he was out the door, I let Bronte out. She bounded over to Willow and greeted her with a thumping tail and tiny little yips.

Neither of us said much as we worked to clean up the broken glass and cover the windows with garbage bags. When we were done, it was close to midnight. I surveyed the room with the dark plastic over the windows.

"Who would do this?"

Willow shrugged. "I've seen worse."

"What do you mean?"

She nodded at the refrigerator. "Let's have a beer and I'll tell you about life around here when both your parents are First Nation."

I opened my last two bottles of beer, and we both settled onto the couch. "And?"

"You remember my dad."

"Of course. He was the groundskeeper for the lodge."

Caleb Grey was darker than Willow and wore his hair in a thick braid down his back, like Rob. He had a graceful walk like the swing of the aspens in a summer breeze. At least that's how I saw it as a ten-year-old.

"He was full-blooded Ojibwe, but he grew up in Killdeer." She gazed at the unbroken window as if trying to pick out the right words. "People don't always live happily together."

"You mean he was harassed?"

"I think today we'd call it bullied. From the time he was little." She paused. "It left a huge scar on him. He drank too much, got into fights, and managed to do everything a stereotyped Indian would do. My mom was a good influence on him for a while. After they got me, he settled down."

I noted a catch in her voice. "What do you mean 'after they got me'?"

Willow sighed. "A bit of a troubled story. I'm glad, at least, that I don't remember the earliest part of it."

I waited.

"My birth mother, whoever she was, abandoned me, of all places, at the lodge. Left me in a box there with a note that said 'I can't take care of her.' I was wrapped in a blanket and she'd tucked a little dream catcher in the box."

"Wow." I pictured a baby in a cardboard box.

"The blanket and the dreamcatcher were all they had to identify her. I don't think anyone tried hard to find her. They put me in a foster home right away. I'm told the foster parents were a really nice white couple who wanted to adopt me. But so many Native American babies were going to white families that back in the seventies, congress passed an act to ensure Indian kids were placed with Indian families. When I was three, they took me from that family and placed me with the Greys."

"Wow, that must have been traumatic." I knew about the Native American Welfare Act because I'd once fact checked an article about a Native American birth father who wanted custody of his son. The white foster parents who had cared for the son since birth were trying to adopt him. It was messy for everyone, and especially for the little boy.

Willow shrugged. "I hardly remember it, except I had a stuffed bunny I wouldn't give up until I was almost a teenager. Slept with it every night and called it Mama. I think the foster mother must have given it to me."

I was at a loss to say anything. The cliché slipped right out of my mouth. "I had no idea."

Willow shifted a little on the couch and smiled. "Well, it's not exactly like I go up to people and say, 'Hi, I'm Willow Grey your veterinarian. Do you want to hear my adoption story?'"

"I guess that might scare customers away."

Willow smiled. "The summer I met you, Mom got sick. We didn't know it, but she had heart damage from rheumatic fever when she was a kid. Rez kids didn't always get the best medical treatment. It didn't take long before she could hardly leave the house because she was so weak. I came home one day to find she'd fallen and couldn't get up." She reached down in a distracted way and patted Bronte.

I thought about my mother and how she'd changed. She fell a lot, too, but it wasn't from a bad heart. It was more like her brain didn't connect with her legs. My dad cared for her in the best way he could.

"God, that must have been hard. I didn't have a clue of what you were going through as a kid."

Willow smiled wistfully. "Until she got so bad, she was a great mom. Well, maybe an okay mom. Dad was another story. Good when he was sober and a mean son of a bitch when he was drunk."

My mother was never what you'd call maternal. She was an artist who often lived in her own world. Dad mothered me more than she had.

"Anyway, the sicker she got, the more he drank." She paused. "Once he was driving drunk and hit someone."

I shook my head. "That sounds bad."

Willow shrugged. "At least he didn't kill anyone. But he spent a couple of nights in jail. Kids teased me at school about it and once someone left a dead cat on our doorstep. When I was twelve, I got up one morning to find they'd broken into the car and dumped dead fish and fish guts all over the seats."

I stared at her. "Why?"

Willow frowned. "He was a drunken Indian. They spray painted the windshield with 'chief mobile.'"

"Chief mobile?"

"A common insult because a lot of the tribe around here were poor and drove old broken-down cars. I was entering my teens and was so embarrassed by him."

"Did you report it?"

Her laugh was more of a snigger. "Oh sure. My poor mom, who could barely talk by then, called Sheriff Fowler. He said he'd get right on it." She finished her beer. "Those were different times. People were pissed off that Native Americans were demanding their treaty rights. It was pretty ugly

81

here for a while."

The broken glass suddenly seemed minor compared to living with a dying mother and a drunken dad.

Bronte stood up and padded to the door. I set my beer on the coffee table and listened through the screen before I let her out.

Willow's voice tightened as if in pain. "I learned early how to stand up to bullies, and I found my support with animals. Helped a neighbor with her horses and learned a lot about what large animals need." She paused, sighing. "There's more, but it's late, and I don't want to get into it."

"Does it have to do with LeRoy Pruitt?"

Willow didn't reply. We sat in silence until Bronte yipped to be let in. She sat at my feet with an expectant expression. It was time to go to bed.

I stood and stretched. "I think all that harassment because of your heritage was awful, but I don't get what it has to do with me."

"You're part Indian, and some people in town know it. They don't like that you own this cabin."

"What?" Her words left me with my mouth hanging open.

Willow also stood and stretched. "It's a long story. Good for another time. Let's just say you should keep your dog with you when you're out on the trail by yourself."

"Seriously?" She made it sound like I was safer walking through Central Park at two in the morning than hiking the Lady Slipper Trail during the day.

I wanted to know more, but Willow was already on the way to the bathroom. "Do you have a spare toothbrush?" she called behind her.

"In the linen closet."

"Thanks. By the way, a couple of years ago I did a DNA test. Turns out I'm not as Native American as I thought. Go figure."

"What?"

"Good night, Jamie."

Once I settled into bed with Bronte comfortably beside me, I wondered what Willow meant about more to the story of the bullying. Was she a victim of sexual assault? I'd once read it was a significant problem for Native

American girls. And what about the DNA test?

"Oh well," I whispered to Bronte. "She'll tell me when she's ready."

With all that had happened that day, I fully expected to toss and turn and not sleep. Instead, I was out almost immediately and didn't wake up until the predawn hours of the morning when Bronte's growl jarred me from a sound sleep.

Chapter Seventeen: Sounds in the Loft

I opened my eyes as Bronte jumped off the bed. She paced by the closed bedroom door and whined.

"What is it?" Haze seeped through the bedroom window, casting deep shadows in the room. I sat up, blinking the sleep out of my eyes, as Bronte continued to pace.

"Did you hear something?" I thought about Willow on the couch and the crappy locks I had on my doors. Would someone try to break in after all the destruction of last night?

"Shush," I whispered to Bronte. I held my breath and listened. Something thudded above me. Or was that my heart speeding up? Again, a soft thud and then the creaking of floorboards. If this was a break-in, the loft would be an odd place to go. I wondered if an animal had gotten in through the broken window. Just what I needed, a raccoon in my loft.

The cabin was built so the front was open to the beamed roof. The back half was a loft that, at one time, had been my bedroom. It had a skylight that, over the years, had pulled away from the frame, leaking onto the floorboards of the loft. Rob had replaced the light as well as the floorboards. When I first moved back, the mice had taken over the space, leaving droppings everywhere. Rob patched up the open places. Now the traps I'd baited with peanut butter were untouched.

All the loft contained were the boxes that made up my earthly goods—boxes I hadn't unpacked and boxes with the only family memorabilia I had left after Dad died.

As quietly as possible, I slipped out of bed and into my moccasins. The last thing I wanted to do was startle Willow after she'd been kind enough to sleep on the couch. "You stay," I commanded to Bronte. I did not want a dog-raccoon fight in my loft.

Bronte whined but sat down. I closed the door behind me and crept out into the living area. With the dark plastic over the windows, the room was nothing more than murky shadows.

"Willow?" I whispered. The blanket and pillow were on the couch, but Willow was gone. "Willow?" This time I said it louder. In the loft, I heard a small thump. Where was she?

As I walked toward the loft, my foot caught on the edge of the rug beneath the coffee table and I stumbled, banging my knee against the edge of the table.

"Damn it!" This time I didn't whisper.

Suddenly, something snapped and Willow cried out, "Shit!" from above me.

I walked through the dark to the loft ladder, rubbing my knee. "Willow, are you up there?"

Willow's flashlight shown in my face, blinding me. I lifted my hand to shade my eyes.

"Oops, sorry." Willow turned the flashlight away.

"What are you doing?"

Willow backed down the ladder, still holding the flashlight. Its beam waggled back and forth in the darkened living area. Once on the main floor, she faced me. I couldn't see her face clearly, but the tone of her voice was sheepish.

"Uh, I woke up and thought I heard a noise." She pointed to the loft. "I was worried it might be a raccoon. They can make a mess, you know."

"And you decided to explore it alone in the dark?"

Willow looked at the floor with a shrug. "Stupid, of course, but I didn't want to wake you." She laughed. "You never told me you had a bunch of mouse traps up there."

Something struck me as odd in her tone, but I let it go.

"Not many people explore my loft in the middle of the night."

"Hey," she touched my shoulder. "Sorry. I didn't want you to worry when I heard the noise..." Her voice trailed off.

The digital clock on the microwave said it was 4:45 a.m. I should have been kinder. I should have asked more questions about the noise. But my body felt heavy and tired. I sighed. "Let's talk about this in the morning. I'm going back to bed." I headed to the bedroom without another word.

The next time I opened my eyes it was to a sloppy kiss from Bronte. She wagged her tail and jumped off the bed. With a couple of woofs, she scratched at the door.

"Want to go out?"

Sunlight eased through the window in my bedroom. Fortunately, the shooters had only hit the windows that faced the lake and my bedroom window facing the woods remained intact. The bedside clock registered 8:00 a.m. Outside, I heard voices, including Willow's. Pulling on a pair of shorts and a T-shirt, I let Bronte out. She bounded to the front door like she was greeting her best friend.

Rob stood outside with his carpenter's apron on. Bronte nearly knocked him over in her enthusiasm.

"Good morning." I blinked away the sleep-blur from my eyes.

He nodded toward the broken windows. "Hear you had some problems last night."

One thing about this community, bad news travelled fast.

"You fix windows?"

"Don't want the rain to get in and spoil my beautiful cabinets."

Willow came out from behind the van, looking cool and refreshed, even though she'd just spent the night rooting through my loft and sleeping on my lumpy couch.

"You called him?"

She smiled. "I wanted the windows fixed ASAP so I wouldn't have to spend another night on the couch."

"Or in my loft."

I expected her to laugh at my comment, but she said nothing, so I let it go. Clearly, she was embarrassed about being up there and hurt by my reaction.

"I'll make some coffee." As I turned to go back in the cabin, another vehicle bumped down the driveway. It left a dusty haze in its wake.

I shaded my eyes, squinting because I hadn't put my contacts in. "Who is that?"

For a moment, I feared it would be LeRoy. Instead, it was a dirty pickup truck that looked like it hadn't been washed since it rolled off the assembly line.

It pulled up behind Rob's van. When the driver switched the ignition off, the engine still sputtered for a few seconds.

Jim Monroe stepped out. "So you had visitors last night."

"What? Was it on *CNN Headline News?*"

He grinned and then his expression turned serious as he noted the broken windows and the sagging tires on my Subaru.

Willow leaned over and whispered, "A new boyfriend?" I wanted to belt her one, but instead, I shrugged her off.

"Join the party. I'm going to make coffee."

Bronte, who had been out in the woods, came galloping back. She stopped when she saw Jim, sniffed, and warily ambled toward him.

He squatted down with his hand out. "You're a fine-looking dog."

She allowed him to give her a scratch behind the ears before she heard a squirrel and went chasing back to the woods.

"Nice dog," he commented.

I wasn't sure what to say, so I turned and stepped back into the cabin to make coffee.

While I was grinding the beans, Willow stuck her head in. "Sorry, I have patients to see. I'll check in with you later."

I was still edgy with her over the loft thing, but I shook it off. She was a friend and was only trying to help. "Thanks. And thanks for staying the night. Sorry I was so testy in the middle of the night."

She smiled. "What are friends for if you can't piss them off every once in a while?"

"Good point."

By the time the coffee was brewed, and I was fully dressed, Rob and Jim were working together on the broken glass from the two frames. They both wore thick gloves and safety goggles.

I watched while they scraped the putty around the glass and pulled out the metal pieces holding it in.

"What a mess."

Rob grunted as the two of them lifted out a large piece of glass. "We'll get this measured and I'll have them cut new panes at the hardware store."

They worked for another half hour, clearing out both windows. Meanwhile, I played Suzy Homemaker and baked some biscuits to go with the coffee. Didn't the women always keep their men fed back in the pioneer days?

It reminded me of Andrew and how I used to cook for him at odd hours because of his auditions and little acting jobs. He never reciprocated when I was under deadline with the magazines. In fact, sometimes I'd get back to our Queens apartment after midnight and he'd be sitting around waiting to be fed. Even Bronte wasn't that demanding about food.

When the two men were done, I invited them in. They sat, drinking coffee and making small talk about household repairs. It was such an ordinary scene, midmorning coffee with Bronte silently begging at Rob's feet. It should have been comforting—all the people who had shown up to help me. I should have been relieved I had friends to call on. Back in the holding cell in Queens, I'd been at a loss as to what to do with my one phone call—if I was allowed one. With Dad gone, Andrew was my only close option. Would he come?

As these thoughts reverberated through my brain, I suddenly felt chilled from the back of my neck on down. The sound of the bullets shattering the glass banged behind my eyes. For a moment, the room, with its warm aroma of coffee and biscuits, closed in on me. My chest felt heavy, like I couldn't get a deep breath.

I stood, barely able to talk. "Excuse me." In the bathroom, tears poured down my cheeks as I gasped to catch my breath. What was this? Some kind of a breakdown? Was I turning into my mother, who once hid in the closet of our Manhattan apartment for an entire day saying the air everywhere else was filled with poisoned gas?

I wasn't much of a crier. In fact, Dad used to call me the stoic in the family. Sitting on the edge of the bathtub, hugging a towel, I tried to make the noise in my head go away. This was one of those moments, one of those flashes of the real world. Someone had tried to hurt me, and my response was to be angry with Willow for investigating a noise in my loft. What was wrong with me?

Rob knocked on the bathroom door. "You all right in there?"

"Fine. Just reacted to the coffee, I guess." Splashing cold water on my face, I wiped away the tears. Time to face the world again and time to find out why Jim Monroe had suddenly shown up.

As I walked into the kitchen, Rob and Jim were engaged in a serious discussion. They kept their voices low, as if to protect me.

"I wonder if this has to do with the murder? Maybe the word didn't get out to some of the yahoos around here they'd caught that kid." Rob brushed a biscuit crumb off his lap.

Jim slowly shook his head. "Could be something else."

I stepped in. "What could be something else?" I stood near Rob with my arms folded.

Jim wrinkled his brow. "Just trying to figure out why someone would want to shoot out your windows."

I decided to make light of it. "They probably wanted to scare me off so they could buy the cabin, tear it down, and build a lakeside mansion."

Did Jim wince?

"Sure," Rob snorted. "No doubt one of those dot-com millionaires who likes to fish." He looked at his watch. "I have to run. Got a sick dog back at the clinic who needs my attention."

I sat down with Jim as Rob headed out the door.

"He's a good friend," Jim commented.

Friends. That was why I moved to the Northwoods.

Chapter Eighteen: The Windows

We sat in an uncomfortable silence, the only sounds the hiss of the coffee maker and the rhythmic thump of Bronte's tail on the wooden floor.

I broke the impasse. "I saw you yesterday at the Loonfeather with LeRoy."

"Oh?"

"Friend of yours?"

He reached down and scratched Bronte. She reciprocated by licking his hand.

It was clear he didn't want to talk about LeRoy. I set my mug on the table and tried to frame my words in a way that didn't sound suspicious. "I'm curious. What brought you out here today?"

He sat up straight and stretched his arms over his head. "I stopped at the lodge this morning for breakfast. Blaine told me about the shots and the windows. Thought I could be of help."

Was he lying? I couldn't tell, but he wasn't meeting my gaze.

"Well, thank you. I appreciate it."

He pushed his chair back and stood. "Guess I'll be on my way. I'll call Toby and let him know you'll need new tires. Don't let him charge you too much."

How would I know what was too much? I almost asked, but I didn't want to get into a conversation about tires with him. I wanted him to leave. Or so I thought. Jim Monroe was a complication in my life I didn't need.

I walked him out to his pickup truck. The summer sun was achingly bright in the spots not shaded by the trees. It would be another hot day.

Close up, his truck looked even worse than when I'd first seen it. It was dented and the wheel-wells were caked with mud. The back was filled with wood. "That poor vehicle needs a bath."

"Guess I'll have to drive her into the lake one of these days."

I laughed, but it felt forced. "Wouldn't hurt. Or you might try the carwash in town."

"Nah. The mud keeps it from rusting in the winter."

I couldn't tell if he was serious or making fun of me.

I changed the subject. "Have you heard any more about the kid they arrested?"

His face was in the shadow of the big pine that stood outside the side of my cabin. I couldn't read his expression, but I noticed how his back tensed up. Jim Monroe knew more about the arrest than he was saying.

"Nope." His tone was abrupt enough I drew back.

Before he climbed into the truck, he turned to me with a serious expression. "Be careful. Things around here might not be as they seem."

I didn't know how to reply to that, so I simply waved and turned back to the cabin.

My solitude lasted no more than an hour when Toby's tow truck rattled down the drive. At the rate the traffic was coming to my cabin, I'd have to install a stoplight.

He inspected the damage. "I brought a couple of tires that should do. I'll get them on for you."

As he walked back to his truck, he muttered, "Damn kids and their rifles."

At least they didn't have automatic weapons with bump stocks to make hash out of my cabin—or me.

***

It was early afternoon, with the cabin heating up, when my next visitor arrived. I had just gathered my insurance paperwork together and was in the process of contacting my agent via email when Bronte ran barking to the door.

Blaine knocked and pointed to her. "She's quite a spitfire—that dog of yours. I brought her a leftover T-bone from the kitchen as a peace offering." He held up the bag.

"Bronte, you're a lucky dog. Now be nice." I let him in the door while holding her collar.

He squatted down with the bag so she could sniff it. With one whiff of the meat, she wiggled her butt.

"Friends?"

I let her outside with the bone, and she trotted off to her favorite spot under the pine for her afternoon appetizer.

"That was nice of you to bring her a bone."

"It's a habit I learned pounding the pavement, or in our case, trotting through the fields to campaign. Most dogs can be tamed with a little love and some rare beef." His eyes sparkled.

I invited him in and offered him some iced tea. "I'd suggest a beer, except Willow and I finished the last ones off last night after the excitement."

"Iced tea would be fine." Something in his voice told me he had accepted many offers like this on the campaign trail. It was a compliment to the hostess to accept hospitality and have people remember when it came time to vote.

"So." He settled onto a kitchen chair. "Any word from the sheriff on who created this mess?"

"I'm supposed to go into his office to file a report." I thought about running into LeRoy and did an inward cringe. "Right now, I'm trying to get things pulled together for an insurance claim."

"Anyone been around to help you with the windows yet?"

The iced tea tasted weak and a little sour. It fit my mood. "Rob stopped by this morning. He'll come back later with the new glass." I set the iced tea down and pointed to it. "That's some of the worst iced tea I've ever made. Sorry about that."

Blaine smiled. "Oh, I've had worse. Once, when I was knocking on doors, a lady gave me a plastic cup with lukewarm lemonade. When I looked in it, I found a dead fly."

"She didn't like your politics?"

He half-smiled. "Naw. She was just a slob. Probably hadn't washed dishes in two years."

I laughed, and it felt good. Blaine looked so comfortable and at home at my kitchen table. It reminded me of the early days after Andrew and I had set up housekeeping. Just a silly chat. Too bad those chats turned to arguments that turned to silence.

Outside, a couple of crows made scolding noises, their babies cawing from the nest. They weren't happy Bronte was out in the yard.

"Jim Monroe also stopped in this morning. He helped Rob with the windows."

"Jim? That's a little bit of a surprise. What was he doing in these parts?"

Hadn't he sent Jim? "He said he talked with you at the lodge."

Blaine wrinkled his brow. "I don't recall talking with him this morning. Must have been someone else."

I tensed. What was going on here?

Bronte let out a happy bark as Rob's van rumbled down the road.

I looked out the doorway. "My window repairman has arrived."

Blaine followed me outside as Rob stepped out of his van. "Hi, Rob. I hear you're helping my neighbor." He extended his hand.

Rob shook it, but I noted a slight frown on his normally stoic face. I watched the interaction with curiosity. In general, the Lady Slipper Group saw Blaine as an ally. This reaction struck me as tense. What was Rob holding back? At some point, I'd ask him, but right now I was interested in getting the windows up. The plastic garbage bags made me feel like I lived in a shack.

Blaine didn't offer to help Rob. Instead, he smiled at me. "Glad you're okay. I'll have my security guy at the lodge keep an eye out for armed vandals."

After Blaine left, Rob carried the glass to the make-shift workbench he'd set up in the yard. He showed me how to put in the window glazing compound on the frames. "Once that's on, we'll put the pane in. I'll tap in the glazier's points and you can caulk over them." He held up the little metal triangles.

It felt good to be outside, with a slight breeze cooling the sweat on my arms as I worked. Since I was a city girl, raised in apartments with caretakers to do repair work, I knew nothing about fixing windows.

We worked together in the quiet of the early afternoon, while Bronte gnawed on her T-bone. After the windows were caulked and installed, I invited Rob in for lunch.

"Can you live with an egg sandwich. It's all I have."

"Better than what Brad makes."

I watched him eat while I drank yet another cup of coffee. When he was done, I asked, "What's the deal between you and Blaine? I thought he was one of the good guys."

Rob shrugged, pushed back his chair, and stretched out his long legs. "It's an old story, well before your time."

"Larissa Lodge and how Blaine's grandfather desecrated the ground?"

Rob's eyes turned weary. "Blaine's father, Mickey, wasn't a saint either. Sometimes history comes back to haunt you."

"What do you mean?"

"The McConnells don't have a history of being supportive to the Indians. Let's just say there's some bad blood."

"And Blaine is part of it?"

Rob didn't answer. Instead, he pushed himself out of the chair. "I'll be back in two weeks, once the caulk has dried, to show you how to paint the frame." He smiled. "The city girl needs to learn some basic skills."

"Oh, come on. I think I can figure out how to paint a window frame."

He raised his eyebrows. "We'll see."

His van kicked up dust as it rumbled down the driveway. Bronte joined me to watch it disappear.

"Does he think I'm a complete idiot?"

She nuzzled my leg in reply and turned to the cabin. She wanted to go in and take a nap.

Ah, the life of a dog.

Chapter Nineteen: The Agreement

My insurance agent emailed me the link to the online forms I needed to fill out. The easy-to-use forms weren't easy to use, and after I filled them out and pressed "submit," the computer went into a perpetual rotating circle mode until I had to do a control-alt-delete and start over.

"God damn it!" When the computer booted up again, everything was gone. I checked my watch. It was time to go into town and fill out a report for the sheriff that would be filed and forgotten. I thought wistfully about that hour spent with Rob in the outdoors doing something concrete.

"I hate computers."

Bronte raised her head then settled back down with a sigh. She didn't have to worry about what happened in cyberspace.

My phone rang as I gathered my keys.

"Jamie, this is Phil from the *Times*. Just wondering what you've decided about my offer."

In the midst of all the chaos, I'd forgotten to call him. "Sorry, I had a little excitement here last night."

"I heard."

Of course, he had.

"I'm still mulling it over." Did I really want to take this on? For a moment, I saw my credit card bill with the charges for new tires. Then I saw my student loan statement. Even if insurance came through, I teetered on the financial edge. Whatever possessed me to take out those huge loans for a useless MFA? Who made money writing poetry, anyway?

A red-winged blackbird trilled and something rustled in the undergrowth outside. It reminded me of how much I didn't want to lose this place in the woods.

I cleared my throat. "You sure this is temporary? I can only commit to a couple of weeks."

"A couple of weeks should get me through the crisis."

I shuffled my feet. "How about if we make it official starting on Monday. I have a few projects I need to finish and some damn paperwork to fill out."

The line was quiet. Did I hear an audible sigh?

"Can you at least come in and write up something quick on the arrest? We have about two hours before it goes to the printer. I'd do it except that I'm struggling with the layout software."

"Adobe?"

"Please tell me you know something about it."

"Only the name. Sorry. I should be there in about forty-five minutes."

Bronte trotted over and nuzzled me as if she understood how conflicted I was.

I stroked her back. "It's okay. I'll fill in long enough to pay for the tires and then I'll come home to you full time."

***

Downtown Killdeer was midafternoon quiet. I parked in front of the newspaper office and walked across the street to the sheriff's office. A pile of dead leaves, signaling the beginning of the end of summer, eddied over the pavement. They landed in the gutter and I thought about how that little action fit my mood. I was swirling. I'd been swirling ever since my life was so rudely interrupted by the law, by the divorce, by the death of my father. What I really didn't want to do at this moment was start a new job. I wanted to sit quietly on the rock by the lake with a mug of steaming coffee and renew my spirit.

Nonsense, Dad would say. You're strong and smart. Hiding isn't in your makeup. Except, Dad wasn't around to give me the pep talk.

The sheriff's outer office was deserted. I looked for LeRoy and was relieved to find an empty desk. The receptionist glanced at me and back at her computer screen. This time I noted she had a name plaque. *Vicky, Office Assistant.* I stood at her desk for a few moments while she ignored me.

"You're Vicky, right?" I broke the silence. "I think we've been seeing too much of each other lately."

She scowled at me. "What?" Vicky was old enough that she wore a pair of reading glasses on a chain around her neck. She had a round face, mousy brown hair, and dream catcher dangling earrings.

"Nice earrings. I have one of those on the wall in my bedroom. It doesn't catch much, though."

Vicky frowned, and I realized that she had no idea what I was talking about. I cleared my throat. "Uh...the sheriff said I needed to fill out some forms because of the vandalism at my cabin last night."

"Oh, sure, that was you." She reached into a drawer and pulled out a sheaf of forms. "Just fill them out and bring them in."

"Will I get some kind of report for my insurance company?"

She shrugged. "Sheriff will get to it when he does."

I took the forms. "Do you think I could talk with him for a few minutes?"

"He's on a conference call."

"I need to write up something for the *Times* about the arrest. Could I give him a call a little later?"

"No. He's not giving interviews." She handed me a printed memo. "This is all he has to say right now."

I walked to the door with the papers as LeRoy stepped across the threshold. He stopped, blocking my exit.

"I hear someone shot up your place. Probably thought you were a murderer, leaving your calling card and all." He made a strangling gesture with his hands.

I stared at him. Really, could anyone be this stupid? I was saved from saying anything when the sheriff called from the doorway behind me. "LeRoy, we've got a situation down south I'd like you to look into."

As he passed me, his hand brushed my breast. I knew it was deliberate. I should have walked away. That was what Dad often counselled. "Choose your battles, honey."

I should have gone quietly. Instead, I stared at his back and said, through clenched teeth, "Don't you ever touch me like that again." I was out the door in two strides.

By the time I reached the office of the *Killdeer Times*, I'd cooled off enough to know LeRoy wouldn't forget what I'd said. Especially since I'd called him out in front of his boss.

Phil sat studying the computer screen, muttering to himself. "No. No. That's wrong. Damn program. Why can't I edit this photo?"

I walked over to him. "Need help?"

"Can you fix this?"

"Nope."

"Well, damn it! Neither can I."

Jilly rescued him. "Move over, Phil. I'll take care of it."

While she worked the mouse and the keyboard, Phil motioned me to Nancy's desk. I showed him the press release.

He scanned it. "Can you make it pretty in less than two hundred fifty words?"

It was filled with misspellings and grammatical errors. "Who taught him English?" Maybe LeRoy had written it.

The release said they were holding Joe Pelletier, no permanent address, for Nancy's murder. The motive appeared to be robbery since several of her items were found in the suspect's possession.

To me, it didn't add up. "I don't like this. I saw the kid in the sheriff's office yesterday. He looked scared out of his mind." Something else about Joe Pelletier niggled at the back of my brain, but I couldn't bring it forward.

"Well, maybe you can dig up a little more on him for next week."

Feeling like I was invading someone else's territory, I sat at Nancy's desk and booted up her computer to redo the press release in decent and correct English. Of course, it asked for a password.

"Shoot!" I would have to get the computer changed over to me. Meanwhile, I dug through the desk, looking for the password. Her desk drawer was a jumble of pens, paperclips, Post-its, and pencils. She also had a drawer with hanging files. I skimmed the topics, looking for one that might say *Passwords*.

Honest, people did that. I guessed they thought thieves couldn't read.

She kept a thick file on Racine Mining. The other files looked typical small-town newspaper topics. They included obituaries, town and county board meetings, high school sports, and one simply marked *The Development*. I assumed it referred to the housing development on the south edge of town that Racine promised when the mining operations started. As Norma, my Lady Slipper friend had aptly said, "And then you owe your soul to the company store."

In my quick scan, I found no password.

Jilly turned to me. "Looking for something?"

"I need to get into the computer."

She chuckled. "Try PASSWORD, all caps."

"Now why didn't I think of that?" The computer opened to a messy desktop with a background photo of a wedding party. I recognized Nancy in an outlandish bridesmaid's dress with big, puffy sleeves. The dress appeared to be a throwback from the 1980s.

I quickly wrote up the information on the arrest and sent it to Phil. He read it, nodded, and pasted it in.

"Voila! Now, how do I send this thing to the print shop?"

"I'll tell you if you promise me a raise." Jilly tapped a key and we all laughed in relief.

"Loonfeather, anyone? I'm buying." Phil slid back in his chair.

"Thanks, but again, home to the mopey teenagers. Lord, when will school start again?" Jilly walked back to her desk. "You go. I'll lock up."

For a moment, I thought about Nancy alone in this building while someone grabbed her and strangled the life out of her. I shook it off. The sheriff had the killer, right?

Phil and I sat at the same table by the window. No one was at the bar, but every time the door opened, I looked up, praying it wasn't LeRoy. Maybe whatever mission the sheriff had sent him on would keep him busy until I got out of town.

"You sure you don't want to start tomorrow?" Phil raised his Diet Coke.

I thought about the package the UPS woman in her brown shorts had delivered on Monday. "I've got a manuscript to work on. I told my client I would have it back to him next week." I cringed a little wondering how much work *Love Story to Alma* entailed.

"Do you like freelance editing?"

I considered the question for a few moments. In New York, all my work had been with seasoned professional writers. They knew how to put the words on paper, how to build a story, and how to keep the reader engaged. The bodice rippers and memoirs I now had under contract were by ordinary people, who wanted to tell stories. They weren't the sophisticates or the writers with an MFA pedigree.

"Some of the writing is really good, but most of it is mediocre, at best. I can't shape the work into prize-winning literature or even writing that might sell. But I can make it better. So, I guess I'd have to say, yes, I like what I do."

I wasn't being totally honest. Some of the writing dragged me down. Some of it was hard to slog through. And some of it, memoirs like *Love Story to Alma*, made me crushingly sad. At least, temporarily, I would trade all that in to cover county board meetings and street repairs. Oh, and murder.

I ordered another beer. "Phil, what can you tell me about Nancy? I'm not convinced her death was a random mugging gone wrong." Again, I pictured Joe Pelletier in the hallway of the sheriff's office looking both frightened and haunted. That was what niggled at me. In that brief meeting in the hallway, Joe looked like someone who had given up.

"Well, I hired Nancy two years ago. These days two years is about the expected life span—sorry, wrong word. Expected employment span for young rural newspaper editors. *Killdeer Times* is usually their first job out of college. They get a little experience under them and move on."

In New York, contract fact-checking and copyediting was about the same. We did it until something better came along that offered a regular paycheck and health care benefits.

"But Nancy was different. Older, with more experience in the world. She'd worked PR and marketing for a company in St. Paul and knew how to put out newsletters and press releases. She said she wanted to get away

100

from the madness of the city. And that's why she wanted to come to Killdeer. How could I not hire her?"

The door opened and a couple of tourists walked in with their small children. The server directed them into the dining room.

One of the kids said, "But, Daddy, I wanted to sit at the bar like you do at home."

Dad grumbled and pushed him through the archway.

"I get the sense you didn't like Nancy much."

Phil looked beyond me with an expression I couldn't read. "She could be short, almost combative, which made me wonder if her 'lay off' from her PR job had actually been a pink slip."

"And?"

"Something happened before she came here that she didn't talk about. Jilly gathered from some overheard phone calls it was quite traumatic and involved her family in some way."

"Ex-husband maybe?"

"Possibly. I had the sense it wasn't a pleasant divorce."

What divorce was pleasant? At least with Andrew we didn't have children or much in the line of possessions. Still...

"Do you think the sheriff looked at the ex as a possibility?"

Phil shrugged. "I would assume so, but he isn't saying much about the investigation, is he?"

I finished my beer and set down the bottle. "I should get back to the cabin to make sure no one has shot it up while I've been in town." The half-laugh didn't work well.

Phil expressed his concern. "Hey, be careful. I need you."

Chapter Twenty: Digging on Joe

That evening I sat on the rock by the lake listening to the gentle lap of the water against the shore. Bronte splashed after the stick I threw for her. Her wet fur glowed as she paddled back to me, the dripping stick clamped firmly in her mouth.

Would I have another shooting tonight? It was hard to think that someone might sneak up again with a rifle in this twilight as a mist rose up from the waters. Was it random vandalism or something more sinister?

Bronte dropped the stick next to me and shook herself with the rattling of her collar. The spray of water cooled my bare legs. I picked up the stick and threw it again. Bronte leapt back into the water, unconcerned that every time she brought it back, it ended up in the water again—a never ending task.

Back in New York, before I had Bronte, I used to wonder why people would keep big dogs in their apartments. To me, it was in a dog's nature to roam, not sit all day in a cramped space waiting for a human to take them outside. Now I understood the need for companionship and devotion. Dogs didn't run off with makeup artists and abandon their spouses. Dogs didn't slash tires, and dogs didn't shoot out the windows in your house. Dogs simply greeted you every day with total love and affection.

My thoughts were interrupted by the annoying buzz of a jet ski doing one more lap on the lake before dark. I hated the noise of their engines ripping up the peace that settled on the lake. Lady Slipper Trail was plagued both summer and winter by motorized vehicles, even though it was posted for hiking and skiing only. In the summer, four wheelers dug up the trail, creating huge muddy ruts. In the winter, snowmobiles packed the snow to the frozen ground, leaving dirt and debris on the trail for the cross-country skiers.

As I pictured the waste of the great outdoors, I speculated on what would happen to the trail if Racine got all its permissions and permits. Would the mining operation cut off the springs that fed the lake? Would the slag and waste seep into the ground water and kill the lake? Would the noise of the digging and the noise of the trucks eventually drive me back to the city?

Bronte bounded out of the water, her chocolate fur sleek, her tail wagging. Rather than drop the stick, she took it back to the grassy part of the lawn, hunkered down, and started to tear it apart. At last, the fetching task was finished for her. Time to go in and tackle the love story.

My internet connection depended on the reception at Larissa Lodge. Sometimes, particularly in the evening, when the tourists were settling in to downloading, streaming, and web surfing, I didn't have enough bandwidth to do much. Tonight, as the day faded into twilight, I had a strong signal.

Before opening the package with the manuscript, I sat at the computer and googled "Joe Pelletier Minnesota." I didn't expect to find anything, but an article from the Duluth paper popped up. It was a two-year-old story about a school shooting in Cascade, a town north of here near the Indian Reservation. Two students and one teacher were killed when a fellow student opened fire in the cafeteria. Four more students were injured, including eighteen-year-old Joe Pelletier.

I wondered if it was the same Joe. I looked for a Facebook page but found nothing for Joe. Then I searched for Facebook pages for some of the others who were listed as survivors. I found one for Betsy Latelle. She'd posted a photo in a hospital bed, with a thumbs-up sign. Several kids stood in the background, including Joe Pelletier, the same boy I'd seen in the hallway in the sheriff's office. His arm was in a sling.

I went back to the article and reread it. It appeared the shooter targeted only the students who were Native. It was listed as a possible hate crime. The gunman was a classmate.

Cascade had a local paper, but when I opened it to look for more information, I found only headlines from the most recent issue. Back issues weren't available online. Or if they were, getting to them was beyond my basic data search skills. I'd have to do what I used to do as a fact-checker. Call the source.

I'd tackle it in the morning.

That night, my sleep was interrupted numerous times by rattling noises in the cabin. Bronte slept on, exhausted from her task of retrieving. At one point, I was sure I heard heavy breathing, but when I sat up in bed, the sound disappeared. Dad used to joke that the cabin was haunted, and when I was a child, alone in the loft, I believed it. Strange crying and moaning and sometimes soft singing sounds wafted up through the rafters. As a grown-up, I looked back at the noises I'd heard and realized they came from my mother. Maybe she had nightmares as her brain slowly died. Maybe she tried to sing away the demons that invaded her.

I didn't want to think about my mother right now. It scared me that I was almost her age when she was first diagnosed. Was it something that ran in the family? I had no one to ask because I knew nothing about her family, other than this cabin. Maybe one day I'd rummage through the papers Dad left behind and see if I could find anything about the Clarks of Killdeer.

I finally fell into a deep sleep just before dawn. I woke up to the sound of rain pelting the window and the smell of fresh-washed air. Bronte stood at the door with an anxious wag to her tail.

"Wanna go out, girl? It's raining, you know."

She was a lab. Water didn't bother her. She bounded out the door and into the woods to do her morning business.

George Slatkin's memoir to his wife sat in a neat pile on the kitchen table. I read through the first chapter, chopping through prose so thick with adjectives and adverbs I felt like I was in a literary jungle. He must have opened up his thesaurus and used every synonym he could find for love.

"Listen to this," I said to no one. "Her lusty, amorous, sky-blue eyes with golden sprinkles met mine on a park bench among the quaking aspen trees shedding their summer coat in preparation for the upcoming winter. Her breasts pressed against the tight red sweater as she leaned to me." This sounded more like Florice's redheaded Constance than a tribute to a wife.

I needed to be careful with how I approached the manuscript, knowing he had written it from the heart. I didn't want to be callous and tell him it sounded like a trashy, self-published romance. Yet, I wanted it to be better for his sake and for the memory of his beloved Alma.

I stared at the manuscript with my blue pencil. It was tempting to rewrite the whole thing in simple language like, "We met on a park bench in the autumn of 1981."

Sighing, I put the pencil down and opened the door for Bronte. She came in smelling of wet dog and tracked her muddy paws over the floor.

"At least working temporarily for the *Times*, I won't have to worry about wounding an aspiring writer." I filled her dish with nuggets of dry dog food.

Setting the manuscript aside, I called the *Cascade Journal* to see if they had more information on Joe Pelletier. When the editor, who was listed on the web page as Ellen Hunter, answered, I identified myself. "This is Jamie Forest. I'm filling in on the *Killdeer Times* and wonder if you can answer some questions for me."

Ellen sounded intrigued. *"Killdeer Times?* My god, the editor was just murdered there. Are you all right?"

I appreciated her concern and explained Joe Pelletier had been arrested for the crime. "Can you tell me anything about him? From what I've gleaned, he comes from Cascade and he survived a school shooting."

"Sorry, I'm new, and I wasn't here when it happened. I'm just looking up what we have on it." She was quiet for a moment while she tapped on the keyboard. "Damn. I can't get this thing to work." She covered the phone and called out to someone.

I waited while she had a muffled conversation. When she came back, she said, "I have someone who knows more. I'm going to turn the phone over to her."

Bronte padded over to me and put one muddy wet paw on my lap. Her look said she wanted more to eat.

"No," I whispered. "Not going to turn you into a waddling fat dog."

"Hello?" The voice on the other end sounded young and uncertain.

I identified myself again and asked about Joe.

"Oh, what a sad story. I was there—well, not exactly there. I was in class at the time." She used upspeak, ending her sentence in a question, like so many teenagers.

"What can you tell me about Joe?"

"Oh, God. He was such a nice guy. On the football team and all. But you know he was shot in the shoulder, and it did some bad stuff. Kinda like it paralyzed his arm or something. I heard he had a college scholarship they took back because he couldn't play anymore."

"Really?"

"It was him and his twin brother Frank. They both played and everyone called them 'Double Trouble' but, of course, with what happened to Frank, it all stopped." She said it with the assumption I knew Frank.

"Tell me about Frank."

"Well, you know he was one of the students that was killed. Died right in front of his brother."

Oh God. And now Joe was sitting in our county jail.

"I'm so sorry." I didn't know what else to say.

"Joe kind of disappeared after that. I don't think he graduated. A bunch of the kids from around the reservation stopped coming to school. Like they were scared it would happen again. I heard he started drinking."

"That must have been a bad time for all of you."

"Our school has never been the same. And now it's all about guards and drills to shelter in place. Kids are still jumpy."

No kidding. "What happened to the shooter?"

"Dead and good riddance. Shot himself, they say." She paused, her voice shaking. "And I hope he's burning in hell."

Her name was Kristy and I asked if I could call her again if I had questions. She was agreeable. "I'm just the summer help here at the paper. I go to college in Duluth, but you can email me any time."

Once I ended the call, I sat at the table with the missive to love stacked in front of me and a sense of overwhelming sadness. Nancy dead. Joe a victim of a school shooting and now a murder suspect. What more could I run into?

I picked up the phone and called the *Killdeer Times* office. Jilly answered. "Is Phil around? I really need to talk to him."

"Sorry. He stopped in to make sure the paper got printed and distributed and said he was going to his 'hiding place' with no cell service. That used to mean he was going to his shack on the lake before he quit drinking. Now I don't know where he goes."

I texted him anyway. **Phil, something is really amiss here about boy who was arrested. Need to talk ASAP.**

I reviewed the photo I had in my head from the Facebook page. Joe's right arm had been in a sling and wrapped close to his chest. Had anyone checked Joe to see if he was physically capable of strangulation?

Chapter Twenty-One: Blaine's Response

The rain stopped midmorning about the time I had macheted my way through two more chapters of *Love Story to Alma.* It would have been such a sweet tribute to her if George had stuck to the script of her perfect beauty and his undying admiration. Instead, by chapter three, he was describing in detail his sexual fantasies and how she fulfilled them in his dream life.

"She comes to me at night, naked and wanting, floating seductively through the air heavy with her scent. I am erect and waiting for her to taste me." I read it with growing alarm as the manuscript veered into erotic romance.

I set it down and rubbed the back of my neck. I would have to cancel the contract with him and refund his deposit if this was the theme throughout the book. Another financial hit.

"This isn't turning into a very good week."

Bronte scratched at the door in response and then started to growl. A car splashed up my driveway.

"Now what?" I tensed, hoping it wasn't someone with rocks to throw or rifles to shoot out my windows.

She let out a happy yip when the car door closed. I stood, stretched, and walked to the screen, watching Blaine approach. He had another white doggie bag.

I let him in while Bronte sniffed at the bag and shuffled her feet.

"If that's another T-bone, you're spoiling her. She'll expect one every time she sees you."

"Naw, it's just a dead crow I found on the road." He laughed, opening the bag to let Bronte grab the bone.

I shooed her out the door and offered him coffee and a day-old donut.

He waved away the donut. "I have enough trouble keeping weight off with all the fish fries and goodies when I'm on the campaign trail. Plain coffee will do."

I stacked the manuscript into "read" and "need to read" piles. "So, what brings you here on this rain-washed day?"

He shrugged with a hint of amusement in his eyes. "Just checking to make sure no one took out more windows last night."

I thought about the evening of terror when Bronte and I sat in the dark as glass shattered and the bullets rained. It led me to imagine the horror for Joe as he sat in the cafeteria with his brother and friends. Suddenly, my hand shook, and I almost spilled the coffee.

Blaine reached over and touched my wrist. "Are you okay?"

I took a deep breath. "I thought I was."

"We'll find out who did the shooting. This is a small community, and people talk."

My hand steadied. "That's not it. Or I should say that's not entirely it."

Blaine wrinkled his brow. "What do you mean?"

I told him about Joe and what I'd found out. "That poor kid. I don't believe he killed anyone, and now he's in our jail. Hasn't he had enough tragedy in his short life?"

Blaine put his arms up in surrender. "Hey, I don't know that he didn't do it. The evidence certainly points that way."

"What do you know?"

He shrugged and wouldn't look at me.

"What?"

He cleared his throat. "I'm not supposed to have any information on the investigation, but sometimes things get leaked."

A small wind rattled the aspens and beads of water from the trees plinked on Blaine's car. The clouds parted, and weak sunshine spilled through the kitchen window.

"Let's just say they've got plenty on the boy—including motivation."

"Really, like what?"

"The day before the murder he was seen arguing with Nancy behind the *Times* office. A passerby heard him say something about the money she owed him."

I scratched my head. "Why would she owe him money? And can anyone verify that it was him?"

Blaine shrugged. "Rick's working on it. He's convinced Nancy knew him."

I didn't say it out loud, but my gut told me none of this added up. What was the connection between Nancy and Joe?

"Has Rick looked into the ex-husband?"

"Says he has a good alibi."

"Oh." This added to my gray feeling about this week.

Bronte barked at the door. I opened it to let her in when I saw she still had the bone in her mouth. "Oh, no. You don't bring bones in." I pushed her back out the door. By now, the sun had disappeared once again, and a steady sprinkle fell from the sky.

"You're going to make the poor creature gnaw on her bone in the rain?"

"Yup."

He laughed. "You're a hard woman."

I wished I believed him.

We talked for a little while about the progress of the trail and also about the progress with stopping Racine Mining.

"It's complicated. It will take them a while to get the permits. Maybe by then we'll have something more to use."

I sensed a lack of conviction in his voice. "You sound defeated."

Blaine pushed back his chair. "As I said, it's complicated."

Just like everything else.

I walked him to the door. "You know that Phil has asked me to fill in at the *Times* until he can get a new editor?"

He shot me the boyish smile I remembered from his lifeguard days. "Very little happens that I don't hear about."

"He asked me to find out more about Joe, which is why I have the information about the shooting. Do you think I could get into the jail to talk with Joe?"

At that moment, the clouds once again parted, and the sunshine poured down.

Blaine's face was in the shadow, but I sensed by the way he folded his arms and stepped back that he wasn't comfortable answering my question. "I'd say, better leave well enough alone. Rick will give you what you need as the investigation proceeds."

This wasn't the answer I wanted. In fact, it sounded more like a friendly warning. Still, I persisted. "Do you know if he has a lawyer?"

Blaine sighed. It was less a sigh of weariness and more the kind of sigh my father used to use when he was tired of answering my questions. "I heard they appointed old Clarence Engstrom. He's the only other lawyer in town besides our part-time county attorney."

"Good. At least he has someone looking after him."

"Sure." Blaine turned away without another word.

I felt like I had somehow alienated him.

After he left, I gave *Alma* one more try. In chapter four, he dropped the fantasy and went back to his thesaurus and all the words for love. At this point, I was wishing his dear Alma had used whips and chains on him like he desired in chapter three. Maybe she would have beaten the adverbs and run-on sentences out of him. I picked up my blue pencil and soldiered on.

By early afternoon, the rain clouds had disappeared, leaving behind heat and high humidity. My hands sweated, leaving damp stains on the manuscript. I didn't dare turn on my overhead fan in the kitchen/living room for fear of scattering the increasingly godawful manuscript on the table.

"I need a break. Wanna go for a walk?"

Normally, Bronte would be up and at the door before I finished the word "walk." Today she lifted her head lazily off the floor with a look that said, it's too hot.

"Well then, I'll go by myself. You can stay here and swelter."

Even that didn't rouse Bronte. Until I sprayed myself down with Deep Woods Off. She sniffed and pulled herself up with a sigh. Once I was at the door, she bounded after me as enthusiastic as ever.

"Good dog. It's your job to keep me company."

I had a little walking path from the cabin to the unfinished Lady Slipper Trail that would eventually cut through my property. Once we had it done, the trail would wind through my woods and eventually end up at the lake about one hundred yards from my cabin.

The insects buzzed around me and the ground crunched as I stepped on fallen sticks and pine cones. As silly as it might sound, I felt a connection with the earth here—almost like it provided me with an anchor. The leaves rustled as Bronte trotted ahead. At one point, I stopped and simply listened to the quiet. In New York, we had no quiet ever. If it wasn't trucks and cars and horns, it was the hum of the heating and air-conditioning and the constant roar of airplanes overhead.

I looked up through the canopy of trees and thought about the day I'd come running to this very spot in the woods that last summer with my parents. I'd been splashing around in the lake, trying to skip rocks, when I thought I heard a strange noise coming from the cabin. I crept up to the front door and peeked in through the screen. Mom was pacing in front of Dad and the sound she made was like nothing I'd ever heard before, something like a combination moan mixed in with a high-pitched wail.

She kept saying over and over, "No. No. I can't see my sister. Patty takes and she takes, and she'll kill me."

I was stunned. Who was this sister and why would she kill my mother? Did I have an Aunt Patty?

Dad talked with her quietly, like he was soothing a baby. "She's sorry, and she wants to see you. Please, won't you think about it?"

Mom stopped in front of Dad, pressing her hands into her head like she was in immense pain. "No! No! She lies! She's not sorry." She swayed, and Dad had to guide her to the couch. "We have to get away before she kills me!"

Up 'til then, Mom had had some strange days, but I had never seen her so worked up. It frightened me, like someone else had taken over her soft-spoken voice. I slipped into the woods far enough that I couldn't hear her sobbing anymore. Two days later, we packed up and left. It was the last time my mother ever set foot in the cabin.

Bronte pulled me from my thoughts when she came running back with a stick in her mouth. "So now you wanna play, huh?"

I threw the stick, still thinking about that scene with my parents. I must have had some family here in Minnesota, but Dad never talked about it. His side of the family lived on the East Coast and my aunts and uncles were all much older than him.

Maybe I should have looked harder for family on Mother's side, but deep inside I knew it scared me. What if I found them and it turned out they all had the craziness that took Mom?

"Geez," I said to Bronte as I headed back to the cabin. "I sure know how to depress myself."

When I got back, hot and sticky and smelling of mosquito repellent, I decided to take a dip in the lake to try to shed the oppressive cloud that hung over me. I'd just wrestled my hot sweaty body into a swimming suit when my cell phone pinged with a text. It was from Willow.

How's it going?

I texted back. **Greased up in mosquito dope and off for a swim.**

She replied with a laughing emoji. **Dog paddle with your dog?**

I replied with that special third finger emoji.

Just before I grabbed a towel to head to the lake, my phone pinged again. I expected it to be Willow replying. Instead, it came from a blocked number.

Drop it or else.

The message was followed by a series of skull and crossbones emojis. Could this day get any worse?

Chapter Twenty-Two: Incident on the Lake

I stared at the message and suddenly I wasn't hot anymore. What was going on? And what did they mean? Was it because of the Lady Slipper Trail? Racine Mining? Nancy Bywater? Or did it go back to the lawsuit in New York that was languishing in the judicial system?

After the article came out in the *New York Times Magazine* about my false imprisonment, I was approached by several law firms who wanted to represent me in a suit against the police department. I shunned them all. The last thing I wanted was to relive the horror. But my finances worsened because I found I was afraid to go out, afraid to go to work, afraid of anyone in a police uniform. I finally broke down, took the advice of one of my father's friends, and contacted a lawyer. He filed a suit against the city. The city's insurance company made a low-ball offer to settle—something like $5,000 to cover the damage to my personal property. The law firm representing me decided to go high—somewhere in the millions. Frankly, I didn't care at that point. I probably would have taken the $5,000 and used it to pay off part of my student loan. But they insisted they could get more.

"Is this my punishment for being greedy?" I pointed to the phone while Bronte watched me pace.

Setting the phone on the counter, I wrapped the towel around my waist, and headed for the lake. I needed to clear my head and a dip in the cool waters of Lake Larissa would help.

I wasn't a very strong swimmer, so I tended to stay close to the shore, mainly dog paddling around, making sure my feet could touch bottom. Today, I decided to be a little bolder. The lake was mirror still, with occasional plops as fish jumped or insects landed. I did an awkward crawl out to where I could barely touch bottom, thinking about Blaine's words, "You're a hard lady."

Well, it was time to be hard. Bronte sat on the small sandy beach area watching me and nudging at a stick.

"No," I called to her. "You want me to throw it? You have to come to me!" As if she would actually try to swim out this far.

Behind me, somewhere near the lodge, a powerboat ramped up. The roar of its engine reverberated across the lake, destroying the serenity of the peaceful waters. I ignored it as I paddled further, doing scissor kicks. I was out far enough that the water was now well over my head when Bronte yipped at me, working her way into a full bark. The sound carried like a warning. The boat was coming closer. In fact, the movement of the water reached me as the boat pushed its way toward me.

"What the hell?" I turned to the engine noise and was blinded by the sun. I started toward shore as Bronte's barking grew more frantic. My arms and legs, like they were parts of separate machines, refused to cooperate. The boat gained on me as I splashed and took in a huge mouthful of water. I gasped and sputtered, flailing to keep my head above water. The noise of the boat and the churning of the water combined as if to pull me farther out into the lake.

"Stop!" I yelled, but it came out as a hoarse croak. Couldn't they see me? But the boat was going so fast and kicking up so much wake that I was invisible.

Swimmers had died in Minnesota lakes after drunken boaters hit them. If the boat hit me, it would either knock me unconscious or the propeller would chop me into pieces. I kicked and splashed with noodle arms as I coughed out water and tried to catch my breath. Then, as if an outside force was driving me, just as I felt the boat bear down on me, a voice in my head said, *Dive! Dive, Jamie!* I took a deep breath and kicked downward, pushing myself toward the sandy bottom of the lake.

Under the water, the sound of the boat was muffled but still there like a leviathan pressing down on me. If I could get close enough to the shore, close enough to the shallows, it couldn't follow me. But, as I opened my eyes, I couldn't tell which direction to go. Where was the shore? If I went the wrong way, I would head further into danger, not away from it.

I stopped my frantic paddling and listened. The engine roared, but, above the noise, I heard the high pitch of Bronte's barks. *Swim to Bronte.* My lungs felt like they might explode. If I could just rise up to the air and take a deep breath. But the voice that guided me said, *No. Swim to Bronte.*

I kept swimming. This time, as the air ran out in my lungs, a languid kind of peace came over me. Yes, I could swim all day. Except, I needed to breathe. Instinctively and desperately, I pushed myself upward. I didn't care about the boat that was trying to chop me to pieces. I didn't care about anything but air.

I broke through the water with a gasp, looked around, and saw the boat receding. With what little energy I had left, I floated, paddled, and kicked my way to shore. As I pulled myself out of the lake, Bronte barreled into me with such enthusiasm that she knocked me down.

I was half-sitting, half-lying in the water as Bronte licked my face, her tail caressing my legs, when a man's voice called out. "Hey, are you all right?"

Jim Monroe, in jeans and a black T-shirt, stood at the shore line with a concerned expression.

"Just glad to be alive," I gasped, thinking about the Winston Churchill quote "Nothing in life is so exhilarating as to be shot at without result."

I pulled myself out of the water, still trying to catch my breath.

He handed me the towel. "I heard a speedboat that sounded like it came pretty damn close to shore here."

"No kidding. It almost turned me into hamburger."

His eyes widened. "Are you sure you're okay?"

"I am now." My legs felt rubbery as I walked up the embankment to the cabin.

Jim caught my arm and held me steady. I was so exhausted that I didn't even question why he had shown up when he did. Before entering the cabin, he took a six pack of beer out of the cab of his truck. Holding it up, he smiled. "I brought you a treat."

"Wow. Thanks." Once inside, I pointed to the beer. "Help yourself. I'm going to take a shower."

I stepped into the hot shower as my body shook and my teeth chattered. Twice, I dropped the shampoo bottle. Twice, it clattered into the tub and I prayed he wouldn't break down the door to make sure I was all right.

By the time I toweled myself off, the shivering had quit, and I felt an unnatural relaxation. It reminded me of sitting in the back of a police van, my hands tied with plastic and a blanket draped over my shoulders. It was like the fight had been wrenched from me.

"Oh no," I said to the mirror. "You're not going to relive that."

I took a couple of ibuprofen and eyed the Xanax prescription bottle. I'd brought the anti-anxiety pills with me from New York with a vow I wouldn't ever get scared or worked up like that again. Now, here I was, in the middle of the quiet woods, with someone sending threatening texts, someone shooting my windows out, and someone trying to drown me with a speed boat. New York suddenly didn't seem so scary.

Jim sat at the kitchen table with a beer in one hand and a page from *Love Story to Alma* in the other. He had a quizzical expression on his face as he set the page down and looked at me. "You okay?"

"You keep asking. Yes, I'm fine."

"Why was that boat after you?"

I grabbed a beer and sat down at the table. It was cold and frothy and just hoppy enough for my tastes. It was all I could do not to chug it. "I don't know that anyone was after me. The sun was bright, and I was out pretty far. Maybe he didn't see me."

His expression betrayed his concern. "I'm not keen on coincidences."

Neither was I, but I was trying to be a "hard woman."

"What brings you out here again?"

He smiled. "Just being friendly."

Cops weren't known for just being friendly. At least not in my experience. "I don't mean to sound impolite, but I don't believe you."

117

He set the beer can down and leaned forward, elbows on his knees. "Okay. To be honest, I heard some talk in town and decided I should check on you."

I gripped the beer can hard enough for it to start to cave in. "What kind of talk?"

"Stupid talk—tree hugger, East Coast liberal, probably had something to do with the murder. Wants to take jobs away with that trail thing. That kind of talk."

I looked at my bare feet. All I really wanted from Killdeer and Lake Larissa was some peace. How had I stumbled into such a hornet's nest?

"Is that why I'm being harassed?" To me, my voice sounded small, like a child's.

Jim scooted his chair a little closer to mine and lightly touched my hand. "I grew up in this part of the state. Most people are decent. But you always have those outliers. Some people are afraid of those who don't look and think exactly like them. They get themselves drunk and do stupid things."

"Like shoot out windows with a BB gun? Or slash tires?"

"Like that."

He took his hand away and sat up straighter. To my surprise, I was sorry about that. I liked the warmth of his touch and the feel of someone looking after me. For this moment, I really wanted to be Florice's redheaded wench, riding off with her knight into the sunset.

I put my elbow on the table and rested my head against my hand, studying him. He had a scar above his left eye that inched into his hairline. His eyes were a deep brown, and he had a lopsidedness to his face. Without it, he might have been considered good-looking. With his dark hair and eyes, it was clear he had significant Native blood in him.

"What should I do?" I felt lost, just like I felt lost in that holding cell two years ago.

Jim took a deep breath and let it out slowly. "I'd say ride it out. Something else will come along to take their attention. Get better locks on your doors and keep your dog healthy."

Bronte sensed the attention and ambled over, placing her chin on his lap. "She's probably the best protection you have."

I offered him another beer, but he turned me down. "I have to get back and change. Night patrol this week." Before he walked out the doorway, he reached in his pocket for a work calling card. "My personal cell is on the back. Call me anytime."

I took it, not knowing whether I'd throw it in the pile with others I'd gathered through the years, or if I'd put the number into my phone.

Chapter Twenty-Three: The Old Lawyer

Life is made up of "should haves." I should have followed Blaine's advice and let the sheriff take care of the investigation into Joe. I should have called Phil to let him know I was declining the temporary job. I should have stayed in New York.

But, after a surprisingly sound sleep, I woke up to a crisp and sunny Friday morning. I decided I wanted to interview Joe. I wanted to be sure he was being represented. I wanted him out of that cell in the county jail.

Recalling how hard it was to reach my lawyer in New York, I called Clarence Engstrom, expecting to have to go through a receptionist or clerk. I was prepared with my credentials and my reason for calling. The phone rang about six times when an elderly voice answered, "Engstrom." Not Engstrom Law Office, just Engstrom.

It threw me off enough that I started the conversation with an "Um. Er. Is this Clarence Engstrom, the lawyer?"

"No other Engstroms around so it must be."

"Oh." I still couldn't find my voice.

"Well? I haven't got all day." Then he laughed. "Or maybe I do. How can I help you?"

"This is Jamie Forest. I'm doing a story for the *Times* on Joe Pelletier. I'm wondering if I can talk with you."

"Well, I'd say you are talking with me. What do you need?"

For the next minute, I stumbled through trying to explain why I was interested in Joe until Clarence cut me off. "Listen, young lady, I'm too old to be doing this. I just had my eighty-fourth birthday and God knows whether I'll make it to eighty-five. Just tell me what you want."

I took a deep breath. "I don't believe he did it, and I want to get his side of the story."

"Finally, a little parsimony." He cackled, and the sound quickly evolved into a coughing spell.

I waited until the coughing subsided. "Do you think I could see him?"

To my surprise, he replied, "Going over to meet the young man at two. If you give me a ride, you can come with me."

"Sure. I can pick you up."

"Can you bring me a sandwich, too?"

Was he putting me on? I didn't dare ask. I took him seriously. "What kind would you like?"

"Something with mayonnaise. And make it with white bread. I hate all that whole wheat, whole grain claptrap. Grew up on Wonder Bread, and I'm too old to change."

After I hung up the phone, I took a few moments to gather my thoughts. Either he was a complete nutcase or simply incompetent. I called Willow.

The phone filled with static. "Hey, friend. Not a great connection."

I held it away from my ear until the static settled down. "Are you out in a barn somewhere? I can hardly hear you."

"Pole building. Sometimes it blocks the signal. Tending to a cow that got tangled up in barbed wire."

"I have a quick question. What do you know about Clarence Engstrom? The lawyer?"

In the background, I heard mooing. Willow muffled the phone while she gave some instructions to a person with a deep male voice.

"What?" She came back on. "Did you say Clarence Engstrom?"

"They appointed him to represent the boy they're holding for Nancy's murder."

"Shit!"

I didn't know if she was responding to the cow or to me.

Her phone muted again. When she came back, over the crackling of the line she said, "Geez, I thought he was dead."

121

"He can't be very dead since I'm taking him to see his client this afternoon."

Was that a laugh or a grunt of dismay? "I think you should leave the investigation to the sheriff, Jamie. I'm just saying, this is a small community."

It sounded like Willow and Blaine were giving me the same advice.

I could have called the old lawyer back and cancelled, but I felt like I had committed myself. While I boiled eggs to mix up an egg salad, I texted Phil once again. He hadn't replied to my text from yesterday.

Going with Engstrom to interview Joe Pelletier

From the freezer, I pulled out a couple of frozen hamburger buns, thawed them in the microwave, and slapped on the egg salad. Phil didn't reply, and I took it as the okay to go ahead with the meeting.

Clarence Engstrom lived in a Victorian style clapboard house two blocks from downtown. The house had a wraparound porch and multi-colored hanging baskets of petunias and zinnias. The lawn was deep green and neatly trimmed. A small sign on the porch announced *Clarence Engstrom Attorney-at-Law, By Appointment Only.*

I parked in front of the house and stepped out into the shade of an oak tree. Two squirrels chased each other up the tree as I walked by. Down the block, a lawn mower buzzed. Otherwise, the street was quiet.

The front doorbell echoed with a musical chime. I waited, noting that a police car cruised slowly down the street. To my relief, it drove by my car without stopping. I was about to ring again when I heard slow footsteps. Clarence Engstrom opened the door with one hand while he leaned on a four-pronged cane with the other.

He looked me up and down. "Kind of young to be a reporter, aren't you?"

At least he remembered why I was there.

I smiled and held out my hand. "Jamie Forest. Nice to meet you."

"Did you bring the sandwich?"

I held up the insulated lunch sack. "On white bread."

"Oh goody. Come in."

He led me down a polished oak hallway to the back of the house. On the way, he pointed to a room just off the central staircase. "My office."

I peeked in to see a wall of bookshelves, several filing cabinets, and a desk bare of everything but a telephone, notepad, and several pens. Without a computer and all the modern tech equipment, it reminded me of a set for an old movie.

He kept walking as he pointed to the kitchen table. "We'll eat first. Never go to the jail on an empty stomach."

The kitchen was immaculate, the counters scrubbed, the floor waxed. He limped to the refrigerator and brought out a pitcher of lemonade, pouring two glasses. I took them to the table. With a contented sigh, he settled on a cushioned wooden kitchen chair and immediately bit into the sandwich.

"Ah, egg salad. My wife made these, but she used some kind of fake mayonnaise that was supposed to be good for you. Didn't work for her."

I didn't know what to say. "Oh?"

"Died ten years ago this winter. Stroke. I thought, to hell with healthy eating. And I'm still here." He cackled, and I hoped it wouldn't end up in another coughing fit.

He ate both sandwiches and appeared to take pleasure with every bite. "I don't suppose you brought some potato chips?"

"Sorry."

"Oh well, my keeper won't buy them for me."

"Keeper?"

"Lorraine. Lives down the street. This is her day off."

The county assigned a lawyer who needed a keeper? I grew more worried about Joe and his legal representation.

When Clarence was done, he wiped his face with a napkin and leaned toward me. "Tell me again why you're interested in doing more than repeating the sheriff's postings?"

I told him about how I saw Joe in the hallway, how scared he looked, and what I'd learned about him.

Clarence leaned back and closed his eyes. For a few moments, I was afraid he'd dropped off to sleep.

When he opened them, he looked at the ceiling. "He's Ojibwe. Full blood would be my guess. Can't get a fair trial in this town."

I was surprised. Not that he couldn't get a fair trial, but that Clarence knew this already.

He must have noticed the expression on my face. "Young lady, I might be old and creaky, and sometimes forgetful, but I've been in this town all my life. I know how things work around here."

"What will happen?"

"First, we need to get him a real lawyer."

I frowned at him. "Aren't you a real lawyer?"

He smiled back at me. "I'm a great lawyer if you need someone to draw up your will." He paused. "By the way, do you have one? I've got a summer special going on wills. Ten percent off. Fifty percent if you make me your beneficiary."

I was so taken aback that I didn't notice the wink at first. "You're kidding me. Aren't you?"

He chuckled. "You youngsters take yourselves so seriously. If you lose your sense of humor, you lose the joy in life. My wife didn't have much of one. Actually, she was pretty dour. But she was good looking until the end."

I didn't know what to say so I sipped on the lemonade. "What did you mean by getting a real lawyer?"

"I'm no good at criminal law. Never was. We'll get him arraigned and have him plead not guilty, and then I'll call some of those old farts at the Bar Association and find a real criminal lawyer for him." He paused. "Sure you don't have any potato chips?"

He finished his lemonade and his expression turned serious. "It doesn't take a rocket scientist to see that something isn't right here. Rick is a good, steady lawman, but he's not the brightest bulb in the bunch, and he does what he's told."

"You think someone else pushed this arrest?"

He stood, a little wobbly on his feet until he got his cane planted firmly on the floor. "Could be. Wouldn't be the first time an Indian has gotten a raw deal around here."

He led the way again, down the hall to the front door. Before we stepped outside, he turned to me. "What did you say your name was again?"

"Jamie Forest."

124

"Not from around here, are you?"

"No. But my mother owned a cabin on Lake Larissa. We used to come here in the summers."

I took his arm as he stepped unsteadily down the stairs from the porch. Once he was settled in the car, he studied me.

"What was your mother's name?"

"Judy Clark."

I thought I saw a spark of something. Or was it a grimace? Or maybe simply a trick of light. But Clarence changed the subject. "Fine day isn't it? Hard to imagine that in a few months we'll be frozen in."

I drove the two blocks to the jailhouse, wondering what he knew about my mother. Maybe after we talked with Joe, I'd ask him.

Chapter Twenty-Four: Joe Pelletier

The county jail was nothing like the holding cells in Queens. It was in a separate building from the sheriff's office and appeared to have been recently built.

As we walked up to the door, Clarence leaned over to me and whispered, "If they ask, we'll tell them you're my accomplice."

I opened my mouth to protest and then decided to let him take the lead on allowing me in for an interview. It was surprisingly easy. The guard took one look at Clarence, nodded as if they were old friends, and waved us through.

"I thought you didn't do criminal cases," I whispered.

"Oh, I've done them over the years," he chuckled. "They like me because I usually lose."

We were put in a small, windowless conference room with a camera mounted in the corner. Clarence pointed at it. "They have to keep an eye on us in case we decide to bust the prisoner out."

"I should have parked closer to the door then."

He slapped his knee. "See. You do have a sense of humor."

Of course, I had a sense of humor, but I tended to lose it around jails and cells and police.

They brought Joe in, wearing an orange jump suit and shackles around his wrists. The jailer unlocked them and pointed to a chair. "Sit and don't give no one trouble."

Joe had deep brown eyes and thick dark hair that cascaded down to his shoulders. He smelled of a medicinal soap. His face had a gauntness to it I hadn't noticed the other day and his lips were dry and chapped. He stared at the tabletop with his hands resting on his lap while Clarence introduced himself.

"Son, I'm your lawyer for the time being, until we can get you someone who knows something."

Not a great way to instill confidence. Joe didn't react.

"This is Jamie. She's here to ask you a few questions."

For the next few minutes, Clarence explained to Joe the charges and what would happen next and how he would appear before a judge for arraignment.

"Arraignment is the first step. It's nothing to be worried about. They'll read the charges to you, make sure you have a lawyer, and ask how you want to plea."

Joe barely nodded.

"Your job will be to say, 'Not Guilty, Your Honor.' My job will be to try to get the case dismissed." Clarence turned to me. "Not very likely, but always worth a try."

Joe remained silent. Nor did he make eye contact. He looked like he'd withdrawn completely within himself.

"Do you have any questions?"

Joe shook his head. I noticed that he had some minor bruising on his face and wondered if someone had hit him.

Clarence looked at me. "How about you? Do you have some questions? It's pretty boring in here when I do all the talking." He smiled, but Joe's expression didn't change.

Up to this point, he hadn't said a word. I wanted to tell him I knew about the shooting in his school and the lost scholarship and the death of his brother. I wanted to connect with him in some way, but as I watched him with his flat expression and the empty look in his eyes, the words wouldn't come.

"Joe." I leaned forward to make closer contact with him. "I'm writing a story on you for the paper so people in the community know who you are."

Again, no response.

Should I tell him I didn't believe he had anything to do with Nancy's death? Should I tell him I was on his side? As I watched him, I took in how young he appeared to be. If they shaved his hair off, he could pass for a fourteen-year-old. "I don't want you to give up. The game isn't over."

He raised his head with a bitter twitch to his lips. "It was over a long time ago."

I studied him, going over in my head the little I knew about him. "I understand you were a pretty good quarterback in high school."

I thought I saw a flicker of interest.

"On your way to a college scholarship. I'm also told you were a good student and you liked to read. Maybe I could bring you some books."

Clarence raised his eyebrows. "I didn't know that."

"Yes. Joe was an honor student in high school until a sociopath showed up with a gun." Now I had Joe's attention. "Isn't that true?"

Still, he said nothing, but he wasn't staring vacantly at the tabletop anymore.

I remembered what Kristy from the *Cascade Journal* said about his arm being paralyzed. "Could you do something for me? Could you raise your right arm up high like you were swearing in?"

Startled, Joe let out a half-sigh, half-grunt of irritation. "No."

"Is it because you can't lift your arm above your shoulder?" I turned to Clarence. "He was shot in the shoulder and it messed up his arm."

This time Joe's voice was low and hoarse. "I can't. I can't lift my arm that high. It's useless. Everything is useless."

"God damn!" Clarence's old eyes lit up. "That, we can use."

I thought maybe I'd opened up the conversation, but Joe lapsed back into silence. I tried one more question. "Did you know Nancy Bywater?"

Joe again stared at the table, but I noticed a small tic in his left eye. Maybe he did know her. The possibility crept into my brain he might be guilty. I wanted to ask him if he killed her but decided it would be best not to ask. I thought about the woman in my jail cell and her advice. "Don't tell 'em nothing, sweetie." Who knew what was being observed on the other end of the camera?

Clarence also didn't ask about his guilt or innocence. Instead, he pointed to the camera. "If you need anything, you talk to those fellas and they will contact me." He winked up at the càmera. "Isn't that right?"

When they led Joe away, I noticed how his right shoulder sagged a little. Could he strangle someone with only one arm?

Clarence and I said nothing as I drove him back to the house. Clarence appeared to be deep in thought. I wondered if he was as troubled by the meeting as I was. When I parked in front of his house, I almost asked, but Clarence didn't give me a chance. As soon as I put the car in park, he flipped open the door.

"No need to accompany inside. I can manage."

I felt like I had been dismissed, but I watched as he used his cane to walk onto the porch. He turned and waved me away.

I didn't know what to do next. I had it in my head that if I met Joe, I could determine right away that he was a wronged party. Now I wasn't sure. He hadn't charmed me or convinced me he wasn't a murderer. Maybe I should stick with the press releases from Sheriff Rick and leave the human interest behind.

What bothered me most as I drove away was the little inkling I had that Joe had a connection with Nancy. Was there some way to find out? Maybe Jilly would know.

Main street in front of the *Times* office was deserted. I pulled over to the curb and looked inside. Lights were on, and Jilly was at the counter, talking with someone.

I walked in to find them in a serious conversation.

"That's what I heard. They want a casino and resort."

Jilly looked at me. "Hi, Jamie. We're talking about the rumors of a big development coming to town."

The woman at the counter turned to me. I recognized her as the desk clerk at the lodge. We'd had a few "Hi, how are you" conversations over the last few months. Her name was Mavis and she had frizzy red hair and a high breathy Marilyn Monroe voice.

"You aren't talking about Racine Mining, are you?" I asked.

Mavis raised a finger to her lips. "I'm not supposed to talk about it."

And, here you are—talking about it. "Oh?"

"Kinda hush hush. Like it might be a partnership with those mining people."

Mavis's phone rang with a jaunty little ringtone. "Gotta get this." She retreated out the door.

"Well." I leaned on the counter. "Do you think whatever it is will have an impact on the Lady Slipper Trail?"

Jilly shrugged. "Who knows around here."

I glanced behind Jilly to see if Phil was there, but his desk was empty. "I was hoping Phil might have stopped in. I've texted him a couple of times and he hasn't replied."

"Sorry. When Phil disappears for the weekend, he doesn't come back."

"I guess he doesn't answer texts either."

Jilly shrugged. "I've never tried."

"I wanted to know if Nancy had any connection with the kid they arrested."

The expression on Jilly's face hardened. "Nancy didn't share much with me. She was more 'do this, Jilly,' 'do that, Jilly,' or 'get me some coffee, Jilly.'"

"The good news is I'm quite capable of getting my own coffee."

"Then we'll get along just fine." She walked back to her desk, sat down, and immediately began clicking on her computer.

It felt like the temperature in the room had suddenly dropped. I had a hard time reading these Minnesotans. In New York, people tended to say exactly what they meant and often said it loudly. Here everyone was so reserved. I'd figured out, over the last months, that if they didn't like something, they'd simply say "That's interesting," meaning "let's not talk about it anymore."

The conversation I'd interrupted about the development reminded me that Nancy had a file called *Development*. I walked over to her desk, opened the drawer and pulled it out. Without saying what it was, I held it up to Jilly. "I'm going to study this over the weekend."

"Fine with me." She kept her attention on the computer.

"Well, have a good weekend. I'll be here on Monday morning."

She waved without looking up.

As I drove home, I reflected on Jilly. It was like something had suddenly changed when I asked her about Joe and Nancy. Very strange, but not my issue to solve. If Jilly and I didn't get along, it was no big deal. My job was temporary. Just a couple of weeks.

I stopped at my mailbox by the entrance to the lodge and my driveway. It was part of a row of mailboxes for everyone who lived on this part of the lake. Mine was marked only with a PO box number. I was glad I had decided to keep it as anonymous as possible, considering the vandalism to my cabin.

A large manila envelope was crammed inside. I assumed it was a manuscript from one of my customers. When I retrieved it, a couple of other letters fell out, including one that looked like a check.

"Halleluiah, I can buy more beer."

Once I was home and had given Bronte her due attention, I opened the manila envelope. Instead of a printed manuscript, the envelope was filled with old newspaper clippings, many of them so brown and fragile they almost crumbled in my hands.

"What is this?" The envelope had no return address and, in fact, hadn't been mailed. Someone had stuck it in my mailbox.

The first clipping showed three men with shovels in a groundbreaking ceremony. The date was June 1935. The headline read *New Lodge to Bring Tourists to Lake Larissa*. One of the men featured was Blaine's grandfather, Mitchell McConnell. The resemblance between Mitchell and Blaine was remarkable—sandy-colored hair and square faces.

I set the clipping down when my phone pinged with a text. Praying it wasn't another threat, I pulled the phone out of my bag. It was from Phil and in all caps.

PLZ HOLD ON DOING STORY ON SUSPECT!

This day was getting weirder and weirder.

Chapter Twenty-Five: The Package

Why? I texted back but didn't get an immediate reply.

Bronte stretched her head to sniff at the manila envelope. It had a familiar hint of a flower scent to it, like the lilac talcum powder Mother used to use after a bath. Where had I smelled it recently? I couldn't remember.

"Please don't eat that. I'm thinking someone put it in the wrong box." I put the clippings back. I'd take it to the lodge tomorrow and see if it belonged to them.

The windowed envelope that looked like it had a check in it turned out to be a mass mailing offering me an instant $5,000 loan. "I guess there will be no beer from this."

The supply of beer from Jim was down to two cans, but I had no desire to drive back into town to get more.

"We'll teetotal it tonight, girl."

Bronte didn't care as long as she had enough dog food.

I sat out on the porch with my head jammed with thoughts that didn't go anywhere. Joe's gaunt face and flatness haunted me the most. What was he hiding, if anything?

"Want to fetch a stick or two?"

Bronte yipped in reply.

At the little beach, I picked up the stick she chewed on yesterday and threw it as far as I could into the water. Watching her paddle out to it brought memories of being under water, desperate for either air or for long-lasting peace. Was I the kind of person who would give up so easily? Was that why

I fled New York to this land of inscrutable people?

Bronte waded out of the lake with her stick and shook droplets of water at me. Suddenly, I didn't want to be here near the water. Was the speed boater an accident? A drunk not paying attention? Or was someone more than rambunctious teenagers after me?

I decided to go back to Alma, the love of George's life.

By chapter six, I had more blue on the paper than the regular ink. George had gone from torrid romance to late 1800s-style with florid writing about the wedding and the guests. I wondered if he had written each chapter after having read a certain kind of book. From *Fifty Shades of Grey* to Charles Dickens. What next? Perhaps a mystery ala Sherlock Holmes?

"Okay. Time to stop."

I stacked the manuscript into the piles of "read" and "to be read," noting, with dismay, the "to be read" was a much larger pile.

"The great mystery here, my faithful pup, is whether I can get this thing done by Monday and still have my sanity when I go into the *Times*."

Bronte, asleep on the cushion in front of the couch, didn't reply.

***

When I moved the stacks to make room for breakfast in the morning, I accidentally bumped the manila envelope. It fell to the floor, spilling its contents. As I retrieved the clippings, a sheet of lined notebook paper caught my attention. It was handwritten in pencil and looked like something had been spilled on it.

I took it over to the couch and turned on the reading light. It appeared to be an undated letter with the only salutation a *Dear Sir*.

Dear Sir,

Please help. They are trying to take my land that has been with my family for many years. I want the lake and the wilderness unspoiled for my children and children's children. But my family is hungry and we need the money. Isn't there some help for us so we won't lose our inheritance? Don't let them scare us off our land.

Even with a magnifying glass, I couldn't make out the rest of the letter or the signature.

Who were the "they" the writer talked about? Did this have to do with Racine Mining? Whoever wrote the letter was definitely literate.

Scare us off resonated with me. Was that what the gunshots and the speed boat and the slashed tires were all about? But judging by the condition of the letter, this was old, not recent.

Suddenly, the newspaper clippings were of interest. I brewed a pot of tea and sat on the couch with the pile of clippings beside me.

Most of them were from the *Killdeer Times* and chronicled the development of Larissa Lodge. I didn't see anything about concerns with taking land. All of the news was focused on how this would help the community by bringing in tourists.

"Well, I don't get it, Bronte. This must have been meant for the Larissa Lodge archives." I was about to stuff the clippings back in the envelope when one piece caught my attention. It was a carefully clipped photo that might have come from the *Times* or from some other newspaper. Even with the fading ink and the grainy quality of the photo, I noted the serious and even angry expressions on the faces of the five people pictured. They stood, lined up, all Native Americans in traditional clothing. The caption said *Indians Accuse Larissa Lodge of Stealing Their Inheritance*. One of the men listed in the photo was John Clark.

I brought out the magnifying glass once again and studied him. He seemed vaguely familiar.

"Do you think he was a relative? Mom was a Clark."

Bronte stood, yawned, and put her head on my lap.

"I guess you wouldn't know."

I thought about the boxes of family memorabilia in the attic. Maybe they held some of Mother's things. I hadn't gone through any of it when I shipped it out here from storage in New York. At the time, in my desire to get away, I'd thought about trashing all of it. But in a saner moment, I'd simply sent it here with plans to someday look through it.

"I'll put it on my to-do list for some time when the weather gets cold and dreary."

That night the half-moon rose above the trees surrounding the cabin.

Bronte snored quietly beside me as I wrestled with the covers and the pillow and the night noises. It was one of those nights when the pillow was too hard and then it was too soft. When I tried sleeping on my side, my ear felt squashed into the pillow. When I tried on my back, my chest felt too heavy.

Above me, something skittered across the loft, followed by the snap of the mouse trap. I slipped out of bed and walked barefoot into the main room. The pile of papers sat untouched on the kitchen table with my laptop by it. I took the laptop to the couch and booted it up. In the search box, I typed in "John Clark, Killdeer, Minnesota." Nothing came up.

I tried "Judy Clark, Killdeer, Minnesota" with the assumption that Mother grew up here. Again, nothing came up. I sat back and tried to remember everything my father had said about my mother.

The summer when I was sixteen and we came here to scatter her ashes, I remembered paddling the canoe, with Dad steering in the back. He wasn't much of a canoeist, and I wasn't much help either. We laughed as the canoe made its wobbly way across Lake Larissa to a small island called Bear Island. It had a lone campsite with four logs around a fire grate. Someone had used it recently and left empty beer cans behind.

Dad looked at the mess and shook his head. "Your mom loved this place. Said she used to come here when she was a kid. I hate to see it like this."

"Mom grew up around here? I thought she grew up in Massachusetts."

Dad shrugged as if he wasn't quite sure. "She didn't talk about it much. As soon as she graduated from high school, she headed East to college."

"You met her in college?" It was surprising what little I knew about them.

"I was a graduate student and she was a freshman."

I laughed. "You robbed the cradle?"

Dad's smile was a sad one. "I guess I did."

We walked a little path to the other side of the island. The sun was waning in the sky and shed a sparkling path of light over the water.

"Let's add her to these ancient waters. I think she'd like that." Dad's voice trembled and, for the first time in this whole journey, I felt the significance of his loss. Yes, I'd lost a mother that I hardly knew, but he'd lost the love of his life.

If only he had written *A Love Story to Judy*, maybe I would know more about her.

What I didn't tell him at the time was I'd felt something deep within me as we released her ashes into the lake. I was connected to this land in a way I couldn't describe. At sixteen, I shook it all off, of course, and tried to forget the cabin and the lake and the island. But sometimes, in my dreams, the place came back to me, as if it were calling me.

"Nonsense, to all of that." I put the laptop away and crawled back in bed with my sleeping dog.

Chapter Twenty-Six: Rob's Story

During the night a low-pressure front moved in, bringing cooler weather and a layer of gray clouds. It looked like the sun would be absent all day. The "you should" nagging voice in my head told me to drive into town and get groceries. However, I had enough to last me until tomorrow.

I was on chapter eight of the memoir to Alma when I heard the thump of Bronte's tail against the floor as she sat at the door. A vehicle rumbled down my driveway. At this point, my author George had settled in on the florid writing, somewhat, to my relief. I was much better with florid than with his steamy fantasies.

Bronte's tail kept wagging. A car door slammed.

"How do you know that car belongs to a friend? It could be LeRoy or someone who wants to burn down this cabin."

Rob knocked and let himself in. "We're going to get some rain."

"Is that your innate Ojibwe sense talking?"

His eyes sparkled as he pointed to his phone. "Nope. Weather.com."

I put the kettle on for tea. "What brings you by?"

As he walked to the kitchen table, I noted a vague scent of wood chips and dog kennel. He must have come from Willow's clinic.

"I wanted to check the windows to make sure they don't leak." Rob's expression appeared a little sheepish, like he had another agenda.

I took two mugs down from the cupboard. "Have some tea and tell me why you're really here."

As soon as he sat down, Bronte settled at his feet. I swore that if she had a choice, she'd leave me in a minute for Rob.

He cleared his throat, studied his hands, and then studied the mess of papers on the table. "I really do want to check the windows, you know."

"But?"

"I think you should skip the Lady Slipper Trail meeting on Sunday."

I poured the tea and handed him a cup. "Why?"

He took a deep breath. "Because I don't think it's safe for you to be there."

I slid into my chair and set my mug on the table. My next question came out in a sputter. "What? Why?"

"There's talk." He didn't elaborate.

"But what has that got to do with me?"

"Jamie, I've lived here all my life. Grew up here, put up with a lot of things. I know this community. Something bad is going on."

This struck me as ironic. I left New York because I was frightened and felt the city was closing in on me. I'd come here hoping to be left alone, and now I was in danger?

"Whatever happened to 'Minnesota Nice'?" I'd been told since I arrived that Minnesotans were always nice and polite. The LeRoy Pruitts of the state didn't fit the description.

Rob cracked a smile. "It's a myth."

"But your concern is more than a feeling, I take it."

"We hear things."

Who else had said that? Jim Monroe was worried about me too.

I felt like we were dancing around something. Thunder rumbled in the distance and the skies darkened. Bronte "woofed" contentedly at Rob's feet.

"Hey, listen, Rob, I know I'm considered one of those 'Eastern liberal tree-huggers,' but I can't imagine that puts me in real danger." Although, someone did slash my tires and shoot out my windows.

"It's more than that, something deeper and darker. I'm really not sure what it is except that you're somehow in the middle of it."

"Sounds pretty dramatic, and I don't buy it."

"Someone shot up your cabin."

"Blaine said someone was shooting up his cabins, too. I think it's stupid, drunken kids."

Rob sighed. "You don't know this community like I do. Just to be clear, you aren't the only 'outsider.' The people with wealth around here aren't Indians, although they made their money from us."

I was surprised by the bitterness in his voice. This wasn't the easygoing artistic Rob I was used to.

"All this land was considered home by my people." He pointed vaguely toward the lake. "First, the fur traders arrived, then the loggers, then the homesteaders. With every wave of white men, we lost more and more."

He leaned on his elbows with an intense look. "Meanwhile, the white men in the wisdom of the time, decided the best thing for the Indians was assimilation." The intensity changed to sadness.

"I've read about that. You mean the Indian schools?"

"They took children from families and sent them to schools run by nuns and other organizations to make them 'Americans.' We were given no choice."

The article I'd read on the Indian schools chronicled terrible conditions. Children, as young as four, ripped from their families, living in dormitories, where many died of malnutrition, disease, or despair.

"There are many unmarked graves of children from my tribe out there." Rob gestured vaguely outside.

"I'd heard there was a school south of here."

Pain etched Rob's face. "Far enough away that it was hard to escape home. My mother was one of the last generation to be put into that school. She survived to come back and marry my father, but she was never right. I remember how she woke up in the middle of the night and paced, singing in our language, as if to ward off the evil spirits."

I thought about my mother and how she paced at night. As far as I knew, though, she was too young to have been in one of the schools.

"Rob, that's all pretty awful. I've read about some of it. I remember in one of my college classes we were assigned *Bury My Heart at Wounded Knee*. It was so sad that I couldn't finish it."

Rob fixed his gaze on me. "Jamie, you know that some of that is your heritage."

It meant so little to me. I was raised in relative comfort in New York City. I didn't say this to Rob, however. "I know my mother was part Ojibwe, but we never talked about it."

With another low rumble of thunder, the rain started with a tapping on the roof. The trees swayed as the wind picked up.

"I still don't know what you're getting at."

Rob exhaled as if I was a bad student. "I've lived through a lot here in Killdeer. My mother died young by her own hand. I made it out to art school but came back. The residents tolerate me and tolerate that I'm queer, mainly because Brad is a hometown boy and so loveable. But that doesn't mean I'm not an outsider to certain people."

"What does that mean?"

"We have to be watchful. The store has been vandalized. Once, Brad found a Swastika painted on the door and a message: 'go home.' I'm careful whenever I'm out at night to listen to what's happening around me. I've been beaten up more than once."

A bright flash of lightning was followed by a dynamite blast of thunder. The cabin shook and the lights snapped off. Bronte sat up with a whimper. Rob patted her on the head, whispering to her in a low voice. She settled down as rain scraped at the windows.

"Whew. That's quite a storm."

"The gods are unhappy." Rob continued to pet Bronte.

"The Ojibwe gods?" I was embarrassed at how little I knew of my heritage. Rob laughed. "No, the Norse gods. You know, Thor and his bunch."

We listened to the storm in the semidarkness. It felt comfortable having a friend and shelter from the raging weather outside. It took about fifteen minutes for the storm to pass. In that time, we sipped our tea and said very little.

As the wind calmed down, I asked again, "So, why do you think I'm in danger. You still haven't told me."

"There are pockets of ugly people in this county. They're ugly because they're afraid. They're afraid someone is going to come and take their livelihood. They're afraid of change."

"Make America great again?" I thought of my conversation with Jim. Rob was telling me the same thing.

"It's not something new. It has always been there. But, Jamie, they see you as part of the conspiracy to take what they have away from them."

In the distance, the thunder had become a low rumble again. The downpour abated into a rhythmic clatter, and a wan ray of sun peeked out from behind the clouds. The storm was over.

"Because I work with you on the Lady Slipper Trail? That doesn't make sense."

Rob was quiet. "That might be part of it, but it's not what has me worried."

"Then what?"

"This murder and Joe Pelletier."

Now that the storm had passed, Bronte sauntered to the door. She looked back at me before scratching at the door.

"Out?" I opened the door and let her out into the wet grass.

A fine mist of rain still came down, but Bronte didn't seem to mind.

"You're not tracking mud in, girl."

She headed for her spot in the woods and ignored me.

I held the tea mug in both my hands. It was lukewarm. "I don't understand what you mean."

"Joe is Native. People want him to be guilty. They want this murder to be wrapped up neatly in a bow and forgotten." He stood. "They don't want you to meddle. And the gunshots and the slashed tires were a warning."

I stared at him. He was so tall and dignified with his weathered face and his long braid.

"Rob, the gunshots happened before I knew anything about Joe. You aren't making sense."

In the darkness, as clouds still obscured the sun, I couldn't read his expression, but I sensed something else was going on.

His tone was grim. "The ugly ones want you gone, Jamie."

Here it was once again—someone wanted me gone. Andrew wanted me gone so he could have his makeup artist. The NYPD Special Task Force wanted me gone so they could cover up their mistake. Now Killdeer wanted me gone. But why?

"If that's the case, what do you suggest? I pack up and run somewhere else?" I moved close to him as the anger built. "I came here to be left alone. This cabin is mine. I love the woods and the lake and the solitude. I am not leaving."

Rob stepped back in surprise, then he grinned. "Atta girl. A person after my own heart. Stick to it."

I calmed down. "So really, what do you suggest?"

"A low profile for a while."

"You mean like step back from the Lady Slipper Trail? Leave Joe to the legal system?"

"Pretty much."

I pictured Joe yesterday, silent and inscrutable. Why was I advocating for him? I didn't know him, and he didn't seem particularly interested in my help. And, it was possible he was guilty.

"Rob, I can't let it go. Something inside me says he didn't do it. The deeper this gets into the legal system, the harder it will be to get him out." My eyes teared up, much to my embarrassment. "I know something about getting stuck in a tangled web."

Rob stepped over and pulled me into his arms. I hadn't had a fatherly hug like that in a long time. It took a while to blink the tears away.

Before he left, Rob asked me to promise to stay home on Sunday evening. "Just for this meeting. Please?"

I wondered what more he knew, but I agreed.

He was halfway to his van when I called him back. "Aren't you forgetting something?" I pointed to the windows. "Isn't that why you came?"

He chuckled as he walked over to inspect the panes. "Looks like they're sealed."

After he left, I thought about the manila envelope with the clippings. Maybe he could have told me something about my family. I decided to hold off bringing the envelope to the lodge. I hoped whoever had left it wouldn't mind.

Chapter Twenty-Seven: Monday at the Paper

While it angered me, I took both Rob and Jim's advice and skipped the Lady Slipper Trail meeting on Sunday. Instead, I stayed home with the memoir and tried to edit it in the kindest way possible. Part of my challenge was to break up the long and convoluted sentences. At one point, he'd literally written a whole page in one sentence, describing how they found their first house. Exasperated, I complained out loud, "I don't care, and the reader doesn't care that you veered slightly to the left onto Elm before taking a hard right onto Bishop Street. If I needed directions, I could look them up on Google Maps!"

***

On Monday I set my alarm for six in the morning. I was out of practice responding to the alarm, and when it went off, I was so startled that my heart pulsated behind my eyes. Bronte leapt off the bed while I flailed around, looking for my phone to turn it off. She sat at the foot of the bed with a confused expression.

"I know. You're not used to me dragging myself out of bed to get to work. Times have changed, girl."

I wanted to look intelligent and professional for my first day as the temporary editor of the *Killdeer Times*. I chose white slacks and a pinkish blouse with ¾-length sleeves. In New York, I would have looked like a tourist from the Midwest. Here, I looked like I fit in. Of course, after my conversation with Rob, perhaps it didn't matter what I wore. I'd always be an outsider.

Last night, Willow called after the Lady Slipper meeting. She was concerned that I hadn't shown up. I explained that Rob thought I should stay home.

She brushed it off. "Hey, he's always super cautious. Anyway, not much happened at the meeting, other than to set up a workgroup for the next section of the trail. I think you'll be safe enough joining us. We'll be armed with shovels and hoes. No word on any progress with Racine Mining. I take that as a good sign."

"Maybe they've run into a roadblock." I pictured Blaine at a land use committee meeting.

"Take care, my friend. Maybe I'll drop by later this week."

"Call first. I'm starting my new job at the *Times*."

We talked a little longer until she was interrupted by a work emergency. "Sorry, pig problems."

That morning as I dressed, I looked forward to a break from poorly written manuscripts. The love story to Alma sat neatly stacked on the kitchen table. Even though I'd devoted the entire weekend to it, to the point of eye strain, I still had about fifty pages to go. Tonight, I promised myself, I'd finish it.

The air outside was filled with the scents of damp leaves and fresh pine. I stood at the back door breathing it in while Bronte finished her morning business. She bounded back to me, her brown eyes alight with anticipation of another fine breakfast of doggie nuggets.

Unsure about what I needed for my new job, I put a blank notebook and several pens in my satchel. I considered bringing my laptop but decided I would designate it as a home office tool. Bronte sensed my energy and followed me around until I pointed to her cushion and said, "I'll be gone all day. Feel free to nap and guard the cabin."

I felt like I was starting school again as I locked the door behind me.

On the drive to town, I visualized the paper and thought about the kinds of improvements I could make. Nancy hadn't been a particularly creative editor or a particularly good writer. Most of the stories read like office memos—straightforward, to the point, and dull as dirt. She must have taken lessons from a high school journalism teacher about sticking with the who, what, and whens. Maybe I could add a little color, like an outdoor column.

By the time I reached Killdeer, I was excited and ready to take on this project, even if it was only temporary. I'd had a number of temporary jobs in the past that morphed into something more permanent. Maybe this one would, too, relieving me from any more memoirs to dead wives.

As I thought about my last permanent job, the one where my editor finally let me go, my enthusiasm dimmed. The stress of the arrest, along with the months of dealing with the aftermath, had taken a significant toll. I'd missed deadlines, turned in incomplete editing jobs, and generally slacked off. I'd earned that pink slip, which was probably why I wrote the article on my ordeal as a way to explain to her why I'd failed.

Fluffy white clouds floated overhead as I drove by the green sign welcoming me to Killdeer, population 3,240. The town had an air of busyness. It was the first Monday in August, and the bank parking lot filled as people deposited their checks and attended to their finances. It amused me how unwired this community was. In New York, my paychecks had been direct deposited. Even here, my little annuity from my father went directly into my account. I was so unused to paper checks that when Florice payed me by check for my first edit of her book, I was at a complete loss as to what to do with it. Willow had to coach me through it.

"Oh, you city folks. Let me tell you, I get paid in cash, checks, and even fresh eggs. I can actually touch the money before it goes into the bank."

I wondered if Phil provided direct deposit.

I parked behind the *Times* in the rutted lot with its shallow potholes. Building and grounds maintenance must not have been one of Phil's strong suits. The back door was open. I walked by shelves of stocked paper for small print jobs and the giant multi-purpose copier. At one time, the back of this building would have held the printing press and the linotype machine.

Dad, on our summer treks, had taken me to the Museum of Printing in Massachusetts, where they had the linotype and the press. We watched as the operator, an elderly man wearing a baseball cap and suspenders, created the type on the machine. I loved the hot smell of the lead pigs that were melted down to make the type and the smell of ink from the small working press.

I walked through the back-room doorway to find Jilly at her computer. She watched intently as Phil and another man talked at Nancy's desk.

"Hi, Jilly. I'm reporting for duty."

She looked startled, as if she wasn't expecting me. "Uh, Jamie. You're here? Didn't Phil call you?"

I assumed she was referring to my text to him about Joe last Thursday. "Call me? No. He sent me a text on Friday." I took out my phone. It had no messages or missed calls.

She pressed her lips together into a thin line. "Phil? Jamie is here for her first day." Her voice rose when she said, "first."

Something weird was going on. Phil's expression as he looked at me was that of a kid who'd just been caught shoplifting.

I walked over to him. "Hi. I'm ready to go."

The man who was sitting at Nancy's desk frowned as Phil gently took me by the arm.

"We need to talk." He nodded to the man. "Excuse us."

He led me into the back room.

"Who is he?" I imagined he was an investigator of some sort. Maybe insurance? Maybe he didn't want the man to ask me questions.

Phil cleared his throat. "Ah, I need to tell you something." He cleared his throat again, looking with great interest at the shelves of paper stock.

"What's wrong?"

"Um. Well, Harry volunteered to come out of retirement for a while."

I glanced through the doorway at the man at the desk. He was in his late fifties, unshaven, with a ruddy face and a shock of white hair. He looked like he'd spent the last twenty-four hours in a bar.

"Yes?"

"He used to edit a paper down in southern Minnesota. He knows the ropes, and I decided he could fill in until I hire another editor."

I stared at Phil and said nothing. He studied his feet, making little circles on the floor.

"I'm not needed then?" A mixture of confusion, humiliation, and anger flooded through me. My cheeks burned, and my mouth went dry. What was this?

Again, he cleared his throat. "I'll pay you for coming in today, of course."

I could have been gracious and walked away. My father used to say, "Honey, don't burn your bridges unless you have to." I should have followed his advice.

Instead, I moved within inches of his face. "This is because of Joe, isn't it?"

Phil stepped back, looking stunned that I had broken into his personal space. "Uh..."

"You are a damned coward." Turning on my heels, I walked away, my back ramrod straight.

I'd just settled angrily into the driver's seat of my car when Jilly came running out.

"Wait!" She bent down by my open window. "I didn't know about this until I came in this morning. I'm sorry."

"He could have called me. Or texted. Or something," I muttered.

Jilly bit her lip. "I've worked with Phil for a lot of years. I know him. He's scared. Something or someone got to him about you."

I raked my fingers through my hair and shook my head. "I don't get it. What does he think I was going to do—an exposé on sexual harassment by the sheriff's department?"

Overhead, a small airplane buzzed its way to the airstrip just outside of town. In the neighborhood, behind the parking lot, someone started a lawn mower. The town felt alive, and I felt like I needed to run away once again. Maybe California this time?

"Listen," Jilly said. "I'll text you. Let's have coffee. I have some things to tell you." She walked back to the office.

Now what?

Steaming, I sat for a long time before I switched on the engine. Beside me, my cell phone pinged. It was another anonymous text. **Go back where you came from.** Again, it included emojis of skulls.

I looked around to see if anyone was watching me. The back lot was empty, other than my car and Jilly's dented pickup truck. Up until now, I'd ignored the texts. Today, as the fury bubbled inside me. I hit reply. **Too much of a coward to reveal yourself?**

I stopped at the grocery store for provisions and the liquor store for beer. I decided my job today was to finish the love story and start a story of my own. The phone was quiet the entire drive.

Once home with Bronte happily dancing at my feet, I made my decision. Opening my laptop, I typed a carefully worded email to an editor at *The New Yorker*, an acquaintance of mine. In the subject line I put "Do they have the wrong man?"

I intended to follow up with the story of Joe Pelletier. I decided I would tell no one about this project, including Rob, Willow, Blaine, or even Jim Monroe.

Perhaps dogs really had a sixth or seventh sense because as soon as I pressed "send" Bronte yipped in her sleep as if she were having a bad dream.

Chapter Twenty-Eight: Nancy and Joe

As promised, Jilly texted me midafternoon. We arranged to meet at the Copper Lake Casino twenty miles north of Killdeer at seven this evening. I took this to mean Jilly didn't want to be seen in town with me. How had I so quickly become such a pariah?

I finished *Love Story to Alma* at six, as the sun was starting to fade in the sky. By the end, I'd run out of enthusiasm for correcting the manuscript. If it had been a Word document on the computer, I would have done a search and replace for all words ending in "ly," along with passion, ardor, and worship. I could have boiled his four hundred pages down to two sentences. "I love you, Alma. You had a fine ass, your cooking was mediocre, and you were good in bed." I might have added, "Oh yes, I cheated on you, but it didn't mean anything."

My thoughts about George's memoir shamed me. Maybe freelance editing wasn't my calling either.

The drive to the casino took me around the west end of Lake Larissa and through a state forest that hadn't been logged out in a hundred years. In my foul mood, I looked at the giant pine trees and wondered when the logging companies would get permits to take them down. I thought about the Lady Slipper Trail and how we planned to have it cut through my land. I owned some of the last virgin acres in the state. Someone had told me that the northern part of my acreage bordering on Lake Larissa had been spared when the loggers came through because it was considered sacred land to the Native Americans. I doubted the loggers cared one way or another. I guessed it had been left alone because the area was so boggy and hard to

149

reach.

The Copper Lake Casino, the only Indian casino within a hundred miles, was a shabby affair. Although the structure was relatively new, it appeared to have been neglected. The stucco on the outside of the building was crumbling, like it had been slapped on haphazardly, and two of the neon lights in front had died. Instead of Copper Lake Casino, it displayed *Cop er Lake Ca ino*. I'd heard from Willow that the management wasn't only incompetent but also corrupt, and that the tribe was getting very little of the revenue.

Willow had noted, however, that the restaurant wasn't too bad. "They know how to turn frozen hamburger patties into cheeseburgers."

Despite the shabbiness of the casino, the gravel parking lot was full, even on a Monday evening. I wondered if that had to do with it being the first of the month, when many pension and government checks came in. I had to park on the outer edge of the lot next to a darkening stand of pine trees. As I made my way to the door, I passed a familiar truck spattered with mud. Jim Monroe was a gambler? Maybe. What did I know about him anyway?

Inside the dimly lit casino, the electronic burble of slot machines lilting up and down the scales assaulted my ears. Someone shouted, "I won!" Others sat at the machines with their gazes fixed on the video screens. I watched someone get a flush on video poker and felt a tinge of jealousy. I liked to gamble, but a little voice, that could have been my father's, reminded me that, in the end, the house always won. Or in the case of Copper Lake, maybe the corrupt management was the winner.

Jilly sat in a booth near the back of the Copper Lake Grill. With all the vehicles in the parking lot, I was surprised that the restaurant was nearly empty. She greeted me by holding up a Bloody Mary. The glass was nearly empty.

"Have you been waiting long?"

"No," she said. "Just desperate for a drink. This has been one hell of a day to go with one hell of a week." She signaled the server for another.

I ordered a draft IPA.

"Not a cocktail drinker?"

"When I was eighteen and a freshman in college, my roommate introduced me to sloe gin fizzes. I got drunk and sick at about the same time. Spent the next day throwing up every hour on the hour. I haven't been much of a hard liquor drinker since."

The server brought my beer in a frosty mug, along with menus. Near as I could tell, the only thing they had here besides variations on hamburgers was a chef's salad complete with ranch dressing. I ordered it.

We chatted a little about the condition of the casino while we waited for our food. "This place was going to make the tribe rich." Jilly pointed to the red duct tape that repaired a rip in the Naugahyde seat of the booth. "My father complained it wasn't fair the Indians would get all the money."

Considering what the tribe had lost through the years, I made a face. "Define 'fair.'"

"Right."

When the salad arrived, it was surprisingly fresh and made with a variety of greens. I realized, as I dug into it, that I had been so distraught by my firing I had forgotten to eat lunch today.

"So, how is Harry working out?"

Jilly's tone was bitter. "He headed to the Loonfeather as soon as Phil left. Didn't see him the rest of the day."

"Who's working on the paper?"

Jilly pointed to herself. "As usual."

She finished her second Bloody Mary and ordered coffee. "My kids would kill me if I got a DUI."

I waited while the server brought us both coffees. "Okay, tell me what you know."

"Well, first, I know that, in the last couple of months, Nancy was hardly doing her job. She was good at delegating—to me. Since I've worked at the *Times* since high school, I know how to do everything except change the masthead to show me as the editor." She stirred two packets of sugar into her coffee.

I thought about how hard it must be for Jilly every time a new editor started. She would have had to train me, too. "Too bad Phil hasn't figured that out."

"No kidding." She leaned across the table toward me. "Could you clue him in?"

"I'm not sure we're on good terms right now. I called him a coward and some other names." The coffee wasn't up to Starbucks's standards. I poured the fake cream in and added sugar. "What was Nancy doing? Do you know?"

"Things changed for her last spring. She covered a county board meeting about Racine Mining and came back to the office with questions about who owned the land around here. She was on to something, but she didn't talk about it. She got calls on her personal cell and went out back to talk. In the last couple of weeks, it had gotten worse. My husband said he drove by the *Times* office on his way home from work at midnight, and he saw her at the computer. But she wasn't doing *Times* business. I know that. Then, last week, she actually asked me to walk with her to her car after work. She said something about her ex showing up, but I didn't see any evidence of him."

"Did you tell the sheriff about this?"

Jilly nodded. "He...or I should say that dope of a deputy didn't seem very interested. Said something about the ex having a solid alibi."

"That's what I heard, too."

The server came with the check, and we agreed to split it down the middle. "I'd like to treat you, Jilly, but my bank account is a little low." Like, if Florice LeMay didn't get a check to me soon, it would be below zero. How had I managed to get into such a financial rut? Maybe I could win at the slots.

Jilly cleared her throat. "But this is what I really wanted to tell you. I was here about a month ago, with my husband, one of my only nights out in a long time. As we left, I saw Nancy talking with someone outside in the parking lot." She leaned forward and whispered, "It was that Joe Pelletier."

"Are you sure?"

She nodded. "LeRoy brought a photo of him over to the *Times* and asked if I'd ever seen him with Nancy—I could hardly lie about it, could I?"

"Do you know what they were talking about?"

"Not a clue. I thought about going over to say hello, but they seemed to be in an intense conversation. My husband yanked me away."

"They must have known each other."

Jilly wiped some crumbs off her lap. "When I asked her about it the next day, she got this funny look, but she didn't say anything. I thought it was weird."

"Curious. Maybe she was having an affair with him and was embarrassed because he was so young."

Jilly hesitated. "Maybe, but Nancy didn't strike me as a cougar who would go after someone that young—especially someone who worked as a busboy in an Indian casino." She stood. "Gotta go. Another busy day tomorrow in the news factory. Sorry you aren't joining me."

After Jilly left, I sat with my coffee and thought about Joe. He knew Nancy. Did they have a relationship? I shivered a little thinking about him with a middle-aged woman. Of course, it was possible.

On my way out, I had five quarters in my pocket and decided I might as well throw them away on a video poker game. I looked around until I found a progressive slot. Why not go for the gold? I fed them in and came up with a full house. My five quarters were now twenty. Wow, five extra dollars. I tried once again and watched as a queen of spades rolled up, followed by a jack of spades, a ten of spades, a king of spades and, at last, an ace of spades. I simply stared at it. "This can't be real." I expected someone to run over and tell me the machine was broken.

"You really should hold all those cards." The voice came from behind me. I turned to find Jim looking over my shoulder.

My hand shook as I pressed the hold button and hit play. Immediately, the bells and whistles started. "I think I won."

"Looks like you did." His eyes danced with amusement. "Never seen one of those show up on the first draw."

I was in a state of shock when the casino manager came over to congratulate me. He needed some information from me before they could pay the $5,000 jackpot.

I slipped off the stool and said to Jim, "Wait for me. I'll buy you a drink if you aren't on duty."

Since I'd never won a jackpot at a casino before, I was surprised they took out taxes up front. I wondered if the money would actually get to the IRS and the state, knowing the rumors of corruption with this casino. I walked out with a check for most of it plus a nice wad of cash.

Jim was already on a stool at the bar when I found him.

"Looks like you have a little playing money."

"Uh, uh. I can pay my electric bill and still eat for a couple of weeks."

"That bad?"

Even though I was in a good mood, I didn't feel like discussing my finances with him. I ordered a beer and paid for his. "You hang around here much?"

"I live nearby, and I like their burgers."

"Oh."

"And you? Gamble much?"

"Every time I get a new manuscript, it's a gamble. I never know what I'm getting into. But no, I don't gamble much. My dad instilled in me the odds. The house always wins."

"Except for tonight."

"I'm sure they're hoping I'll put it all back into a machine. But they don't know how desperate I am to keep my electricity on and my dog fed." Immediately, I was sorry I had let him know my poverty-stricken status because his expression turned from amusement to a serious look.

I was spared questions when Jim's attention switched from me to something in the casino. I turned to follow his gaze and immediately a chill ran down my neck. LeRoy, in uniform and armed, was talking to the manager, who had just given me the check and the cash.

"Something wrong?" I asked.

He slipped off the stool. "Thanks for the beer. I've got to go. Maybe we can do this again?"

If he was spending time with his buddy, I wasn't interested, even though, close-up, he smelled like Irish Spring soap. Like the old commercials, I liked Irish Spring. He sauntered toward LeRoy, and I took it as my cue to leave.

Outside, the partial moon cast a sickly glow on the poorly-lit parking lot. It was emptier now than when I had arrived. I wondered if the casino got an after-work crowd that cleared out before the evening got too late. I heard a peal of laughter, followed by the closing of a car door. Otherwise, it was quiet and shadowy. Why had I parked so far from the door?

With my purse filled with bills and the check, I made my way into the darkness, cursing myself for not taking all the money as a check. It was a stupid decision, one based on wanting to actually see cash. What if someone saw my winnings and followed me?

Behind me, I heard a light crunch on the gravel, followed by eerie silence. I looked back at the casino and thought I saw movement behind a white van.

"Not good, you dope. Why didn't you ask for an escort to your car?" The answer, of course, was we were in the Northwoods of Minnesota, where the crime rate hardly registered—except for a recent murder.

I felt more than saw a presence. Clutching my bag, I sped up.

Chapter Twenty-Nine: The Attack

Over the years, I have been indoctrinated about personal safety. Dad enrolled me in a self-defense class when I was fourteen. "It never hurts to be prepared, honey."

I learned kicks and jabs and all sorts of ways to do physical damage to an attacker. However, the instructor, a female ex-marine, who was built like a tank, told us that being prepared was the most important thing we could do.

"Know your surroundings. Pay attention and be aware. If you think it's a threat, treat it like a threat. Your biggest enemy is denial."

As I sped up my pace to my car on the edge of the lot, away from the lights of the casino, her words came back to me. I used to be prepared at night when I was out alone in New York, but I'd grown lax since the move to the cabin.

My heart raced, and my mouth turned dry as if all the saliva had been sucked out. I couldn't hear the footstep anymore because my feet were making so much noise as I hurried on. In my hand, I had my keys with the car fob. With a sense of relief, I pressed the fob and heard the door unlock. I was safe.

Then behind me, arms reached out and grabbed me in a suffocating bear hug, jerking me back away from the car door. The instructor's military drill voice came back to me. "Kick, pinch, use your elbows. Go for the eyes, the balls, the knees. Surprise them. Do something they aren't expecting."

He expected me to fight. He expected the kicks and the elbow jabs. Instead, I wheezed, "Heart! Having a heart attack!" With that, I went limp against him, like I was going to faint.

"What the fuck?" In his surprise, he lost his balance as I fell against him. He loosened his grip. It was enough that I thrust my elbow as hard as I could into his belly, and as soon as I heard the "oomph," I took my keys with the little container of pepper spray, twisted around, and sprayed into his face.

Unfortunately, the spray also got into my eyes. I coughed and sputtered as he howled and put his hands to his face. Maybe I should have taken this opportunity to kick him in the balls. I would have made my instructor proud, but I was now completely in flight mode.

Through my tears, I didn't get a good look at him before I took off running back to the casino, yelling the whole time, "Help! Somebody help!" By then, an elderly couple walking to their car were also yelling.

"Help that poor girl. She's been attacked!"

I didn't look back. Ahead of me, in the blur of the tears pouring out of my pepper-sprayed eyes, I saw Jim running toward me. Behind him was LeRoy and an overweight security guard, who looked like he was halfway to a heart attack.

Jim got to me first and gave me a quick hug. "Get inside. We'll go after him."

I stood in his embrace just long enough to see LeRoy over his shoulder. In my blurred vision, LeRoy didn't look concerned; he looked disappointed.

Once inside, my cheeks wet with tears, the manager ran toward me. "Are you all right?" Beyond me, the slot machines continued to sing their eerie tune.

Grabbing my elbow, the manager escorted me to his office.

I sat down on a hard chair and wiped at my eyes with the back of my arm. "I need to wash off my face. The pepper spray got to me."

In the bathroom, I rinsed my eyes in cold water. My hands shook as I pulled down a paper towel. In fact, my whole insides were shaking. The stinging in my eyes abated with the cool water, and I wondered what it felt like to get a direct hit. I hoped it hurt like hell for hours and hours.

While I waited in the manager's office with a small glass of brandy, he called the tribal police. "We're on the reservation, so it's their jurisdiction."

I felt comforted that I wouldn't have to talk with LeRoy and discomforted that I was once again talking to the law.

The policeman arrived within ten minutes. He was older, maybe in his fifties, with longish salt-and-pepper hair. He looked more like a college professor than a policeman.

"Hi." He pulled up a chair beside me. "I'm Charles LaDuke."

For the next few minutes, I described to him what happened. "After he grabbed me, I was able to spray him with this." I held up my key fob with the pepper spray.

He nodded his approval. "Did you get a look at him."

Should I tell him I didn't see him, but I smelled him? My attacker wore Drakkar Noir cologne, just like Donald Pruitt, LeRoy's cousin. I weighed it for a few moments, noticing how Charles was studying my expression.

"You recognized him. I can see it on your face."

I cleared my throat, a chill rising in my chest. "Uh, no. I didn't see him that well. But I smelled him."

Charles's mouth twitched into a little smile that he quickly erased. "Smelled him, eh?"

"He was wearing Drakkar Noir. I recognized it because my husband…ex-husband used to wear it." I realized as soon as the words came out of my mouth that I sounded stupid. The attacker smelled just like my ex? Really?

"Was it your ex-husband?"

"No. He's back in New York." Probably screwing his makeup artist.

The manager, whose name was Craig something-or-other, piped in. "Whoever it was must have seen you win. Probably tried to snatch your purse. You really should have asked security to escort you to your car."

I didn't feel like being scolded right now and was about to say so when I decided silence would be more prudent.

In New York, I'd had a couple of purse-snatching attempts, which was why I always wore my bag cross-shouldered. This wasn't a purse snatching. I felt it deep inside. This man wanted to hurt me. But I didn't argue with the manager.

Charles asked me where I lived by first saying, "You aren't from around here, are you?"

How many times had I heard that? "I live here now, but I grew up in New York. Some of my family came from here."

I told him I was living in a cabin my family owned on Lake Larissa, near the lodge.

"Really? You're the one who moved into the Clark place?"

I'd never heard it referred to by that name. "I guess. At least, my mother's maiden name was Clark."

He studied me again. "Oh, yes. I can see a little bit of resemblance. I went to school with the Clark sisters—Judy and Patty."

"My mother died when I was sixteen," I murmured. "We lived in New York, and I didn't know the family here."

Charles sat back and nodded. "Yes, most of that family is gone now. But I remember your mother. She was a little older, of course. Really smart. I think she was the class valedictorian. We thought she would go places. Same with Patty. Their mother, Arlette, pushed them. She was one smart lady, too." He opened his eyes and gazed beyond me. "Too bad about Patty."

I stayed quiet while Charles reminisced. This didn't seem like a good time to admit I knew so little about my family. I flashed on the memory of Mom crying and talking about her sister Patty. Aunt Patty. Why hadn't I asked more questions back then? Maybe because I was scared, scared by her reaction, scared by what was happening to her. Scared of losing my mother who thought Patty wanted to kill her.

When he opened his eyes, a look of sadness filled his face. He shook his head and repeated. "Too bad about Patty."

We were interrupted by a knock on the door. Jim and LeRoy walked in. Jim had scratches on his face and a bead of sweat rolling down the side of his face. LeRoy looked as clean and pressed as ever.

"We think he disappeared into the woods. I tried to follow, but it's too thick and dark in there."

LeRoy said nothing but kept his gaze on me as if I was about to jump up and escape.

Charles cleared his throat, and I waited for him to tell LeRoy I had smelled my assailant. Instead, he said, "Doesn't appear that whoever it was got anything. Jamie, here, is okay. It's late, and I'll continue to pursue any leads."

Jim's expression was one of skepticism. "We might be able to catch him tonight."

Charles simply smiled, and I said nothing. I was grateful he hadn't mentioned the Drakkar Noir.

I pushed back my chair, slightly giddy from the brandy. "I'd like to go home now, if that's okay."

Immediately, LeRoy responded, "I can walk you to your car."

Charles saved me from having to figure out how not to be alone with him when he smiled at LeRoy. "Not necessary. I'll escort her. I'd like to see the scene of the crime."

As we walked out into the casino, he leaned over and whispered, "I don't trust any of the Pruitts. Still haven't figured out why Rick hired him. But I've learned to stay out of the county business."

"Thanks."

The casino was nearly deserted. A few people sat glassy-eyed in front of the slot machines. I glanced at the archway leading to the table games and was surprised to see Phil talking to someone. His back was to me and the other man stood hidden in the recesses of the game room. Phil's posture told me he was in a serious conversation.

At this point in my life, I hardly cared what he was doing. Maybe Phil was a high-stakes gambler. Maybe he moonlighted as a dealer. My thoughts stopped there as a deep exhaustion crept through me. Even my knees felt weak, like I'd just run a marathon. I was so looking forward to climbing in bed with Bronte snoring beside me.

"Are you okay to drive? I can get my deputy to take you home."

All I wanted was a little solitude. "I'm fine, thanks."

I wasn't fine, of course. I paid little attention to my surroundings as I drove home through the darkened road. The trees were hulking shadows alongside the road, but overhead, the stars shone through a thin haze of clouds. I didn't notice the headlights of a car following me until I turned off at the lodge to my driveway. It followed me.

When a car followed you, according to my self-defense instructor, you should drive to the nearest well-lit convenience store. As if we had such a thing out here in the wild. I could have stopped at the lodge, but I was tired, achy, and fed up. I wanted no more confrontations—ever.

I drove to the cabin. In less than thirty seconds, the vehicle that was following me came bumping down the road. I clutched my pepper spray and watched my rearview mirror. The headlights were growing brighter as the vehicle approached.

"Oh God," I said aloud. "Please not a Pruitt, someone with a rock, or someone with an air rifle."

Bronte barked at the back door. If I made a dash for it now, I could probably get inside before my follower could get to the cabin. With a burst of energy, I threw the car door open, grabbed my bag, and ran as fast as I could to the cabin. Bronte's bark was filled with joy. I had a concrete step that led up to the door and, in my haste, my toe caught on it, causing me to lurch forward. The keys went flying into the flower bed beside the door.

I should have been scared. I should have run. I knew these woods and the paths. I could head for the lodge or the water or the not-yet-completed Lady Slipper Trail. Instead, I chose to grovel around the flower bed for the keys. I was tired of running.

"Lost something?"

I looked up to see Blaine. In the low light, it seemed like he was smiling.

"I've had a helluva evening. Can you help me find my keys?"

When I found them and got the door open, Bronte came tearing out with her teeth bared. "No!" I grabbed her collar. "Stupid dog. She doesn't remember you're her T-bone man."

Blaine stood back while I restrained Bronte. "I'll remember to bring one next time. I was at the casino, and they told me someone tried to jump you. I said I'd make sure you got home."

"Thanks. I'd invite you in, but I need to shower and crawl in bed. How about a raincheck."

What I really wanted to do at that moment was shove Bronte aside and fall into his strong and virile arms—just like Constance in *Knight of Lust*. Instead, I yanked Bronte inside and bid him farewell. At least someone was looking out for me.

Chapter Thirty: Patty Clark

I treated myself to a long soak in the tub, using bath salts left over from our days of visiting the cabin when I was little. When I stepped out, the room smelled of roses and old ladies.

Pouring myself a glass of wine, I settled on the couch in a long-sleeved nightshirt. Bronte tried to join me, but I pushed her down.

"This is my space, girl."

The cabin was the perfect temperature for lounging. This was the vision I'd had of the peace I would find when I moved here. Sadly, I wasn't feeling particularly peaceful as I sorted through everything from the day.

In one of my student jobs in college, I had been an administrative assistant to a dean. He loved to use flip charts to make lists to present to the faculty. Even though we were fully equipped to use computers and PowerPoint, he insisted on them. To this day, if I smelled a marker, it brought me back to stuffy conference rooms with paper taped to all the walls.

"I could use a flip chart tonight."

Bronte lifted her head, as if she was interested, then nuzzled her nose back onto her paws.

What did happen today? I went through a mental list: fired from the paper, yelled at Phil, finished the love memoir, had dinner with Jilly, won a bunch of money, attacked in the parking lot, and surreptitiously escorted home by Blaine.

"Oh yes, found out my mother and my Aunt Patty were smart. You know what, old girl, that's too much information." I finished my wine and went to bed.

After a restless sleep, I woke up early to a sunny sky with a few high streaky clouds drifting lazily overhead. I walked down to the lake with my mug of coffee and sat on the smooth rock near the water, hoping the morning sun soaking into my skin would relieve me of this haunted feeling that weighed on my shoulders.

Bronte, contrary to my mood, galloped around fetching a stick with a look of puppy joy. When was the last time I had felt joy? Or had I ever? Maybe it was time to sell and head back to New York. For a moment, as the lake water lapped at my bare feet, I longed for the anonymity of the big city. I wanted to be in a place where nobody knew my name.

I was so lost in my thoughts I didn't hear the pickup truck or the door closing or the footsteps behind me.

"Good morning. I brought you some breakfast," Jim greeted me.

His voice startled me. I spilled coffee on my lap, staining my only clean pair of shorts.

Bronte, who was out in the woods stalking a squirrel, finally noticed him and barked.

He joined me on the rock, handing over a white bakery bag. He was dressed in a red T-shirt and khaki shorts. His legs had the tanned muscular look of a bicyclist, and he exuded a freshness that my ex-husband Andrew never had.

"I didn't hear you. Did you sneak up through the woods?" I took the bag and opened it, my hand still shaking. The aroma of fresh-baked bagel wafted out. "How did you know I love bagels?"

"Wild guess. You're from New York. I hear that's all they eat."

Although I still didn't quite trust Jim—he kept showing up at odd times—I did feel my sour mood lift as I pulled off part of the bagel and savored it. I offered him half.

"Where did you get these? The bakery in town doesn't make them, and the grocery store sells something so doughy and filled with preservatives I feel like I'm getting embalmed every time I eat one."

Jim laughed. "Embalmed, huh? The casino bar and grill has a little bakery."

With the mention of Copper Lake Casino, one of the white clouds drifted by the sun, putting us in sudden shade. The temperature dropped for a moment, and I shivered.

Jim took another bite of the bagel. "I'm just checking. How are you doing?"

What could I say? I was contemplating fleeing this Eden for the heat and stink and congestion of the big city?

I shrugged.

"We didn't find the guy. I'm guessing he knew the woods and the area."

Should I tell him I recognized the man? Or at least his scent. Could I trust him? Bronte sat nuzzling Jim's leg. Maybe that was a sign he was safe. I stared at my shorts now spotted with dribbled coffee.

"Did you recognize him?" Jim looked out at the lake, like the question made him uncomfortable.

I almost told him I thought it was Donald Pruitt—almost. But something held me back. I shook my head. "I didn't see him."

"Even when you pepper sprayed him?"

I tensed, sensing he was pushing it. Was he fishing to find out if I recognized LeRoy's cousin Donald? Maybe he was a good friend. Suddenly, I was chilled, like the sun had gone out of the sky. Jim wasn't to be trusted.

I moved a little farther from him. "Listen, I'm going to be honest with you. I told Charles LaDuke everything I saw. I feel like you're interrogating me. Go ask him!" The viciousness of my tone surprised me and caused Bronte to lift her head off Jim's lap to look at me.

Jim raised his hand. "Now wait a minute…"

I stood and turned away from him to squeeze back the tears welling up.

Because he was sitting with his back to the sun, I couldn't make out the expression on his face.

"Please go." I pointed to his truck. "I need some space."

He slipped off the rock and, in a quiet voice said, "I just wanted to see if you were okay and share a bagel." He shrugged and walked away without another word.

Bronte followed him then came bounding back like she expected me to join him.

I stayed, my feet massaged by the gentle waves of the lake, until I heard the pickup truck fade down the driveway. "No wonder Andrew left you. You're a bitch." I walked back to the cabin, wiping the tears that dribbled down my cheeks.

The rest of the morning I reviewed George's love memoir. I sat at my computer trying to come up with a letter that would include positive remarks as well as suggestions. I drew a blank. My mood was too foul to work on this right now. I hated myself for disliking the love story and for insulting Jim. The more I sat and thought about it, the more I realized I owed Jim an apology. I was about to text him when Bronte growled her deep, threatening sound.

Blaine stood at the back door holding a doggie bag.

"Hey," I greeted him. My late-night stalker.

He smiled, but his eyes looked tired. "At your service." He let Bronte sniff the bag and then emptied the steak bone onto the front step.

She grabbed it and ran off to her spot under the aspen.

I invited him in for coffee and as I brewed another pot, I watched him read a page from George's manuscript. He was softer and wider than his days as a teenage lifeguard. His cheeks had a sag to them, as if either gravity or the world had pulled them down. Still, his eyes were that greenish-brown hazel and his hair, though short, was still the sun-bleached blond of those days gone by. I wondered, for a moment, what he looked like naked.

God. What am I thinking? And then as quickly as the thought ripped through my brain, I pictured Jim's tanned and muscular legs. Time for a cold dip in the lake.

I handed him the coffee.

He pointed to the manuscript. "Sounds like this poor guy really misses his wife."

I didn't tell him about the sex fantasy chapter, although, as I sat down, I thought about it.

He put the manuscript page down and looked at me with concern. "I hear they didn't find the guy who attacked you."

This was my moment to tell him who it was and my suspicions about LeRoy and his cousin. This was a perfect time to share my angst and anger.

166

Instead, I said, "I had a nice talk with the reservation policeman."

"Charlie?"

"He told me something interesting."

Did I note a tightening of Blaine's grip on the coffee mug? Or was I being silly.

"Oh?"

"He said he remembered my mother and her sister."

I stirred a little sugar into my coffee. In my distress, I'd made it far too weak. Dad used to call bad coffee "Minnesota Coffee." He said it tasted more like dishwater.

Setting down the spoon, I looked at Blaine. "You've lived here all your life. Do you know anything about my family?"

Outside, Bronte woofed to be let in.

Blaine pushed his chair back. "I'll do it. You sit."

Bronte trotted into the kitchen, directly to her water dish, and slurped at it, leaving a wet mess on the floor.

When Blaine sat down again, I thought I detected a wariness in his voice. "I don't know much. When I was a kid, I didn't pay a lot of attention to the adults and their stories."

"But there were stories?"

Blaine pushed his chair back, folded his arms, and stretched his legs. He looked at the ceiling. "What I heard—and you have to remember I was a teenager with my mind filled with thoughts of girls, not gossip—is that this cabin and the one next to it belonged to sisters."

"There was another cabin on this road?"

"I'll get to that."

Bronte sauntered over and collapsed at my feet but kept an eye on Blaine.

"There was some dispute between the sisters. Patty Clark, who was your aunt, hooked up with some guy who pushed her to claim all the acreage when the girls' mother died. She contested the will, claiming her full-blooded native status meant the property belonged to her."

"Wait. Did you say Patty was full-blooded Ojibwe? My mother wasn't. Even though I don't know much about my family, I do know that."

"Patty and Judy had different fathers, from what I understand."

"Oh." This sounded too much like a soap opera. "What happened?"

"It ended up in a legal battle, I guess. We acquired the property a couple of years ago, after Patty died."

"Patty is dead?" I felt a momentary sense of disappointment. She wouldn't be able to tell me about my mother or my family.

"Sad story. She had a serious drinking problem, and it looked like she set the place on fire and burned up in it."

I shivered. "That's bad." I pictured the forested land between my place and the lodge. "So, that overgrown logging road between here and the lodge was a driveway?"

Blaine nodded. "Dad wanted to use the land to add cabins. I wanted to leave it alone. Since Dad died, I haven't done anything with it." His tone turned solemn, like he was giving me a sermon. "It's important to preserve the land." He hesitated. "And if you ever decide to sell..."

"Thanks. I plan to hang on to this for a while."

Outside, in the distance, I heard the ugly sound of a pair of jet skis on the lake. Inside the cabin, the only sound was the occasional burp and hiss of the coffee maker.

Blaine sat up straighter and reached for his coffee. He grabbed it a little askew and it slipped out of his hand, spilling onto the manuscript. We both moved at the same time to keep the papers from getting soaked. In doing so, we bumped arms. With the warmth of his arm against me mine, a little zing went through my chest.

"Oh shit! I'm so sorry." He pulled a handkerchief out of the pocket of his khakis and swiped at the spill, breaking the contact.

Between the two of us, we mopped up the mess. The coffee had laid waste to chapters seven and eight. Unfortunately, the ink George had used to print the manuscript was water soluble. I had my work cut out for me this afternoon trying to put it back together.

After I cleaned the table, Blaine stood. "I am so sorry about this. Can I make it up to you? Maybe dinner at the lodge? I'll buy."

I laughed. "You sure you can afford it? The prices are quite steep."

168

Before he left, he took me in his arms and hugged me. No kiss, but a warm, lovely bear-hug. Bronte growled but stayed on her rug.

I watched his SUV disappear down the road and decided I needed to explore the old logging road. But first, I had to figure out what to do about the manuscript, and I needed to get to town to deposit my big casino check.

Chapter Thirty-One: Patty's Cabin

As I drove down the road to the lodge, I stopped where the fence and the *No Trespassing* sign guarded the overgrown driveway. I remembered the other day when the crows had gathered. A shiver ran down my back. I would take Bronte with me to explore it later that afternoon. A walk in the woods might help me think about my future.

Town was Tuesday-noon active with tourists in baggy shorts strolling down the sidewalk, pushing kids in strollers. I used to be one of those summer people, window shopping with my mother on the days when she felt she could be out. Looking back, the last year we came as a family, I didn't think she left the cabin except to sit on the rock by the lake. Dad had hovered around her, which gave me the opportunity to grab a towel and walk to the lodge's beach.

At the bank, I deposited my casino winnings into my checking account. The teller took the check and said, with a note of envy, "I've never had much luck at the slots."

For some reason, I wanted to assure her I didn't spend all my time gambling. "It was a fluke—really. I hardly ever go to casinos."

"I hear it's not safe there. They say that some woman was attacked in the parking lot."

My cheeks burned. "That's too bad. Did she get hurt?"

"They say he tried to drag her to the woods, but she got him good with Mace or something."

"Smart woman. I'll remember that next time I go." I was glad my keys with the pepper spray were in my purse where the teller couldn't see them.

I was tempted to stop at the *Times* to see how Jilly was doing, but when I walked by, I saw Phil was engaged in a serious conversation with her. Jilly wore an angry expression and her hands flew as she gestured at him. Nancy's desk was empty. Perhaps Harry was doing his afternoon coffee break at the bar.

It was nearing five before I had all my errands done, including loading up on groceries. In New York, I had a little grocery store right on the corner across from my apartment. For a moment, I missed my fractured Spanish conversations with Juanita, the clerk. Here, the clerks were polite, but they didn't give me advice on making empanadas or the best salsa to go with chips. In New York, I could stop at the store almost anytime. Here, it involved getting into the car and driving ten miles. I'd learned to stock up.

By the time I reached home, the clear, sunny skies had darkened as deep gray thunderclouds rolled in from the west. The clouds brought an oppressive humidity and trapped it in the torpid air. If I gauged my weather correctly, we were in for another storm.

Bronte greeted me as I hauled all the grocery bags in. George's coffee-stained manuscript covered the kitchen table and the counters, drying out. I looked at it in dismay.

"When we get all this food put away, let's go for a long walk. The weather be damned."

Bronte wagged her tail with enthusiasm.

I changed into a lightweight T-shirt and sprayed myself down with Off. Once out on the road, I was pleased I'd covered myself in it. The air was still and heavy, and the mosquitos whined around my ears. I wondered how the Ojibwe survived the insects. I'd read somewhere they smeared themselves with bear grease. Would it be worse to smell like a dead bear or be eaten by the mosquitos? At least the mosquitoes here didn't carry malaria. However, the deer ticks had Lyme Disease. Maybe another reason to pack up and move back to New York. If I decided to give it up and go back to the city, at least Blaine was interested in buying the cabin. I could sell it to someone who wanted to preserve the land. The thought gave me some comfort, although at this point I wasn't ready to think about selling.

As we walked, the forest took on an unnatural calm. Even the birds quieted. The loudest sound was the crunch of gravel beneath my feet and the rustle of leaves and underbrush as Bronte bounded in and out of the woods.

The closer I came to the old driveway, the heavier the air grew. Sweat dripped down the inside of my T-shirt, and the wet cotton clung to my back. I stopped at the abandoned road and slapped at a deerfly buzzing my head. Another fly joined it, and as I stood, a heaviness filled my chest, like someone held me in an unfriendly bear hug. It reminded me of the attack the night before. On instinct, I reached into my shorts pocket to make sure I had my keys with the pepper spray. It seemed silly in these quiet woods, but this road spooked me.

Bronte sat down and looked at me with her liquid brown eyes as if to say, *are we really going in there?*

"Nonsense," I said aloud. "Let's explore." I looked up through the trees to see clouds roiling. Maybe Bronte was right. We should go back. Otherwise, we might end up getting drenched.

I shook my head at her. "I didn't put all this awful mosquito spray on me to chicken out. We're going in." I didn't know what propelled me down that road. It certainly wasn't Bronte urging me on.

She didn't run ahead like she usually did. Instead, she stuck by my side as I slipped through a gap in the barbed wire fence with its faded *No Trespassing* sign. I thought about what Blaine had said about preserving the wilderness and wondered how long he could hold out on not developing the land. He might have been an environmentalist, but he was also a businessman.

The road was overgrown with tall weeds and underbrush. I was surprised that, after several years of lying fallow, little trees hadn't sprouted up. Perhaps the dirt had been packed too hard. But, as I made my way down the road, another thought crossed my mind. Perhaps nature knew something about this land and had chosen not to renew it.

I realized, as I swatted at the deerflies, that I was being a little dramatic, but the heaviness stayed in my chest, and Bronte stayed at my side. The woods were thickening alongside the abandoned road and casting dark shadows. Overhead, thunder rumbled.

About one hundred yards in, I reached a clearing with the charred remnants of Patty's cabin. A fragment of the wall facing west still stood, along with the fieldstone fireplace. The rest of the cabin was nothing more than blackened rubble.

I walked around the foundation, drawn by a sense of loss. The cabin sat, like mine, on top of a rise that sloped down to the water. In front of it, through the wild shrubbery and underbrush, I saw a glint of the lake. I took in a long breath of the heavy, heated air and let it out with a shudder. It was as if I was standing by a twin. The foundation looked to be the same size as mine and the view similar. Except that this place felt wrong.

Stepping inside the foundation, a chill ran up my legs, like I'd walked in ice water. Bronte stood outside the foundation and whined. How could a place feel so cold in the middle of this sweltering heat? Nothing remained in the cabin to indicate a person once lived there. I studied it, not sure what I was looking for. Maybe something that would tell me about my aunt? All I saw was blackened rubble.

I thought about my mother. At least her ashes had become one with the lake she loved. What had happened to Patty's?

Bronte whined and turned toward the road. "Want to go home, girl?"

The sky through the trees grew darker, but the air stayed still and stagnant. For a few moments, I was glued to the place, like it was holding me in an embrace. Bronte whined again and broke the spell.

"Looks like a storm is coming. Guess we'd better find our way back."

As I passed the side of the foundation, the side that, in my cabin, held a flower bed with a climbing rose that Mother had planted years ago, I noticed something red. I stooped down to examine it, even as the sky grew darker. It was a lone rose clinging to its thorny vine. When I reached down to it, a thorn stuck my finger and a little bead of blood formed.

"I'll take that as a sign to get the hell out of here."

As if the spirit of the storm had heard me, the air went from dead and silent to a sudden rush of wind ripping through the treetops. At the same time, a bolt of lightning tore across the sky. Rain came in large splats. I turned toward the road. Bronte was already running ahead of me.

The thunder crashed, and something reached up and grabbed at my ankle. I tripped, falling forward on my knees, scraping the palms of my hands across the grass and brush and dirt. Bronte barked with an urgency, and the rain came down, pushing its way through the canopy of pines and aspens. When I tried to pick myself up, I was tangled in the rose vine.

"How the hell did that happen?" Yet, something deep inside said it was no accident. The cabin was trying to pull me in. I brushed the thought away. Clearly, I'd been reading too many gothic romance manuscripts by authors like Florice.

Bronte ran to me, barked, and ran back down the road. If she could have talked, I think she would have said, "Hurry! Hurry!"

The wind swept in like a gale and suddenly a flash of green white light lit up the cabin area. The thunder was loud, like a bomb exploding next to my ear, and a jolt of electricity shot through the ground. Lightning had struck a tree about twenty feet from me. The top of the tree swayed and toppled.

I picked myself up and ran as the tree came crashing down. The rain was like a waterfall. I barely saw the abandoned road as the rain poured from the sky, but Bronte's bark kept me on track. I followed the sound. Behind me, I felt as if something was reaching out to pull me back.

My chest ached from running and stumbling and picking myself up. Bronte kept barking. I was soaked through, my T-shirt and shorts clinging to me, restricting my movement. When I reached the road, the rain came down so hard I felt I had a sheet in front of me. I almost ran into the barbed wire fence. Headlights of an approaching car saved me. Someone was driving away from my cabin. I hoped they hadn't vandalized it or stolen my laptop while I'd been on this exploration from hell.

If the driver saw me, he didn't stop. I stood at the fence, gasping for breath, as the car drove away. I recognized it by the rusted, dented fender and the faded red color. I'd seen that car parked in front of the *Times* last Friday. What would I find when I got back?

Chapter Thirty-Two: Mitchell McConnell

B y the time I reached the cabin, the storm's fury had abated. The rain was a gentle patter on the leaves of the trees, rather than a gushing waterfall. My hair was plastered to my scalp, and water dripped down my face and off my nose.

In Florice's romance, the redheaded maiden's hair always flowed saucily onto her shoulders. Mine stuck to my chin and neck. There would be no knight on a steed to rescue me from this storm.

The sky lightened as I approached the cabin door. I had forgotten to lock it and the door stood slightly ajar.

"Oh please, not some kind of a robbery." If someone wanted me to leave, to head back to New York, this would have been a good time to vandalize the place. I had enough money in my checking account to get a one-way ticket East and never look back.

However, when I walked in, the cabin looked the same, with George's manuscript still scattered over every flat surface. Perhaps the car I'd seen was someone who had taken a wrong turn.

Except, Bronte pawed at something just inside the door. On the floor was a thin manila envelope with the words *You should know* scrawled in block letters across the front.

"What?" I stared at it, not daring to pick it up. Could it be some kind of poison, like the anthrax someone sent people years ago?

"Can you tell me whether it's safe to open this?"

Bronte shook herself, sending water spraying across the floor, and walked away, having lost interest in anything but her own water dish.

After I toweled off and changed into dry clothes, I picked up the envelope and brought it over to the kitchen table. Sliding George's manuscript aside, I set it down and opened the clasp. Holding my breath, I slipped the envelope flap open. No suspicious powder. Inside were more old newspaper clippings about Larissa Lodge.

"Curious." I poured them out on the table. A mildew smell wafted out, mingling with the flowery fragrance. It was as if these clippings had been stored in a basement for many years.

"Why would I care about this?" I sighed, wondering who thought I would be interested. I shoved the contents back in the envelope suddenly tired of all this intrigue.

***

That evening, with the skies cleared, I sat on my porch with an ice-cold amber ale and wondered what to do next. I'd focused the weekend on George's memoir so I could start a job on Monday. Monday, I was hired-fired at the same time. Monday, the casino temporarily saved me from financial ruin, and Tuesday, Blaine nearly wrecked all the work I'd done over the weekend on the manuscript when he spilled coffee on it.

Should I fix the coffee-stained mess? Spend more time with the mystery clippings? Do more research on Joe? Check to see if Racine Mining had produced more propaganda? Text Jim to apologize? Or simply pack up and move? With the sun setting gently over the lake, I did none of the above. Instead, I did what I used to do when I was avoiding something. I grabbed *Jane Eyre* out of my bookcase, curled up on the couch, and read.

That night I dreamed a voice called to me from across the lake, except I was in my grandmother's house in Boston—an old, drafty Victorian with a sagging porch. The voice was neither male nor female, merely a hoarse whisper. I couldn't make out what it was saying and the closer I got to it, the farther it faded away. When I stepped into her dark, stuffy living room, the floor gave way, and I plunged into the holding cell in Queens. All the people around me were enveloped in the shadows, except one near the open door

176

of the cell. *Come,* the voice beckoned, but when I tried to reach the door, I found my ankle was shackled to a metal eye on the floor and the floor was awash in something thick and putrid. *Come.*

I woke up with a start to the darkness of my bedroom and Bronte sleeping peacefully at my side. My pillowcase was damp with sweat. Taking deep, calming breaths, I slid back under the covers. When would those nightmares go away? When I closed my eyes, I saw the ragged open space that once held Patty's cabin. I tried sleeping on my side and my shoulder hurt. I tried the other side and my hip hurt. Finally, still wide awake, I got up and stumbled to the bathroom, where I kept the prescription for Xanax. For the first time since I moved to Lake Larissa, I took one.

The next morning, I woke up feeling groggy and slightly hungover. The voice in the dream followed me around as I fed Bronte and made coffee. I felt surrounded by unfinished business, unable to focus on any of it. I might have stayed in that state of ennui except, when I checked my email, I had a reply from the editor at *The New Yorker*. "Hi, Jamie. Of course, I remember you. Yes, I'm interested in your proposal. Please send an outline and a 1500-word sample."

I stared at it. What a coup to write for *The New Yorker*. But, did I have the talent to do this? I walked down to the lake with my coffee to sit on the rock and think about how I would research the article and who I would need to contact.

The wind blew across the lake, creating whitecaps that crashed rhythmically against the rocky shoreline. I'd brewed the coffee so strong it had sludge in the bottom of the mug. Instead of thinking through an article about Joe, my thoughts strayed to the previous morning and how nasty I had been to Jim. My first order of business today was to text him and apology. Then, I needed to fix the memoir. After that, I could concentrate on an article for *The New Yorker*.

"*The New Yorker*," I called into the wind. "Imagine that!"

A van rumbled down the driveway while I was singing to the wind. I didn't hear it until Bronte squealed and loped up the hill to the cabin.

Rob called out, "Hello down there. Don't let the wind blow you away!"

22222222

He joined me on the rock like Jim had the day before, except he didn't have any fresh bagels. He did have fresh paint on his coveralls.

I pointed to it. "What have you been up to?"

"A little work for the lodge."

"I thought they had their own staff."

"I don't generally help them out, but the price was right."

I'd sensed Rob wasn't a big fan of the lodge or its management.

A cool gust of wind sent shivers through me. "Let's go up to the cabin. I'm a little chilled."

On the way up, Rob told me he'd heard about the attack at the casino and also heard it was LeRoy Pruitt's dumbass cousin who'd done it. "That whole family of Pruitts are bent. Bad folks going back many generations."

"But how did anyone know it was Donald Pruitt. I didn't identify him."

Rob smiled and flicked his gray braid. "Injun sense."

"You know Charles LaDuke, don't you?"

I made a new pot of coffee without all the sludge. While we drank it, I showed him the package that had been delivered under my door. "This is the second one that has found its way to me. Strange. Why would anyone think I was interested in old clippings about the lodge?"

Rob leaned back and regarded me with his deep brown eyes. "Do you know the story about this land and the lodge?"

"What story?"

He pointed to the clipping of Mitchell McConnell. "He wasn't a righteous man."

I thought it a strange way to describe Blaine's grandfather.

"Before McConnell came along, all the land around Lake Larissa belonged to the tribe. Each member was allotted twenty acres for their home and livelihood. It was during the Depression, and we were desperately poor. Grain didn't grow in the heat and the drought, and, even though we had plenty of fish and wildlife, people in power restricted what we could take. They wanted us to leave the land."

I thought back to *Bury My Heart at Wounded Knee* and all the other abuse Native Americans had suffered. I remembered what Rob had said about

McConnell unburying the dead here.

"McConnell came in with cash and started buying the acres that weren't part of the reservation. The families weren't sophisticated and didn't know how they were being taken. He stole the land from the rightful owners to build the lodge."

Rob's fingers tensed as he set down the mug. "My parents sold to him. He promised they could live on the land, but then he started charging rent, and when they couldn't pay, he had them evicted."

"And the burial ground? I heard he had it moved."

"Moved? Shoveled it up and dumped it in the lake."

Bronte sensed Rob's distress and ambled over to him, placing her head on his lap. Rob stroked her.

"But what has this got to do with me?"

"McConnell wanted the Clark land. But your grandmother wouldn't sell. When she died, it was divided between her two daughters—your mother and her sister, Patty."

I held my hand up. "Wait. I heard about this. Patty tried to get Mother's piece of the land. This is where it's so weird for me. All my life, I thought my relatives on Mother's side were either dead or scattered. Now I hear that my Aunt Patty lived just down the road and died in a fire."

"No one talks much about her—she had a sad life. I'm told she, too, sold to McConnell in the end. Only your mother held out."

I thought about the burned-out spot, the twin of my cabin. What kind of a story did it have to tell?

"Jamie, you're an island in the middle of McConnell land. They own most of this side of the lake now."

"Blaine told me he wanted to preserve the land."

"Don't believe everything you hear." Rob looked at his watch and stood. "I have to go. The puppies at the clinic are calling." He walked to the door. "I apologize for being so downcast. I get into moods like this whenever I step on lodge land."

I smiled at him. "Well, you're safe here. I have no intention of selling."

After he left, I wondered if the McConnells had ever talked with Dad about selling the cabin. He'd told me it was important to my mother that the land stay in the family.

I poured myself another cup of coffee, reflecting on that conversation. It had taken place before Dad had his first stroke. I'd finished my bachelor's degree and was thinking about graduate school. We were sitting in his apartment in Manhattan. Dad had lived in it long enough that it was rent controlled. The building had been sold and the new owners were offering incentives for the residents to move. I asked him why he didn't take the money. The place was too big for him, since by then I was living on my own.

"It's my anchor," he'd said. "Just like that land in Minnesota was your mother's anchor. Even when we went through times when money was tight and I had trouble paying for her care, I couldn't sell it. Until the last couple of years when she didn't know me, she always asked about it."

He had such a combination of sorrow and passion in his voice that I stopped myself from asking if he would be willing to sell the cabin to pay for graduate school. From then on, I thought of this place as my obligation to my mother.

Was it time to give in? Both Mom and Dad were dead. I was barely making a living here, and I was being harassed. I looked at Bronte wagging her tail as Rob's van pulled away. No, it wasn't time. Bronte wasn't a city dog, and, in the end, I didn't think I was a city person anymore either.

I sat down with the pile of old clippings and sorted through them. In the middle of the pile was a note-sized envelope stamped and addressed to Judy Clark, my mother, at her university address in Boston. The mailing address had been Xed out and *Refused* written in large letters. The return address was P. Clark, Rural Route, 2 Killdeer. A note from the dead to the dead.

Chapter Thirty-Three: The Letter

I studied the envelope for a few moments, debating whether I had the right to open it. Did I want to know what my aunt wrote? I thought about the mother I knew as a child and couldn't picture her writing "refused" across a letter. She was quiet and kind and usually distracted. Dad said it was the artist in her. I didn't think she ever raised her voice to me.

The last time I saw her, I had just turned fourteen. By then her dark hair had become wispy and lank, as she rocked back and forth in her chair making chewing motions with her lips. I hadn't wanted to take the trip on a weekend to see her because it meant missing a sleepover with friends. Dad insisted I go with him just before Thanksgiving. The sky was slate gray, and the wind blew with the damp rawness so typical of November in New York. We caught the Metro North to Poughkeepsie and then walked several blocks to the Fair Oaks Nursing Home. The trees were barren, and the leaves swirled in little eddies on the street.

I thought, for a moment, when I bent down to say hello that she recognized me, that she had a little spark in her eyes. But, when I said, "Hi, Mom," she rocked a little harder, and her eyes emptied.

Now, as I held the returned letter, I also remembered she'd said something to me that day. At the time, it made no sense. "Oh, no. Patty." Then she started to cry, and the crying quickly escalated into a howl. The nurse had to come and take her away. She must have thought I was her sister.

When I asked Dad about it, he shrugged. "Who knows what's happening in her head. She's very sick."

I cried on the way home—perhaps because I felt sorry for her, perhaps because I was tired, or perhaps because I wanted my real mother back, not this ghost.

"Well, Bronte, what should I do? Should I leave well enough alone or should I open the letter?"

Bronte sighed from her cushion on the floor and provided no canine advice. I hesitated for a moment then sliced the envelope open. Of course, I was going to read it. What naturally curious person wouldn't?

The one sheet of stationary had the image of a pink Lady's Slipper orchid in the upper right-hand corner. The writing was in a careful cursive, but the sentences slanted downward.

> *Dear Jude,*
> *I am sorry. It was a BIG mistake about the land. I wasn't thinking right. M was pushing for it. But you shouldn't have left me. It won't happen again. Please come home. I was bad, but I'll be good. Please come!!!!*
> *Love always,*
> *Patty*

I set the letter down. I recalled how Patty had wanted to see Mother the last time we came to the cabin. Clearly, they'd had a big falling out over the land. Was that what she was talking about? And who was "M"?

The words sounded so desperate. It saddened me that Mother had refused the letter. It saddened me that Patty became a drunk and died in a burning cabin. No wonder that place gave me the creeps.

I slipped the letter back in the envelope and thought through all the people I knew in Killdeer. Someone must remember the details of what happened between the two sisters. Charles LaDuke, the reservation policemen, knew them. I needed to talk with him.

As if by the magic of some spirit, my focus on the letter was averted when the phone rang.

"Jamie Forest?"

I recognized the wizened voice of Clarence Engstrom. "Hello, Mr.

Engstrom. What can I do for you?"

"First, you can call me Clarence," he chortled. "Then you can come over and take me to the jail. I need a ride to see that boy of yours."

Joe had become *my boy*. I noted that Clarence didn't even ask if I wanted to give him a ride.

"You know I live by the lake. It will take me a little time to get you."

"Yes. I know all about where you live. Did legal work for your family."

"Really? Did it involve my mother's sister, Patty?"

Clarence cleared his throat. "Could be. But that's a story for later. What time can you come?"

We agreed I would pick him up in an hour. I wondered why he had decided I was his Uber service, but, at this point, I wasn't going to argue. This would be a good opportunity to gather information for *The New Yorker* article.

***

Killdeer was mid-week, mid-afternoon quiet. As I drove down the main street past the *Times*, I wondered how Harry was doing with the deadline for getting the paper to the printer. A piece of me hoped he had made a mess of it, and another piece was relieved I wasn't under the pressure to get it out.

I glanced at the empty parking space in front of the *Times* and it triggered a memory. A car had been parked there last Friday with a damaged fender. It was the same car that had passed me on my road in the rain storm. The driver must have left the second packet of clippings at my cabin.

Mavis, the receptionist from the lodge, had been talking with Jilly. Was that her car? I'd have to take a look when I drove by the lodge on my way home. If it was, why did she drop off that packet?

My thoughts were wrenched away from Mavis and the envelope when Donald Pruitt passed me in his pickup truck. He looked straight ahead and wore dark glasses. Good. Maybe I had done damage to his eyes.

As I parked in front of Clarence's house, I had a millisecond flash of the previous night's dream. I couldn't remember much of it, but I did know it had taken place at my grandmother's in Boston. Or had it? The houses were remarkably the same except Grandma Forest's house was old and unkempt.

Clarence greeted me at the front door and led me once again to the

183

kitchen. He hadn't asked for a sandwich and, for a moment, I wondered if he had expected me to bring one. However, the kitchen table was set with a hamburger casserole still warm from the oven and a green salad.

"Have some lunch before we go off to that snake pit of a jail." He chuckled. "I guess it's not a snake pit. I've seen worse."

"So have I." It came out before I could stop.

He raised an eyebrow. "I read your story."

Who in this town hadn't read it?

We sat down, and he dished out a generous helping of the steaming hamburger, noodles, and cream of mushroom soup. "My wife tried to interest me in what she called 'healthier eating.' She snuck spinach into everything and refused to cook with hamburger." He pointed to the casserole. "At least my girl understands this is what I like. Good old hot dish."

I grew up in New York with an incredible variety of food, and none of it involved hamburger and cream of mushroom soup. Yet, the casserole was quite tasty.

"So," Clarence said between bites of food, "we need to get our young man to talk to us."

"Have you found him a different lawyer?"

"No luck with that. Those young, earnest kids just out of law school aren't interested in a five-hour drive to the wilderness. Until I find someone, I'm it, and I'm assigning you as my assistant."

I squirmed in my seat like a little kid. "Um, I'm not sure I can be of any help."

"Oh, I'll pay you."

"Pay me?"

"You can be my investigator. I read that article. You're smart, and you figured out how to research information on false arrests. I believe this is a false arrest. I think Joe is a fall guy for someone else."

I put my fork down and looked directly at Clarence. "He knew Nancy. He was seen with her."

"So what? He murdered her for what? I talked to the sheriff. They found some things of hers in his pickup truck, but her purse, with all the money and credit cards, were still in a drawer in her desk."

This was information I hadn't heard. "Oh."

He grinned at me. "It's the senile old lawyer and the Yankee tree hugger against the world." His expression turned serious. "This is a community with deep divides. Even though they were here first and even though we stole their land, the powers that be have a strong bias against the Indians. Plain and simple. Justice does not favor Joe."

"What about the tribe? Won't they help him?"

"Who do you think is paying for the defense? But don't tell anyone I told you."

I didn't know what else to say.

When we finished eating the casserole, Clarence put a little green salad on his plate and grumbled, "Nothing like eating silage."

I bussed the dishes. We drank a cup of coffee and Clarence filled me in on what he knew.

"I looked at the charging papers. It's pretty thin. The sheriff received an anonymous tip Joe had been seen with Nancy on Sunday at the *Times* office. Joe had been working at the casino as a dishwasher and living pretty much out of his camper truck. When they searched it—and I'm not convinced it was a legal search—they found some items that belonged to the Bywater woman."

"What did they find?"

"A jewelry box with a diamond necklace and earrings, an iPad and five hundred dollars cash."

"And this belonged to Nancy?"

Clarence looked amused. "That's what the sheriff says."

I switched to fact-checking mode, remembering the scut work I'd done in New York. "It sounds like we need to confirm these were Nancy's items. We also need to check to see if he has an alibi for the time they say Nancy was killed."

"That's why I need my tree-hugging assistant. I'm no good with those computer searches, and I haven't got the legs to find people."

He named an hourly wage for me that was far too low, even for Killdeer standards. "Wait, are you trying to scam me? That's not even minimum wage." Heat rose to my cheeks. I would not be taken.

He laughed. "Just kidding." His next offer made far more sense.

"What would you have done if I'd agreed to your paltry first offer?"

He winked at me. "Maybe added the difference to my estate."

"Then I hope I'm your sole heir."

He checked his watch. "Looks like we need to head out pretty soon."

Before we left the table, I put my hand up as if to stop him. "I do have a question for you."

He raised his eyebrows. "Okay, Counselor."

"You said you did legal work for my family. Can you tell me about it?"

He sat very still for a moment, not looking at me. When he finally spoke, his voice had a sad note. "It's a long story. Let's worry about the boy first. Then I'll tell you about it."

I felt a sudden let down. I could tell he knew something pretty important but was putting me off.

"Are you sure we can't talk about it now."

He didn't reply. With a groan, he pushed himself out of the chair. "Got to use the facilities before we go to the jail. Finish your coffee. I'm an old man and this might take a while."

I was left at an empty table wondering what he knew about my family.

Chapter Thirty-Four: Joe Talks

The sun cast a bright light over Killdeer, and the leaves of the hardwoods shimmered in a slight breeze. I took a deep breath of the fresh air before going inside. We were ushered into the same conference room at the jail. It was as damp and dreary as ever, like we had been transported from the beauty of Northern Minnesota into the subways of New York.

Joe looked even more gaunt than last time. I wondered if he was eating. He had deep shadows under his eyes and a bruise on his cheek that was turning greenish yellow as it healed.

Clarence shook his hand in a formal way and reintroduced himself. "As you recall, I'm your lawyer. Good thing you remember because I sometimes forget what I'm doing." He chuckled, but Joe looked uncomfortable.

"He's kidding," I added. "Clarence is sharper than he lets on." At least I hoped he was. I also reintroduced myself. "I'm helping Clarence investigate. I'm his computer person and his legs."

Again, only an uncomfortable expression from Joe.

"Son, I've read what they have on you. It's pretty thin. An anonymous tip, some possessions in your camper that might belong to the Bywater woman. Not much else. I need you to tell me what you know."

Joe looked at his lap. The orange jumpsuit they had for him was too big and he again looked far too young to be sitting in this place. We waited for him to speak. The silence of the room was broken only by the ticking of a clock on the wall and voices beyond the conference room.

In the culture I was raised in, silence was a rare beast. I grew more restless

187

by the second, but Clarence simply sat with his hands clasped on the table and a serene expression. His eyes were closed, and I hoped, after a big lunch, that he wasn't napping.

Finally, Joe spoke slowly and hesitantly, like he wasn't sure of his voice. "I didn't hurt her."

Clarence opened his eyes and smiled. He had a radiance to his face that seemed to melt all the aging wrinkles. "Now we're getting somewhere. Tell us about Nancy Bywater."

I worried Joe would lapse into another long-termed silence, but he looked beyond Clarence at the wall behind him, where the clock ticked away.

"She found me."

"What do you mean?" I jumped in. Was he a long-lost relative? Was she Native American? I pictured her dark hair but couldn't tell if she had Native blood.

Clarence put his hand on my arm to warn me to stay quiet.

"She was writing a book." Then Joe lapsed into silence.

I had to clamp my teeth together to keep from yelling, "Spit it out. Spit it out."

Again, Clarence's hand touched my arm. I fidgeted but stayed quiet.

When Joe spoke again, it was with resignation. "She wanted to know what the shooting was like and what happened to the people who were shot. She said she had a publisher who was interested."

Oh my God. That was Nancy's side project. I still wanted to jump in with questions, but I followed Clarence's lead and said nothing.

"She talked to some of the others. That's how she found me."

Clarence took his hand off my arm and leaned forward. "What about the things they found in your truck? The jewelry? The iPad?"

Joe wouldn't look directly at Clarence or at me. Instead, he gazed down, as if studying the tabletop. "Stole them from her."

"When?"

He reached up with his left hand and rubbed his eye. "Sunday."

"Why?"

He shook his head. "I don't know." His voice was a mere mumble, and it

188

was hard to understand him.

"So, you did see her on Sunday?"

He nodded. "Her house in the afternoon."

"Could someone have seen your truck at her house?"

Again, he nodded. He fidgeted, picking at the jumpsuit, wriggling in the chair. His sudden restlessness alerted me he was holding something back.

Clarence let the silence fill the room again. After the clock had ticked away long enough that I thought I might explode, Clarence spoke. This time the gentleness had gone out of his voice. His gaze bored into Joe. "You aren't telling us everything, are you?"

"I should go." Joe made a move to stand up when Clarence suddenly pounded his fist on the table. Startled, both Joe and I flinched at the same time.

"No. You need to tell us!" The old-man quaver disappeared from his voice. He sounded hard and commanding, like a military general.

Joe sat back down. His hands shook. "She discovered I'd taken stuff and texted me to bring it back. She said she was at the *Times* office and I should meet her there."

"And did you?"

"I drove there. The back door was partly open and a light was on. When I called out to her, no one answered. She was in the front on the floor. I could tell without touching her she was dead. I panicked and ran out. Someone must have seen my truck." He stopped and, for the first time, looked directly at us. "I didn't do it!"

"Oh hell," Clarence said. "I knew that."

All the questions I had for Joe drained out of my head as I watched the interplay between the two of them. Joe didn't need a different defense lawyer. Clarence, the octogenarian, was both capable and wily.

"Did you see anyone else? Another car? Anything?" I leaned forward and looked directly into his eyes.

He blinked as he fought back tears. He shook his head. "I don't know."

Clarence was quick. "What do you mean, you don't know?"

Again, a long, long pause. "Just that her text about the stuff I took was strange. It was full of abbreviations. Like 'u' for 'you.' She never texted like that."

I mulled that over. Nancy wasn't of the texting and messaging generation, with all the shortcuts. "Could she have been in a hurry?"

Joe shrugged.

"Or maybe someone else sent the text."

Clarence looked at me with a satisfied smile. "That's why I need you to investigate. Now we have more to go on."

I noted that Joe's shoulders relaxed as he took in a deep, shuddering breath.

Clarence explained the next steps. "I'm going to have my detective here check some things out. Meanwhile, don't talk to anyone, including the jailers, except to ask to use the bathroom. Jails have ears." He turned to me. "We need to know more about what the Bywater woman was up to and establish her relationship with Joe here. See what you can find."

He stood, reached across the table, and took Joe's hand in a firm two-handed grasp. "We'll figure this out, son. Leave it to us."

I wished I had the same confidence. It seemed to me Joe's presence at the *Times* office on that Sunday night had condemned him. Was he lured there? I wasn't so sure, but I thought I could find out more about his connection to Nancy.

Once outside, I stood on the sidewalk to the jail and let the breeze cool me off. I felt contaminated by the conference room and the hard-concrete grayness of the jail. We walked slowly to the car.

"Is he telling the truth?" I asked.

"Don't know."

When we reached the car, Clarence slid in with a groan. "With age comes oldness. It's a hazard of outliving your bones. I need a nap."

On the two-block drive back to his house, I glanced over at him. His head was tipped to his chin and he looked like he had nodded off. As soon as we reached his house, though, he was wide awake.

"Do your detective work, and we'll talk tomorrow."

After I dropped him off, I drove by the *Times* again but saw no evidence of Harry the temporary editor. I was tempted to stop at the Loonfeather to see if he was at the bar but decided it wasn't any of my business anymore.

The weather was Northwoods perfect that afternoon—a good time to take a swim in the pristine waters of the lake. I shoved all the drama of Joe out of my head and pictured myself sitting on the rock by the lake, enjoying the solitude and the gentle wash of the water. Would the development of the copper and nickel mine destroy the lake? I'd been so distracted by all the things happening that I had forgotten about the mining dilemma.

"Some tree-hugger you are."

When I pulled up to the cabin, it occurred to me Clarence had managed to avoid telling me about the legal issues with my family. I wondered if it was simply forgetfulness or if it was deliberate. The more time I spent time with Clarence, the less I believed he forgot things.

Chapter Thirty-Five: The Manila Envelopes

The cabin smelled stuffy and of garbage that needed to go out. Although I lived in the country, I still had garbage pickup. Organics went into a compost box by the shed. The rest I hauled to a garbage and recycling can at the end of the driveway by the turn-in to Larissa Lodge. It was a pain to do, so I avoided it as long as possible.

"You know," I said to Bronte as I loaded up the back of the Subaru with stinky bags of garbage, "in the city, I dumped all this down a chute and didn't worry about it."

Bronte jumped in the car for a ride down the driveway.

I waggled my finger at her. "Not today. Remember the last time I took you with me? You jumped out of the car and ran over to sniff some male poodle's butt?" I directed her back in the cabin.

As I passed the abandoned road to Patty's cabin, I wondered what Clarence knew about her. Had he represented my mother when the question of who owned the property came up? He was a crafty old guy, and I'd bet that, in his heyday, prosecutors rued going up against him with his homespun humor and the sparkle in his eyes. I wished I'd had him when they locked me into that cell in Queens.

The lodge parking lot was full for a Wednesday afternoon. It appeared they were hosting a conference. Larissa Lodge wasn't big enough for major meetings but often held smaller weddings and celebrations. I wondered what could be happening midday.

As I dumped my garbage bags, I recognized some of the Killdeer elite, the two bankers, the school superintendent, and the mayor. Several of the public relations people from Racine Mining joined them as Blaine stood out on the lodge veranda and welcomed the group.

A wave of disappointment washed through me. I thought he was on the side of the Lady Slipper Trail. Why was he hosting a meeting with the enemy?

And to think I'd let myself imagine him naked. To my surprise, a highway patrol car pulled into the parking lot. Jim stepped out in full uniform and walked into the building.

Rather than stand there and gawk, I decided to take a casual stroll into the lodge to do some spying. As I neared the front door, I noticed the red car with the dented front fender. Maybe I could kill two birds with one stone.

Mavis, with her frizzy dyed hair, stood at the reception desk. The lobby was empty. All the Killdeer notables had disappeared into the conference room at the back of the dining room.

"Hi." I smiled at her.

She squinted over her glasses at me for a moment, as if trying to place me. Then she smiled. "Oh, Jamie. Sorry. I didn't recognize you at first. I broke my regular glasses. Damned middle-aged eyes."

So far, my eyesight was fine, but I worried that if I had to edit more manuscripts like George's, I'd be headed for the glasses with the chain around the neck. Or the nut house.

"What brings you here?"

I leaned casually on the counter. "I was just dumping my garbage and saw all the bigwigs walk in. Just wondering what's happening."

Mavis tsked. "They got some expensive architect here to show them drawings."

"For the mine?"

The color rose on Mavis's face. I was sure she knew my stance on the mine. "Uh. Well..." she stammered. "It's something to do with Larissa Lodge. Remodeling the cabins, I think."

Mavis was clearly rattled by my question. Why would all the heavy hitters in the community, plus the state patrol, care about cabin remodeling?

"Oh, that's interesting. Big plans, I guess?"

Mavis busied herself, shuffling some papers, and didn't reply.

"One other question for you."

Mavis concentrated on the papers in front of her.

"Did you drop off a manila envelope at my cabin?"

Once again, she blushed. This time her cheeks turned almost the same color as her hair. "Uh."

A father with a boy about ten walked in and stood behind me. The boy had tears rolling down his face. "I didn't mean to lose it, Dad."

I leaned over to Mavis and said in a low voice, "I'd like to talk to you about the envelopes."

Mavis cleared her throat. "Let me see if Ronnie can handle the desk. We can go outside and talk."

"Thanks."

I stepped aside so the dad could talk with Mavis. As I walked out the doorway, I heard the sad tale of one of the lodge's volleyballs ending up in the lake. "I told Adrian not to hit it that direction."

If only lost volleyballs were the biggest problem adults had to deal with.

I sat at a wooden picnic table beneath an oak tree. It might have been the same table I used to sit at with Willow when I was ten and she shared her peanut butter and jelly sandwiches with me. I remembered how she told me about the night animals that came around the cabins and how she'd found a rabbit's nest with babies. Willow's interest in animals went back a long time. Funny, though, she hardly ever talked about people in those days.

When Mavis came out, she looked around like she was afraid someone might see her.

"I told Ronnie fifteen minutes. That's about all she can handle before she loses someone's reservation." She slid in across from me.

Behind her, the high-pitched voices of children wafted up from the beach. I waited for her to talk.

"Um. So. About the clippings and such. Patty Clark and I were friends when she worked here. She did housekeeping, you know."

I nodded, even though I knew nothing about my aunt.

"Well, one day she asked me to hold on to those envelopes. She said I was supposed to give them to her sister's family so they'd know the story."

"The story?"

Mavis shrugged. "I don't know what it was all about. But she used to talk about her land and the lodge land as if it should all be hers. 'They stole it,' she once said."

I thought about what Rob had told me. "I heard Mitchell McConnell bought people out at low prices and kicked them off the land."

"I heard that too. I've also heard the lodge and the cabins are haunted by spirits." She looked at the tree. "Who knows? I hear funny noises sometimes and wonder if it's the dead getting their revenge."

"You thought I should have the clippings?"

Mavis blushed. "Well, I kinda forgot them until I heard about the shooting at your place. I guess I never thought anyone from Judy's family would come back."

I leaned forward. "Did you know my mom?"

A frisbee whizzed by the table and clattered to the ground about five feet away. Two boys came running by to retrieve it, their cheeks pink with sunburn. They reminded me of Bronte—joyous and playful.

Mavis took a deep breath. "I didn't really know your mom. She was older than me and very different from Patty. Patty was wilder."

"It sounded like she tried to get Mother's cabin at some point."

"I guess. But your mother hired old Clarence Engstrom, and the suit didn't go anywhere." She pushed her hand through her frizzy hair. "Things changed for Patty after that. I heard she was sneaking around with a married guy and he dropped her. She disappeared to Minneapolis for a while. A lot of the Indians headed there because they couldn't find work here. But she came back. The rumor was she'd gotten pregnant by the married guy and had a baby."

I sat up straight. If she'd had a baby, then I had a first cousin somewhere. "Really?"

Again, Mavis shrugged. "Patty never talked about it."

DEATH OF AN EDITOR

"I'm still not clear why she wanted me to have all those clippings. They don't tell me much."

Mavis leaned forward and lowered her voice. "About the time Blaine got his divorce, Patty started acting really nervous. Like she was nipping a lot from a bottle she kept with her. I asked one day if something was wrong and she said the oddest thing."

I waited while Mavis cleared her throat.

"She said, 'It's unholy what they're doing. If Mickey was alive, he would put a stop to it.'"

"Wow, do you have any idea what she was talking about?"

Mavis shrugged. "I thought maybe Blaine was having an affair and that's what the divorce was all about. It was real hush, hush."

"And the clippings?" I prompted her.

"She gave them to me two weeks before she…uh…died."

"And it was suicide?"

Mavis nodded with a grave look. "That's what they say."

A car door slammed in the parking lot. Mavis glanced at her watch and stood. "Oops, gotta go. Ronnie can really mess things up. I never let her handle the front desk for long."

Mavis walked away, her hips pushing against the polyester of her dark pants. Once I got home, I planned to take a closer look at the clippings.

On my way back to the car, I met Jim as he walked down the steps of the lodge.

I raised my hand with a little wave. Suddenly, I felt sheepish. I'd been rude to him, and it was time to make amends. "Hi."

His brow was knit as if he were in deep thought, and he looked at me with a startled expression. "Oh. Jamie. Hi."

"I'm sorry I was so rude to you. I meant to text an apology…"

He blinked, still distracted. "Oh sure. No problem." He paused to study me. "Listen, we should talk. But I have an emergency out on the highway. I'll get back to you."

He was gone in a flash. Did he really have an emergency or was he desperate to get away from me?

Once home, I called Clarence. His housekeeper answered and said he was napping. She would give him a message to call me, but I shouldn't wait by the phone for him to do it. I sensed Clarence wasn't good at returning calls. I'd try him again tomorrow.

I pulled out the clippings from the two envelopes and spread them out on my coffee table. Other than the sealed letter from Patty to my mother, they were all taken from the *Killdeer Times*.

"I don't get why she kept them and why she wanted my mother to have them. What was so 'unholy'?"

Bronte sniffed at the browned newsprint and settled back on her cushion.

I sifted through them, noting they were all stories about Larissa Lodge and all featured photographs of Mitchell McConnell or his son Mitchell "Mickey" Junior. Mickey must have been Blaine's father. Still, nothing jumped out at me.

Arranging them in chronological order, I went through them again. And again, nothing. I read through the latest ones to find out that thirty years ago, about the time I was born, they'd added five more cabins to the resort and expanded the beach area. None of the articles mentioned the tribe or the burial ground.

"This isn't telling me anything." I put the most recent clippings down. "What did Patty want?"

The most recent one, from the summer I was born, had a group photo of the Larissa Lodge staff. All the people were identified. Mitchell McConnell and his son stood in front, wearing short sleeves and ties. Though the photo was a little blurry, I noted the resemblance between Blaine and his father, Mickey. Standing behind Mickey, and slightly obscured by his head, was Patty Clark.

"Okay, Bronte. This is interesting."

It was hard to tell because of the poor quality of the photo, but I saw immediately she had the same face shape as my mother. Something else about her was familiar, but I couldn't put my finger on it. I studied it until my eyes started to water.

"Enough." I slipped it back into the envelope with the other clippings.

I reread the letter from Patty to my mother. The only thing that piqued my attention was the letter "M." Who was "M"? Who was pushing her? Could it stand for McConnell? Mitchell? Mickey? Perhaps Clarence could tell me. I would call him in the morning.

This was interesting, but not very important in the scheme of things. I needed to get working on the connection between Joe and Nancy.

Chapter Thirty-Six: Nancy's Book

"It's like I'm in school again and have all this homework." I set the envelopes with the clippings aside.

Bronte put her paw on my leg, as if to comfort me. "You remind me of Dad when I used to complain about schoolwork. He smiled and nodded and expected me to get it done."

I sorted through George's coffee-stained manuscript pages, and, to my relief, all were essentially intact. It was time to write the letter to him that outlined my comments.

"Do you think he'll send me another manuscript if I start the letter with 'Dear George, take your laptop and bury it in the backyard. Get on an airplane and tour Europe. Get a job. Keep Alma in your heart but stop writing about her?'"

Bronte ventured no opinion except to wag her tail. She probably thought I was telling her about the rawhide chew I had for her.

For the next hour and a half, I composed, erased, edited, and rewrote the letter to George. I praised his passion and told him how his love for Alma shone in his writing. I suggested he take out the sexual fantasy because it wouldn't appeal to the audience who read these memoirs. I also suggested he make it shorter. When I was done, I felt I'd been as kind and objective as possible. I also decided to save it on my computer and let it simmer for a day.

Willow called shortly after I had finished the letter. "Hey. Sorry I've been too busy to check up on you. I heard you had a little 'incident' at the casino."

"I'm fine. Pepper spray is a great antidote to mugging." I opened the door and threw a rawhide chew out for Bronte. Life was so easy for her. "Do you want to come by this evening? I've just stocked up on beer."

She must have been calling from her clinic because I heard a yipping noise in the background. "Can't tonight. I have a speaking engagement with the Women's Aglow group."

"Don't they gather to read the Bible and sing praises or something?" For a moment, I realized I didn't know that much about Willow. Maybe she was an evangelical Christian.

She must have sensed my thoughts because she started to laugh. "They do their singing and praying after they have a little educational presentation. I'm talking to them about heart worm and Lyme Disease."

"Oh."

"How about we get together tomorrow?"

We talked for a little while. I filled her in on the Pruitt cousin who I thought was my attacker.

"Pruitts are the scum of the earth. No doubt about it. I'd guess he was after your money and your body."

"Yuck." I shivered.

I also told her I had a temp job helping Clarence Engstrom with his defense of Joe Pelletier.

"Really? That ancient gasbag. So, he is still alive."

I was taken aback by her tone. "You don't like him much?"

"Long story that I'll tell you when you're old enough to understand."

Again, her coldness surprised me.

I decided to change the subject. "Do you know anything about a meeting today with the Racine people, some of the Killdeer bigwigs, and an architecture firm?"

Willow hesitated. "A meeting?"

"I saw a bunch of them go into the lodge when I took my garbage down the drive. I stopped and asked Mavis at the front desk. She was kind of cagey but finally said they were meeting with architects about remodeling the cabins. Seemed like a bigger deal to me than a cabin remodel."

The line was silent for a moment. "Uh, listen, I have to go. I'm getting another call. See you tomorrow." The call ended abruptly. Her response struck me as strange. Did she know something about Racine that she wasn't telling me?

I brewed a cup of tea and walked down to the lake. I needed a few moments with the rhythm of the water to think about the phone call. Two things were off. First, Willow's reaction to Clarence Engstrom. I sensed something bad had happened with him. But it was the second that puzzled me more. My gut said Willow was lying about the meeting at the lodge. She knew more than she was telling me.

I considered driving back to the lodge and demanding to know from Blaine what the meeting was about. Maybe they were conspiring against the Lady Slipper Trail. Maybe they were making deals that would hurt the environment. Plus, I wanted to know what Jim Monroe, in full uniform, was doing with them.

Bronte joined me with her saliva-soaked rawhide. She dumped it at my feet, looking at me with her puppy enthusiasm.

"No, I'm not going to pick that slimy thing up and throw it for you. Find yourself another human."

Rather than ponder all these things for long, though, I resolved to work on my assignment from Clarence. Was Nancy really writing a book about the school shooting that had killed Joe's twin?

I called Jilly at the paper. I shouldn't bother her on deadline afternoon, but I thought she might have time for a short conversation.

"*Times.*" She answered in a curt tone.

"Jilly, it's Jamie. Do you have a few minutes?"

She sighed. "All hell is breaking loose here. Harry stormed out and Phil just crashed the layout program...so, sure, I have a few minutes. I need a break."

She stepped outside and called me back on her cell phone. "I heard about the casino attack. I saw Donald Pruitt slinking around the casino earlier and heard you identified him. Any arrests?"

"No."

"Well, don't hold your breath."

"As long as he stays away from me, I don't care. He didn't get my money or my maidenhood." I knew I should pursue it, but, with everything else, it didn't seem that important.

I could tell Jilly was in the back parking lot of the *Times* building because of the sound of a car crunching on the gravel.

"Jilly, I called because I'm trying to find out if Nancy's side project had to do with the school shooting in Cascade. Did she say anything to you?"

"Nancy and I weren't exactly pals. She kept me at an arm's length. But that doesn't mean she wasn't working on something. Like I said, the last few weeks she seemed edgy and distracted."

I wasn't sure if this was proper to ask, but I forged ahead. "Uh, would you be willing to do something that might not be above board?"

"What? Like shoot Phil?"

I chuckled. "Not that illegal. If you get a chance, could you look at Nancy's computer and see if she had a file or something saved about the shooting incident?"

In the background, I heard a voice that sounded like Phil's. "Jilly, I'm in a jam. Can you get back in here?"

Jilly said, "I'm coming. Just a minute." When she talked to me it was in a lowered voice. "I'm not sure I can do that."

I tried to hide my disappointment. "I understand. But thanks for talking with me."

After I hung up the phone, I pictured Nancy's computer and the electronic files she'd saved. Unfortunately, I hadn't paid much attention to them. Then I remembered I'd grabbed a file from her desk to review for my now former job as temporary editor. It was still in my bag. Maybe I could use it as an excuse to go back to the *Times* when Phil wasn't around. Maybe I could convince Jilly to look the other way.

I ran out of maybes when it occurred to me I was writing a television script rather than dealing in reality. If I wanted to know what Nancy was doing, I needed to contact some of the other victims of the shooting.

"Time to fire up the computer, girl."

Bronte didn't even raise her head. She'd worn herself out chewing on a rawhide. Oh, to have such problems.

I reviewed the notes I'd taken on Joe and the school shooting. They included the phone number for Kristy, the summer intern at the *Cascade Journal*, who had been in school the day of the shooting. I called and got a perky voice mail asking me to leave a message.

"Hey, Kristy, this is Jamie Forest from Killdeer. I have a few more questions for you about Joe Pelletier. If you have a chance, can you give me a call?"

I reread the article from the Duluth paper about the shooting and wrote down the names of the victims and the survivors. As I studied the list, my reluctance grew to contact anyone to see if Nancy had talked with them. They'd already been through so much. Would I be opening a wound? Did I really want to do this? On the other hand, it might work as background information for *The New Yorker* article.

One name stood out. The teacher who was killed was named Tony Vincent. The article said he was in his second year of teaching math and science. For some reason, the name tickled something in back of my head, but I couldn't bring it forward. Vincent wasn't a common name around here, and I was sure I'd seen it somewhere.

My phone rang before I could dig deeper.

"Hi, this is Kristy. Did you just call me?"

I told her I was following up on a story about Joe and wondered if she knew whether victims of the shooting had been contacted by someone who was writing a book about it.

Kristy hesitated. "Well…I don't hang around with those guys much."

"Have you heard anything, though?"

I tried a few more questions, but Kristy didn't have more information to share. I changed tack. "What about the teacher who was shot? Tony Vincent. Have you heard anything about him?"

A small plane droned overhead, and Bronte yipped in her sleep, as I waited for Kristy to answer. When she did, she lowered her voice to almost a whisper. "Please don't tell anyone I said this, but there were rumors."

"Rumors?"

"Well, like he was interested in this girl, and she was Neil's sister."

"Neil?"

"Yeah. You know, the shooter—Neil Kavanaugh."

I sorted this out in my head. Maybe this wasn't a hate crime but a crime of passion. "But why would he shoot everyone?"

"Well, it's just what I heard—like Mr. Vincent did something to Neil's sister and Neil was after revenge or something."

It didn't add up to me, but I wasn't talking with her to solve the unsolvable. My job was to verify Joe's story about his relationship with Nancy. We talked a little more about how it felt to have to go back to school after the carnage. She said that even though it happened two years ago, she was still nervous when she was in the classroom at college. "Honestly, I try to take as many classes online as I can."

Before we hung up, she said she'd ask around and see if anyone had talked to a writer about the shooting. I stared at my notes and thought about Nancy. She was probably ambitious, working to establish herself as a journalist, and saw this story as a gold mine—especially if it turned out the slain teacher had sexually assaulted the shooter's sister.

"Well, girl. The plot thickens. But I'm not any closer to knowing whether Nancy was indeed investigating the shooting."

Chapter Thirty-Seven: The Shooting Victim

Hunger pains pulled me away from my research on Nancy. I craved the empanadas from the little hole-in-the-wall bodega a block from my Queens apartment. Senora Juanita made them in her kitchen above the store on Thursdays and Saturdays. My stomach growled as I thought about how Andrew and I used to pick them up and bring them back to the apartment. We talked about the future with so much enthusiasm. Andrew dreamed of scoring a big role on Broadway, and I dreamed of becoming the poet laureate for the nation. At least he had some success. I hadn't written a poem since getting my MFA.

I made a quick stir fry using frozen shrimp and soy sauce. It was too salty, but I didn't care as I wolfed it down, wishing I had green tea ice cream to go with it.

The sun glowed a reddish yellow as it sank behind the trees on the other side of Bear Island. I sat on the porch with a beer and thought more about Nancy. In some ways, she was like me. She'd had a job in Minneapolis but fled to the hinterlands to start her life over, following a divorce. She was a foreigner in this town, just like me. She had writing aspirations and few connections in the community. I wondered what she had left behind in the city.

Back in the kitchen, I logged onto my laptop and googled her name. Her obituary from the *Minneapolis Star Tribune* popped up. The information was standard format for an obit. Born, preceded in death by, survived by, and a note on when the service would be. I scanned it quickly and almost missed the most important point. Tucked in amongst the survived by names was a sister named Melanie Vincent. I had seen the Vincent name before.

The day I sat at Nancy's computer, she had papers scattered over the desk. An envelope with a card in it had slipped to the floor. When I picked it up, I noted a return address in Minneapolis with the name Vincent on it. At the time, I'd wondered if it was from a relative or a friend. I'd put it in the box of things for her family to pick up.

Was that box still in the *Times* office? It was too late to drive into town, but perhaps I could go in the morning with the excuse I had to bring back the files from her desk.

Next, I googled Melanie Vincent and found the same obituary. I tried Facebook and found several Melanie Vincents but only one living in Minnesota. Instead of a headshot, her page had a photo of a rocking chair with a teddy bear. The teddy bear wore a black ribbon around his arm. The feed was filled with messages of sympathy.

I clicked onto her shared photographs. Most of them were of her children, who looked to be in the preschool and toddler age. As I skipped through, I finally found one of her. It was a wedding photo. She looked radiant in her white dress and headband made of flowers. Next to her, looking a little dowdy in the long purple bridesmaid dress, was Nancy, along with two other bridesmaids. Another photo was a formal shot of the wedding party, including her husband, Adam Vincent, and the best man—Tony Vincent. Moreover, both Tony and his brother had distinct Native American features. In fact, while the groom wore his hair in a short stylish cut, Tony wore his dark hair in two braids.

"My God, Bronte, she was related to the teacher who was shot."

Did someone kill Nancy because of her investigation of the shooting? I sat back with my eyes closed to take it all in. What did I know about Nancy? She started working at the *Times* about two years ago. Was this before or after the shooting? Either Jilly or Phil had mentioned she left her job in Minneapolis after some "incident." Was it the death of her brother-in-law's brother?

Even if someone could answer my questions, would they be relevant to Joe? If nothing else, maybe I could establish that Nancy was truly writing about the shooting. I thought about where I would keep files if I was writing about the massacre. Since it was a private project, I'd probably keep them on my own computer and possibly back them up on a work computer. If she was writing about it, she had to have files somewhere.

I almost called Clarence to ask if the police had a laptop or computer of hers. When I looked, though, I realized it was after ten. Clarence probably went to bed when the sun went down.

I was wide awake, though, and wondered what else I could find. I googled Tony Vincent and found his obituary. It confirmed he was survived by his brother, Adam, and sister-in-law Melanie, along with nieces and nephews. He was born in South Dakota and came to Minnesota for college. Graduated with honors and Cascade was his first teaching job. The obit didn't list a wife or children.

Before I went to bed, I opened up Facebook and sent a message to Melanie Vincent asking her to email or call me. I lied and said I worked for the *Killdeer Times* and had some questions. I hoped she wouldn't call the *Times* instead.

I didn't sleep well. I felt as if the cabin was surrounded by people like Neil Kavanaugh, who wanted to hurt me. As I was finally dropping off, the wind picked up and a branch scraped against the wall outside the bedroom. If that wasn't enough, a rabbit squealed in fear and agony as a predator of some kind attacked it. Bronte woke with the sound of the shriek and leapt off the bed, barking as she headed for the door.

When I finally did sleep, I had vague dreams about the newspaper clipping photo with Patty Clark in it. In the dream, I was trying to warn her that her cabin was burning. Something dark rolled in behind me. I tried to call 911 for help, but I couldn't see the keyboard on my phone.

In the morning, my eyes felt like I had sandpapered them, and my brain felt waterlogged. When I let Bronte out, she came back with a mouthful of bloody rabbit fur.

"Oh, for the calm of the big city."

After breakfast, I checked my email to see if Melanie Vincent had responded to my Facebook message. Although I wasn't surprised, I was disappointed not to have a message from her. Putting myself in her shoes, I remembered all the messages I'd received after my article came out. I concluded that she probably wouldn't respond. I needed to get a phone number for her.

The *Times* should have an emergency contact for her in Nancy's personnel file. If they kept a personnel file. I was about to call Jilly when an email from Kristy from Cascade popped up.

Hey, just wanted you to know I heard that Nancy talked with Betsy Latelle, one of the kids that survived the shooting. Here's her number.

At last, some confirmation.

I recalled the photo from Betsy's Facebook page with Joe in the background as I punched in the phone number. After three rings, a sleepy voice answered, "'Low?"

Realizing it was eight thirty in the morning, I apologized right away. "I'm sorry to call so early, this is Jamie Forest from Killdeer."

"Oh, sure. Kristy said you might call. Give me a minute—I was out late last night." I heard the sound of the bed creaking and a whisper to someone.

While I waited, I felt a sweep of sadness that my only bed companion was a snoring canine. Back before my marriage went bust, Andrew and I had a little ritual. He was an early riser and would come in, kiss me on the cheek, and declare, "Morning breath. Quick, brush your teeth and hop back in the sack." And we would.

"'Kay, I can talk now. What was it you wanted?"

I decided to be honest. "You know that Joe Pelletier has been arrested for the murder of Nancy Bywater?"

"Yeah, I heard. That's pretty bogus."

"I'm working for his lawyer. Joe said he knew Nancy because she was doing a book on the shooting. I'm trying to confirm it."

Betsy's hesitation concerned me. "Sure, I guess. She did talk to me about a month ago. But..." She stopped.

I decided to wait her out.

"Okay, like yeah, she talked to me. She asked a lot of questions about the shooting, but I wondered if she was after something else."

"Oh?" Through the kitchen window, I watched Bronte launch herself at a crow that had landed on the lawn. The crow flew up into the tree and scolded her from a distance.

"She wanted to know about Mr. Vincent and the things he was doing. Like maybe she wanted to do a book on him as a teacher or something."

"What else did she ask about?"

"She wondered if Neil Kavanaugh had been in Mr. Vincent's class."

Bronte sat at the foot of the tree and barked at the bird. *You're wasting your time.* I watched the dog. *You'll never win against a crow. They're too smart.*

"Did she talk with anyone else?"

Betsy cleared her throat. "I heard she talked with a couple other kids and she tried to talk with Kavanaugh's sister."

"Do you know if they talked?"

More whispering. "Um, I've gotta go now. But I don't know about Kavanaugh's sister. My friends and I don't have much to do with them—you know?"

We finished the conversation with an agreement that if I had more questions, I would call back. Joe was right that Nancy was doing research, but it looked like she was trying to uncover something else. Perhaps the rumors that something was going on with the shooter's sister were true. Did I want to pursue that angle or simply leave it alone and let Clarence know Joe was telling the truth?

I thought about the possible article for *The New Yorker.* Investigating Nancy's investigation would certainly add substance to it. But, really, did I want to do the article and expose myself once again to criticism and hostility? I imagined how the Killdeer community would respond if I authored a piece in a national magazine that made the sheriff's department look like a group of incompetent rural hicks. As LeRoy Pruitt had said, people knew where I lived.

Chapter Thirty-Eight: Sewing Patterns

I called Clarence to tell him I might have found proof of the connection between Joe and Nancy. He answered on the fifth ring.

"Engstrom."

"Clarence, it's Jamie."

"Ah, yes. My investigator. I hope you're keeping track of your time."

I laughed. "You can count on that. I called because I think I've verified what Joe told us." I filled him in on what I'd uncovered about Nancy's project. "I'd like to have something concrete, though, like her notes or a manuscript. Do you know if the sheriff found a laptop?"

"Let me check my paperwork."

I pictured him shuffling his way to his office and expected a long wait.

Instead, he came right back on. "Not listed in what they took in as evidence."

"Damn. Could you recheck with the sheriff?" I was sure Nancy had her own computer. In this day and age, who didn't?

Clarence chucked. "Yes, ma'am."

We talked a little more about next steps. Before I hung up, I asked him about my family. "As long as I have you on the line, what were you going to tell me about my mother and her sister?"

Clarence hesitated. I heard the sound of a spoon stirring a coffee cup and some wheezy breathing. "I remember it was a nasty fight. Divided some of the people around here."

"Why?" A dispute between sisters hardly seemed like something that would upset the general public.

"Economics. The general thought was that if Patty got the property, she'd sell it to the McConnells so they could expand the lodge. Bring in more tourists, that kind of thing. It happened around the time when the mine wasn't doing well and people were out of work."

"Did my mother know this?"

"She was in college, but she was one smart woman. She knew that if the McConnells got ahold of the land, it would be developed into cabins, condos, and a golf course."

A chipmunk chattered in the backyard. Bronte lifted her head and woofed at it with little enthusiasm. I shuddered, thinking about what would happen if the land was developed.

"What happened with the lawsuit?"

"Oh, Patty had an expensive Twin City law firm handling the case. They didn't understand the culture here. In the end, she dropped the suit."

I fingered the letter Mavis had given to me. "Patty sent my mother a letter that she never opened. It mentioned someone with the initial "M." Do you know who that was? Could it have been one of the McConnells?"

Clarence coughed and cleared his throat. "Possible, but I'll tell you, Patty certainly didn't want anything to do with the McConnells later on."

"What do you mean?"

"She called me shortly before she died. Wanted to know if there was a way she could make sure they didn't get the cabin if she died."

"What did you tell her?"

"She needed to have something specific in her will about it."

"Did she?"

"Not with me."

I sensed that he knew something more than he was saying, but I decided to let it go. "One other thing, and I'll let you get back to lawyering."

He laughed. "The schedule is full."

"I heard the McConnells own her property now. Do you know if that's true?"

"I haven't kept up on it, but I wouldn't be surprised. Old Mitchell and his son wanted that property. She might have sold it to them in the end after all."

I slid the letter away from me. "Well, I guess they got what they wanted then. Except that Blaine says they plan to preserve the land."

Clarence was silent. When he spoke, he changed the subject. "Let me know if you find out anything more about Nancy and Joe. I'll sit by the phone and await your call."

I laughed. "You might have a long wait."

After I hung up, I stared at Patty's refused letter for a long time, as if it would suddenly make sense to me.

"Time to move on," I finally said to Bronte.

She took it that we were going for a walk and galloped to the door.

"No, not that kind of move on."

I needed concrete proof of Joe's connection with Nancy. Would her work computer hold the key? A tiny evil voice inside me whispered, *go hack it. You have the password.*

"Sure." I poured coffee into a mug and walked out to my rock. A gentle breeze rippled across the lake. The air smelled of fresh water, and the dewy grass was cool on my bare feet. What if I could get into Nancy's computer at the *Times*? Maybe I could convince Jilly to look the other way.

Why not give it a try? If I got caught, at least I knew a lawyer.

Back in the cabin, I changed into clean khaki shorts and a sleeveless blouse. Bronte watched me with anticipation.

"Sorry, girl. I'm going to town, not for a walk." I knew it would be tricky, but I needed to get into Nancy's computer.

The temperature was rising. This would be another hot, sticky day. I hoped to get my errand done before the heat became stifling. We were entering the dog days of summer.

The car kicked up dust as I drove down the rutted road. I thought about late summer and my dad. When we visited the cabin, he would say, "It's time to leave when we reach the dog days." I assumed it meant hot sticky days when all the dogs lazed around panting with their pink tongues dripping saliva. But Dad explained that it was an ancient Greek saying that referred to the time that Sirius, the Dog Star, was the brightest. I liked the idea of lazy dogs better.

On my way out, I passed Larissa Lodge and noted the activity as people checked out with their roller bags and their sunburns. Did the McConnells really plan a big expansion if they could get the land north of the lodge? I wondered what my cabin and twenty acres would be worth to them. Would I sell if the price was right?

Unless I could figure out a better source of income, I might have to consider that possibility.

In Killdeer, I turned into the alley behind the *Times* and parked in the rutted lot. I honestly wasn't sure exactly what my plan would be to get into Nancy's computer. Jilly's car was the only one parked behind the building.

I knew it was a hairbrained mission. Nevertheless, when I stepped out of the car, I closed the door as quietly as possible. It was a silly act, considering it was midmorning and anybody who wanted to could see me. The back door to the *Times* was unlocked, and when I opened it, I expected to hear a buzz of activity. It was Thursday, publication day, and Jilly had told me people often stopped in to buy a paper.

"Stupid day to decide to break into someone's computer," I muttered. My half-baked plan was to beg Jilly to let me take a quick look at Nancy's computer. I knew she would be reluctant based on my previous call to her, but I thought if I sounded desperate enough, she'd look the other way. Chances were slim she would allow it, but I decided it was worth a try.

I walked through the back room, inhaling the aroma of paper and fresh ink from several bundles of the latest edition of the *Killdeer Times*. I was puzzled that they were still there. In my understanding, part of the editing job was to haul them to various stores for sale. Maybe Harry hadn't gotten around to it yet.

In the front office, Harry stood behind the counter, reading the new edition of the paper. His eyes had a bleary look, and his hand shook as he turned the page. He barely acknowledged me when I walked in.

"You here to take those papers? Phil says they've got to get out."

Jilly's desk was unoccupied. I pointed to it. "Where's Jilly?"

He shrugged. "Delivering down the street. She should be here soon." He turned back to the paper.

I guessed he wanted to head to the Loonfeather as soon as he could. I peeked out the window to see if Jilly was in sight. A pedestrian jaywalked across the street to the bank. Otherwise, the sidewalk appeared deserted.

A plan quickly formulated in my larcenous brain. "Uh...I'll take care of those papers in the back as soon as I've looked up the...uh...drop sites." I pointed at Nancy's computer. "I'm new to the delivery."

Harry nodded.

Holding my breath, I sat down and entered PASSWORD. Thank God Harry hadn't changed it. The files popped up on the desktop. I looked over at Harry before I pulled a thumb drive out of my pocket. Would he notice?

I read the listing of files and folders on her desktop, searching for one that might be labeled "Personal" or "Cascade" or "Joe." All of them appeared to be newspaper related, just like the files in her drawer. I remembered I had taken the paper file for something called "Development." She had a folder for it along with a folder labeled *Racine* in her computer. Quickly, I copied them to the drive. Now what?

Out the window, I saw Jilly walking on the other side of the street. She was talking to the clerk from the sheriff's office. She gestured in a way that made me suspect she was angry. I didn't want to face her, and I definitely didn't want to face her if she was worked up. I had to hurry. I peered at the desktop for anything that was unusual, panic growing as the words blurred in front of me.

"Finding what you need?" Harry interrupted my concentration.

"Uh, yes. Just have to email it to my phone," I lied.

I glanced out the window to see Jilly wave goodbye to the clerk and step onto the street. A couple of cars passed by her, halting her progress. I prayed for a traffic jam so I could concentrate on the screen.

"Shit!" I didn't realize I'd spoken out loud until Harry grunted at me.

"Need help?"

Just before Jilly reached the sidewalk on this side of the street, I spied a folder with the unusual name "Sewing Patterns." Without opening the folder, I copied it. The copy finished just before Jilly reached the door. I grabbed the thumb drive and retreated toward the back as the bell over the door jingled.

"Got it!" I called to Harry and nearly tripped over a stack of papers as I ran out the back. I hoped that Jilly hadn't seen me and that Harry was too hungover to describe me.

On my way out of Killdeer, I half-expected to hear a siren as LeRoy chased me down. The sun was high enough in the sky to be eye-achingly bright. Weeds in the ditch alongside the highway swayed gently in the breeze and no one followed me. By the time I reached my turnoff, my shoulders had relaxed, and I felt a little giddy. I'd just completed my first illegal heist. I hoped it wasn't going to turn into a pattern.

Chapter Thirty-Nine: What Nancy Knew

By the time I pulled up to my cabin, the giddiness of my caper had worn off. It occurred to me, as I unlocked the door, that the files I had obtained might now be inadmissible in court. What did I know about the law? Perhaps I had just totally screwed up the case for Joe.

The humid air smelled faintly of skunk. Sweat rolled down the inside of my cotton blouse, and I felt slightly soiled. I let Bronte out and stood outside, with the sun beating down on me. What had I done?

I busied myself packaging up George's manuscript, along with the sheet of comments. While Bronte lolled on the back step, I stared at the thumb drive. Maybe if I returned it without looking at it I would be okay.

Carrying a tall glass of iced tea, I walked barefoot out to my thinking rock. The grass was soft under my feet and reminded me that I needed to mow the lawn. Maybe I could talk Rob into doing it.

The rock was hot on my legs as I sat on it. The breeze had died away, and the lake stood glassy still, like it was trying to reflect the heat back to the sun. Bronte found a shady place near the rock and settled down, her pink tongue lolling like the dogs of the dog days.

Across the water, light glinted off an aluminum canoe. Someone was visiting Bear Island. I turned to Bronte. "Someday we'll paddle over there. I think the island holds the spirit of my mother."

I might have spent more time wallowing in regret about hacking into Nancy's computer, but the rock was too hot and the ice in my iced tea had melted and turned it into tepid tea. I knew, as I made my way back to the cabin, that I would open that thumb drive and find out what Nancy had to say about "Sewing Patterns."

The cabin had heated up but was still cooler than outside. Bronte followed me in and flopped down on the bare wood floor. I fished out the thumb drive and popped it into my laptop. When I opened the folder labeled "Sewing Patterns," several sub-folders appeared, including one titled "Jamie Forest" and another titled "Joe." I opened the Jamie file to find only three sentences.

Talk with Jamie about what Joe overheard in the casino. Might be in danger. How to know? Maybe need to go to the source.

A chill crawled down my back as I recalled her voicemail message to me. What was going on?

Next, I opened the "Joe" file. It looked to be transcriptions of interviews, including at least three with Joe and several with other shooting survivors. They described the details of the time before the shooting and what happened during the shooting. Nancy had made annotations like "subject cried during this part," or "no eye contact while talking."

The transcriptions were in chronological order. The project had started two months ago in early June. Wasn't that when Jilly said Nancy had become more preoccupied?

I found it hard to read through. Yes, I'd suffered a major trauma with my arrest, but I hadn't seen my friends killed in front of my eyes. Or for Joe, his twin brother. This was all the proof I needed that Joe had a reason to know Nancy. As I scrolled through, I felt like a voyeur, like this wasn't mine to see. I should stop. The description of the blood and the screaming was too real.

The screen blurred as the tears welled up. I blinked them away, took a deep breath, and let it out with a shudder. It was time to close the computer and take a rest.

Outside, near the border of my yard, where the forest started, I saw a stag. He was young, with the early growth of his antlers. He stood calmly chewing something in the undergrowth. He looked so sleek and natural that my tears dried up. I watched him for several minutes before he melted into the woods. Bronte stayed quiet. Either she hadn't sensed the deer or understood I needed those minutes of silence.

I turned back to the computer and the last entry in the file. It was a transcription of Nancy's final interview with Joe, the day she died. She must have typed it up immediately after she talked with him.

I overheard about it when I was working at the casino. Those guys were standing by the kitchen. They said they were trying to get that woman out. Needed her to sell or the whole thing would fall through. They ain't good people, Nancy. You gotta tell her...

The file ended there, like the recorder had run out of tape or like Nancy had stopped it. I gaped at it. What did he mean? Did this have anything to do with me? Who were "they"?

I took a sharp intake of breath, so sharp a pain stabbed my side.

Up until now, I had wondered if Nancy's death had something to do with Joe and the shooting. Maybe she had uncovered some kind of incriminating evidence. Maybe the shooting wasn't what we all thought.

But now, I wondered if it was something totally different. Did the clippings that Mavis left for me mean anything? What about the meeting yesterday at the lodge?

"What do you think?"

Bronte lifted her head with a sigh. She was stretched out on the floor near the couch. My bag was leaning against the coffee table. I hadn't touched it since Phil fired me. It still had the file in it that I'd taken from Nancy's desk to review.

I brought the bag back to the table and pulled out the file labeled *Development.*

Inside was a large sheet of paper folded to fit in the file. I unfolded it and laid it out on the kitchen table. It was a sketch of the proposed Larissa Lodge Resort and Casino. The sketch included a new casino, a new lodge and hotel, an 18-hole golf course, and a condominium development. The condos had lake views with the golf course behind them. Studying the notations, such as "site of current lodge," I was able to picture the layout. The condos started at about the place Patty's cabin had stood and stretched through my property and into the swampy acreage next to mine.

What? a small notation on my property said, *acquisition pending.*

I knew from the clippings that the McConnells wanted to expand the lodge and cabins, but nothing had indicated such a grand development. No one had spoken about this at the Lady Slipper meetings. I'd seen nothing in the paper. It was like this was a secret plan known only to a few. But who were the few? Clearly the tribe had to be part of this in order to build the casino.

A note in the corner said these plans were prepared for M&G Associates, LLC. Did the land really belong to the McConnells or did they have other investors? In order to create something on such a large scale, they would need significant money. And they would need my land. Was that what the anonymous texts, the BBs through my windows, and the slashed tires were all about?

If they wanted my land, why hadn't they simply approached me with an offer? Why go through such nonsense? Maybe they thought they could get a better price from the city girl if they scared me. What did Blaine know? Or Jim, for that matter?

"I don't get this, Bronte, but I'm going to do a little investigating."

Bronte flicked her tail but didn't move.

I once fact-checked an article by a landowner who lived next to several vacant acres. He wanted to buy the acreage but found it nearly impossible to contact the owners. The land was listed as being owned by a defunct LLC, and the article detailed the detective work he had gone through to discover the people who actually owned it. My fact-checking included a call to the secretary of state's office.

I opened my laptop and looked up the Minnesota secretary of state. They had information on all the LLCs in the state. When I typed M&G, I found several names as part of the organization. The one that stood out was Blaine McConnell. The other was Dorothea Grey. Could she be someone related to Willow?

I called Willow and immediately got her voicemail. "This is Dr. Willow Grey. I'm unable to take your call. Please leave a detailed message."

"Willow, it's Jamie. I've just discovered a weird thing—a plan for a resort and casino that includes my property. Please call me back. I'm confused."

"Confused" was probably the wrong word. "Furious" might have been a better one.

I looked at Bronte. "Someone is trying to get my land." I pictured my mother sitting serenely on the rock absorbing the sun and the wind and the rhythm of the lake. She would want me to fight.

Willow didn't call me back that night.

Chapter Forty: Bronte Crisis

That evening as the setting sun shot its last rays across the lake, I sat on my rock trying to put it all together. Maybe M&G had tried to buy the property back when it was still in Dad's name. Maybe the paperwork in the boxes in the loft would give me a clue.

I checked my phone for a call or a text from Willow, but the screen remained blank.

I walked back to the cabin in the twilight. The air remained warm and humid. It would be one of those sweltering nights, like the night of my arrest in Queens. I thought about climbing up to the loft and going through papers but was filled with a heaviness that told me to go to bed and deal with all of this in the morning.

That night, as I lay naked on top of the covers, wishing for a hint of a breeze to come through the bedroom window, I slept fitfully. Bronte stayed on the bare floor by the bed and occasionally yipped in her sleep. I dreamed I was in a dark, smothering closet and couldn't find the door to get out. I was desperate for fresh air, but I couldn't find the door. When I fumbled with my phone to call for help, it dropped. When I stooped to pick it up, I was back in the dank holding cell surrounded by shadows.

I woke up with a gasp. "Time for another pill." I stumbled to the medicine cabinet and took the Xanax before I could talk myself out of it.

The morning dawned hazy and humid, as if the earth was being held hostage under a dank, moldy blanket. I arose, groggy from the pill and in a foul mood. I needed to shake the mood and get my thoughts organized. I took my coffee out to the rock. When I sat down, I was overwhelmed with the smell of dead fish. Floating near the shoreline were at least a dozen crappies and perch.

"What?" I caught Bronte by her collar and tugged her back from the shoreline. She'd like nothing better than to roll in them.

I'd had dead fish wash up before, but never so many. I hoped this wasn't a sign that something was happening to the lake water.

"Well, this certainly fits the day and my mood. I guess I know what I have to do." If I didn't get them buried, the stink would infiltrate the cabin, and Bronte would need to be tied up to keep her from playing with them.

"Damn it, Bronte. I came here to get away from controversy. Now I feel like I'm up to my eyeballs in it. Plus, I'm going to have a bucket full of dead fish to deal with. What else can go wrong?"

As the sun rose, the stink of the dead fish rose with it. Sighing, I headed for the shed for a pail and shovel. Time to bury the carcasses.

Wearing yellow rubber gloves and oversized rubber boots, I sloshed through the water, picking up dead fish and dropping them in the bucket. At first, I thought they had been blown in by the wind last night. But it had been a still night, with no hint of a breeze. Now I wondered if someone had dumped them off a boat to contaminate my beach.

Bronte frolicked in and out of the water. She seemed amused every time I dropped another fish in the bucket. "This isn't fun, you know." I watched her carefully to make sure she didn't sneak off with one.

I had my back turned from the cabin and was squatting down to get another fish when Bronte started barking. It wasn't her playful bark. It was her warning bark. Before I could call to her, she tore up the bank to the cabin, her bark reaching a hysterical pitch. I dropped the bucket and ran after her.

"Bronte! Who's there?"

I stopped dead when I saw the sheriff's car. LeRoy stood with the door open, pointing his gun at Bronte. She stood stock still five feet away, growling at him with bared teeth.

"Bronte, stay!"

"Goddamn dog! Back off!" Fear filled his voice.

"Stop!" I yelled. "She won't hurt you."

I opened my mouth to call her to me when he pulled the trigger. I don't know if the bang of the gun or my wail was louder. Something stung my side as Bronte howled and collapsed. I rushed to her screaming, "Bronte! Bronte!"

LeRoy stood with a dumbstruck expression, the gun shaking in his hand. I skidded to a halt by my dog, my companion, my soul mate. She lay on her side with blood coming out of a wound in her shoulder. "Oh God! You shot my dog!"

I could have killed him with my fists and my feet. The fury rose so fast, but Bronte was bleeding on the grass, and something hurt just below my ribcage. I ignored it and reached down to stroke her head. "It's okay, girl. Stay still. We'll get you help."

Working on autopilot, I grabbed for my phone, ignoring the ache in my side that caused my breath to catch. I didn't care if LeRoy towered over me with a Neanderthal expression. I didn't care that he still had his gun in hand. I hit the speed dial and continued to stroke Bronte. "Stay still. You'll be okay."

She whimpered as if she knew something bad had happened.

Willow answered after what seemed like hours.

"Oh God, Willow. He shot Bronte. You've got to come! Now!"

Willow's voice was soothing but professional. "Jamie, are you all right?"

"No," I insisted. "It's Bronte. You must come." The words came out in choked spurts like I'd added a period behind each one.

"Slow down and tell me."

I described the wound and the blood and that Bronte was still awake but something in her eyes told me she was fading.

"I'm on my way. Put pressure on the wound if you can and keep her still."

LeRoy stared at me as if he, too, was in shock. "She attacked me. I didn't have a choice."

"Go to hell!" Something was sticking in my side, like a thorn. Except the thorn was leaking maple syrup.

I grabbed the kerchief I'd tied around my hair and pressed it against the wound. Bronte shuddered but stayed still. I was too busy tending to her to hear the sound of a car coming up the driveway.

A car door slammed, and Blaine shouted, "I heard gunshots. Is everything okay?"

He rushed to me. "Oh my God. What happened?"

"Willow's on her way."

In my panicked haze, I heard him say in a tight, angry voice, "LeRoy, put that goddam gun away. What the hell were you thinking?"

The next few minutes were a blur. For some reason, I was having trouble catching my breath. While I talked to Bronte and kept the pressure on her wound, the world grew fuzzier and fuzzier.

Blaine knelt at my side and gently lifted my hand away from Bronte. "Here, I'll do it."

"I can't let go. Please." But my voice grew fainter as it became harder to get enough air. In the distance, as if in a tunnel, I heard the sound of another vehicle and voices around me.

"My God, she's been shot."

"Help her!" The voices all faded as I fought to catch my breath.

When I opened my eyes again, I was in the back seat of Blaine's car as he sped down the driveway. Every bump knocked more breath out of me.

"Bronte? Where's Bronte?"

"It's okay, Rob and Willow have her. I'm taking you to the hospital."

I tried to push myself up, but dark clouds filled my peripheral vision. It was hard to breathe, as if all the air had gone out of the SUV. When we reached the highway, I heard the sound of a siren and then everything faded once again.

Looking back on it, I had fragments of memories. The siren, being put on a gurney, the pinprick of something in my arm. Bright fluorescent lights and the urge to fight. I needed to get to Bronte.

***

Several hours later, I woke up to a thick bandage around my side and an IV line in my arm. I was in a hospital bed. For a few moments, I couldn't remember why I was there. It felt warm and nice, with my head on the pillow. Low voices talked outside my room. Then a faint odor of dead fish rose up and I remembered.

"Where's Bronte?" My throat was so dry, the words came out in a croak.

Jim Monroe stepped inside the room. "Jamie, are you awake?"

I blinked away the grogginess that encased me. "What happened? Why am I here?"

Jim bent down, a deep concern reflected in his eyes. "You got shot. The bullet that hit your dog grazed you."

"But Bronte. Is she okay?" I watched for uncertainty in his expression or in his voice. I didn't want him to tell me she was gone.

He stroked my cheek. "Willow and Rob are tending to her. She's in good hands."

I tried to take a deep breath, but the bandages held me back. "Am I okay?"

"I'll let the doctor tell you."

I reached over and touched his face the way a child might touch a parent. "Thank you."

The doctor came in. "You're going to be fine. The bullet didn't hit anything vital, but it did cause your lung to collapse a bit. We had to insert a tube to get it inflated, but you should be fine."

"Can I go now?" I tried to sit up straighter but felt a strong kink in my side.

"We'll keep you until tomorrow."

"But...what about Bronte?"

"You rest now."

Norma, the nurse who worked with the Lady Slipper Trail, walked in with a syringe. "This will help you sleep. I know Willow will take good care of your dog." She patted my shoulder before she injected the medication in the IV.

I slept. When I woke up, it was dusk, with the sun casting a pinkish red glow behind the oaks outside the hospital window. I still had the vague odor of dead fish on me. My room was shadowed, except for a light in the bathroom. If I could use the bathroom and get the fish smell off me, maybe they would let me go.

I felt a hundred and ten years old as I crept barefoot to the little hospital bathroom, pushing the pole with the IV on it. My exhaustion told me the doctor was right. I needed to spend the night.

When Norma came in, I asked for my cell phone. She brought it to me from the nurse's station. "Don't spend the night playing games on it." She smiled.

I assured her I would behave and quickly hit the speed dial for Willow. When she didn't answer, I texted her. Then I called Rob. He didn't answer either. Finally, in desperation I called Rob's partner Brad.

When he answered, I told him I needed to speak to Rob about my dog.

"Oh," he said. "I heard about that. He's with Willow now. I'll have him call as soon as he gets back."

I wanted to jump out of bed and rush to the clinic. I needed to be with my dog. Would the sheriff try to pick me up if someone reported a barefoot woman in a hospital gown barreling down the street pushing an IV stand?

"Not funny," I said aloud.

The "ping" from my phone woke me an hour later. My room was completely dark, and the sliver of a moon cast a faint light on the parking lot directly by my window.

Bronte holding own. Sleep tight. W.

I read it several times before tears trickled down my cheeks.

***

The next morning, the doctor okayed me for discharge, with a warning to keep the dressing dry and come back to the clinic in a week to have the stitches taken out. I hardly listened. I was so anxious to get to Willow's clinic. Sometime, while I was having an X-ray taken, someone—probably Willow—had dropped off some clothes.

Jim was waiting for me when I returned to my room. He was in full uniform and cleared his throat in an official way. "I need to ask you some questions."

He told me the highway patrol had been assigned to investigate the shooting.

"Good. Put that deputy in jail. He's a menace in more ways than one." In the back of my head, I heard the voice of my jail mate in Queens. *Don't say nothing.*

Well, she wasn't going to stop me from trying to get a gun away from that idiot.

I told him all I could remember. "Yes, Bronte was barking at him, but she wasn't anywhere near him. In fact, she'd stopped because I called for her."

"She wasn't lunging at him?"

"No." My voice was emphatic. "No, she wasn't. She sounds scary, but she's never bitten anyone."

He asked a few more questions before he put his notebook down. "Jamie, I'm so sorry about this."

I was afraid that if he said anything more, I'd start to cry. I turned away for a moment.

"I'll drop you at home, if that's okay."

I took as deep a breath as my side would allow me and forced a smile. "Thank you."

First, Jim took me to Willow's clinic. Inside, the waiting area was empty and smelled like disinfectant. I rang the bell and Rob came out, wearing a crisp white lab coat. He looked at me with concern. I must have been a mess, greasy hair, a bulging bandage under my T-shirt, and dark circles under my eyes.

"How is she?"

Rob took my arm and led me to a chair. "I'm sure Willow would want me to be honest. She lost a lot of blood. We've got her on an IV and antibiotics, and she's sedated. I'll stay with her, but you need to go home."

"I want to see her."

He hesitated, first looking at Jim and then back at me. Jim must have given him a nod. "Okay. But only a peek. We need to keep her as quiet as possible. Unlike people, we can't tell her to be still. Best if she doesn't see you."

He led me back and let me look through a window in the door. She was on her side, with a warming blanket pulled up to her neck. Her mouth was partially open, and her tongue was out. I could see the rise and fall of her body as she struggled to breathe.

I turned away. I knew what I had to do. One voice screamed in my head, *no! no!* The other said, *it's the right thing, Jamie. You know it.* Without looking at Rob, I whispered, "Tell Willow I don't want her to suffer. You won't let her suffer, will you?" These were some of the hardest words I'd ever uttered.

He pulled me into a careful hug and said nothing.

I couldn't talk as we drove back to the cabin. When Jim opened the car door for me, I slipped out, wondering if my legs would hold me up. I thought for a moment about that long walk to the subway from the hospital after my father died. Even surrounded by hundreds of people, it was one of the loneliest moments of my life.

I felt the same way today as I crossed the threshold of my home and no one greeted me.

Chapter Forty-One: The Development

J im fixed a cup of tea for me as I settled onto the couch. My side hurt, and my throat felt constricted, like the tears would come at any moment. If he said anything about Bronte, if he said anything kind, I wouldn't be able to stop them. He set the mug down and took my hand. "I'm sorry. I have to go, but I'll check back with you."

I wanted the anger to rise up. I wanted to yell out, "Find LeRoy and shoot him!" but I didn't have the energy.

"Thanks. I'll be fine." I pointed to my cell phone. "I've got you on speed dial." I didn't really have him on speed dial. Nice as it was to have him around, I still didn't totally trust him. Why did he spend time with LeRoy? What was he doing at that meeting with the Racine people? Did I really care right now?

I sat for a long time, my head a jumble of thoughts, until an ache in my side told me it was time to take one of the pain pills the doctor had given me.

"Just a three-day prescription," she'd said. "After that you should be okay with Tylenol."

The drug took away the physical ache but not the rest. I might have sat all day feeling bad except, with the pain gone, I remembered dropping a bucket of stinking fish on my lawn. Like an arthritic old lady, I pushed myself off the couch, found a pair of yellow rubber gloves in the kitchen, and limped out the front doorway to the lawn.

The bucket was still there, and the smell of rotting fish contaminated the air. Flies swarmed around it. Trying not to breathe through my nose, I picked it up and lugged it across the lawn behind the cabin. By the time I reached the weed-infested garden to bury the fish, I had broken out in a cold sweat. My side ached and my hands trembled from exhaustion. I realized I wasn't in shape to dig a hole to bury them.

As I stood wondering what to do, the stink from the bucket surrounded me. It was like the stink from all the things that had happened since Nancy was strangled enveloped me. Was it time to pull up stakes and move? M&G would probably be willing to give me a good price for my land. And without Bronte? What would hold me back?

Tears dribbled down my cheeks as I stared at the bucket of fish. How could everything turn so rotten?

The sound of a car coming up the driveway pulled me out of my self-pity. I pondered whether it would be polite to ask the visitor to bury the fish and decided to wait to see who it was. If it was LeRoy Pruitt, I'd dump the bucket over his head, assuming he didn't shoot me first.

The car door closed as I made my way slowly around the cabin. My heart began to beat faster. What if it really was LeRoy? Would he risk hurting me again? I should have grabbed the hoe that leaned against the shed in case I had to defend myself. Of course, in my current state, I couldn't lift it enough to do any damage.

When I came around the corner, I recognized the pickup from the parking lot behind the *Times*.

"Jilly?" I rasped.

Startled, she turned and regarded me. I must have been a sight, considering I had on baggy shorts so they wouldn't rub on the bandages, flip-flops, and yellow rubber gloves.

"Fish," I said, as if that explained everything.

"What?"

"Dead fish. I'm trying to bury them."

Jilly wrinkled her brow with an expression that said "you must be on drugs." I didn't have the energy to explain. Instead, I invited her in.

Once inside, I eased myself onto the kitchen chair, trying not to groan. "Sorry. I'm a little sore." I pointed to the coffeepot. "You can have some coffee if you'd like, but you have to make it."

She tried to smile. "No, that's okay." She must have noticed how haggard I looked. "Unless you want some. I can make a pot."

My stomach was unsettled, and I still smelled dead fish on me. "I'm good for now."

Jilly sat down with an uncertain expression. "Uh, I didn't mean to disturb you. I heard about LeRoy." She fiddled with something in her hand. "I didn't think you'd be home, but I wanted to drop this off."

She handed me an envelope. Inside was a thumb drive.

"What is this?" I stared at it like I'd never seen one before. My brain wasn't operating at optimal capacity.

"I know you tried to get into Nancy's computer yesterday. Harry told me and then he told Phil and I think Phil told the sheriff. That's why the scumbag LeRoy Pruitt came—to investigate."

"He shot my dog over a stupid thumb drive?"

"I'm so sorry. I should have given you access to her computer when you asked."

"No. You did the right thing." I fingered the drive. "I did get some of the files, though."

We sat in silence while a woodpecker knocked on a tree near my yard.

Finally, she said, "Please keep digging. Something bad is going on in Killdeer. You need to find it."

I couldn't speak for a few moments. My throat closed up, and I gritted my teeth, trying not to totally break down. My voice was a hoarse croak. "Thank you, Jilly. I know how much trouble you could get into with this."

I looked at the thumb drive and wondered why, all of a sudden, I was the person to fix it. "I don't know. I'm not sure I can dig anymore."

Her look turned fierce. "LeRoy Pruitt is up to his ears in something. Someone has got to put a stop to him."

If I had been feeling better, if I'd had more energy, if Bronte hadn't been shot, maybe I would have asked her what she meant. But I was tired, my body ached, and my heart ached. I let it go.

Abruptly, she pushed her chair back. "I've got to get back. Phil fired Harry and now he's bringing in some poor new guy he just found. I have to give him an orientation."

I shook my head. "Can't he see you're perfect for the job?"

She sighed. "Underneath it all, I think he's a little afraid of me and what I might do with his paper."

"Like tell the truth?"

***

When I could no longer hear her car on the driveway, I took two more pain pills and settled onto the couch. I wrapped myself in the warmth of my grandmother's afghan. It smelled like Bronte: mildew, and wood smoke. I took comfort in it. As my eyelids drooped shut, images from the day before flashed through my mind. Bronte barking. The sound of the gunshot. The voices. People shouting. People whispering...

An hour later, I woke up with a start. The cabin had heated up from the afternoon sun, and I was damp with sweat. Sometime during the nap, I'd thrown off the afghan. It lay in a heap on the floor.

I blinked away the grogginess and recalled the dreams. The voices—something about the voices stuck in my head. What was it? I remembered being down on the ground, struggling to get air. I remembered that someone picked me up. Was it Blaine? Was it Jim? Why would Jim be there? But again, the voices.

I sat up slowly as the fragment of a voice came back to me. It was male, and it was a whisper to someone. The word "idiot." Then the phrase, "Supposed to scare her not shoot her."

It felt like a piece of ice had been jabbed in my belly. What had Jilly said about LeRoy Pruitt? Up to his ears? Someone had sent LeRoy to scare me. The punctured tires, the speedboat, the attack at the casino—they weren't coincidences. They were planned. Who did that voice belong to? Was all of this because I opposed Racine Mining? Or because my cabin was in the way of a grand development?

"This doesn't make sense." When I realized I'd spoken out loud to an empty cabin, I was overcome with a sense of loss. Even though she never replied, Bronte always listened.

Another car came rumbling down the driveway. Who would it be this time?

With effort, I pushed myself off the couch, tottered to the kitchen table, and grabbed the two thumb drives. As the car neared, I stuck them in a drawer under the kitchen towels.

Please, please, don't be a sheriff's vehicle.

Chapter Forty-Two: The Boxes

Blaine stepped out of his SUV. A part of me was grateful that he cared. That part of me also wanted him to take me in his arms and hold me and keep me safe. Just like Constance and her Sir Eddard. But the words M&G Associates floated through my head. What was he up to? I decided to take a light tone with him, at least until I could ask about the LLC.

I walked to the door, concentrating on ignoring the ache in my side. I wanted him to think I was fine.

"Hey," he called. "Looks like you're up and about." He held up a plastic container. "I thought you might like someone else to do the cooking."

I opened the door for him and worked on turning the grimace of pain to a smile. "Blaine. It's so nice of you. Thanks."

He set the container on the table. "Chicken soup."

I motioned for him to take a seat while I eased myself onto a kitchen chair. "I didn't know you were a cook."

He shook his head with a smile. "If I set foot in the lodge kitchen, the cook would throw me out. But I guarantee, this was made from scratch. She might have even plucked the chicken."

"Thank you. I feel bad about making a mess in your car." I closed my eyes, thinking about the jolt of the car as it raced down the driveway and how hard it was for me to breathe.

"I'm glad you're okay, Jamie. I heard they put LeRoy on desk duty until they can sort out what happened."

"Jim told me the sheriff asked the highway patrol to investigate."

It could have been the lighting in the cabin, but I thought I saw an almost imperceptible flinch when I mentioned Jim. However, I didn't pay much attention to it. I wanted to ask Blaine about M&G.

Blaine pointed to the soup. "It's still warm. Can I dish some up for you?"

I didn't want to appear to be ungrateful, but my stomach was so agitated that the thought of putting anything in it made me nauseous. "I just took a pain pill. I'd like to wait a little. But I'm sure it will cure me."

What would cure me was to have Bronte at my feet asking for dinner. I pushed the thought out of my head.

Blaine fiddled with the key fob he had in his hand. He didn't quite make eye contact. "That whole thing with LeRoy doesn't make sense. Did he tell you why he was here?"

It sounded to me like he was fishing for something.

I dodged the question. "Really, Blaine, I don't remember much of what happened, except I was suddenly gasping for breath and you were there to take me to the hospital."

It seemed as if he relaxed with my answer.

We talked a little longer about the injury and recovery. He told me that a college friend had gotten a pneumothorax like mine and the doctors thought it was caused by playing a strenuous set of tennis.

I tried to laugh, but it came out as a hoarse gasp. I had to hold my side as I coughed. "Sorry. Didn't know tennis was so dangerous."

Blaine leaned in toward me like he was going to give me a kiss. Under other circumstances, I might have been ripe for it. Today was not the day.

I drew back. "Blaine, I need to know about the resort and casino development."

His eyes widened and a little color rose under his tanned face. For a moment, there was something familiar in his hazel eyes, but with the pills and the pain, my brain wouldn't take me there.

Recovering, he said in a smooth voice, "It was a pipe dream of my father and grandfather's. Nothing ever came of it."

"I don't believe you."

Before he could respond, we were interrupted as another car rumbled up the road. This old driveway hadn't gotten this kind of traffic in years. I winced, thinking about how big the ruts were getting. But then, maybe I didn't care. Especially if I decided to leave.

Blaine leaned over and took my hand. "Jamie, whatever you've heard about the resort development is just talk. You know how rumors fly around here."

I pulled my hand back. "What about M&G Associates? I saw your name as part of it and someone named Dorothea Grey. Who is she?"

We were interrupted as Jim walked through the doorway. I wrapped my arms tightly around my chest. I felt, more than saw, the tension between the two men as they greeted each other.

Jim stayed by the door. "I'm checking to see if you're all right. Maybe I can come back later. I have a few more questions for you if you're up to it."

He was still in uniform and his voice had a formal tone to it. I wasn't sure if it was meant for me or for Blaine.

"Thanks, Jim. I'm feeling a little tired right now. How about if I call you after I take a rest. Would that be okay?"

He nodded before he walked out the door.

I looked at the floor. "I don't mean to be rude, but I really have to lie down. Can you please go?"

"Listen, Jamie, I really am on your side. I can explain M&G when you're feeling better." He stepped over to me and kissed the top of my head like I was a child.

I felt both hot and cold with his gesture. He had me completely off balance.

As I listened to his car disappear down the road, my head felt like it was in a vise and nausea rose up into my throat. Who could I trust? I stumbled over to the couch, wrapped the afghan around me, and called Willow.

She answered after the third ring. "Oh my God, Jamie! I'm so sorry I haven't talked with you. I've been...well, as you know...busy." Someone was in the room with her. She told them she'd just be a minute. "Listen, first of all, Rob told me what you said this morning." She paused. "We're keeping her comfortable."

Keeping her comfortable. That was what they said after Dad had his last stroke. For a moment, I flashed on being at his bedside and remembered how he opened his eyes only once. I thought he recognized me because he squeezed my hand. That was our last communication.

"Jamie? Are you okay?"

No, I wasn't, but I needed to know about the Lake Larissa Resort and Casino and M&G. "I really need to talk with you."

Willow started to tell me in clinical terms what she was doing for Bronte. I stopped her. "I want to talk with you about the Lake Larissa Resort and Casino. I'm hoping you know something about M&G Associates. Blaine is mixed up with them and maybe the Racine people are, too."

The silence on the other end of the line was long enough that I wondered if we'd been cut off. Willow's voice had something in it when she finally talked that gave me pause.

"Um, we can talk about it when I come out?"

"You know something?"

"I'll come when Rob gets here. He's in the middle of a remodeling project. I'll be there around seven."

When she hung up, I stared at my phone, wondering why I felt so uneasy.

After another pain pill, I tried to nap. My brain was too full of images. One that kept coming back to me, though, was a discussion I'd had with Dad after his first stroke. He was still able to get around and, even though his speech was affected, he seemed as alert and smart as ever.

It was just before Christmas and before I found out about Andrew and his affair. Dad was still independent, but I saw what an effort everything was. Stacks of bills and statements were piled unopened on his desk.

"Dad, I want to take care of all of this." I pointed to the desk.

He looked so tired and so shrunken sitting in his chair, with the cane beside him.

"Honey, we can get that all figured out. But I want you to remember one thing—the cabin in Minnesota—it was important to your mother. When she was still well enough for us to talk about it, she said, 'It's my family's legacy. I almost lost it to my sister. Don't let it go.'"

At the time, the cabin wasn't my priority, but as I lay bundled in the old afghan, I wondered if something had triggered him to say that. Had someone contacted him about selling it? For years, he'd used a local real estate agent to manage renting it in the summer. Were they after him to sell?

I sat up and looked at the ladder that went to the loft. Despite my pain and tiredness and sadness, I knew it was time to find out if those boxes held any secrets.

Chapter Forty-Three: Papers in the Loft

My body ached and begged to stay on the couch as I crawled up the steep stairs to the loft. I snapped on the light, recalling that Willow had been up here less than two weeks ago because she'd heard an animal. I hoped the animal was gone and hadn't left droppings behind. Boxes were stacked against the wall on either side of the loft. I could stand up, but someone like Jim would have to stoop in order to be up here. By the time I reached the top and stood up, I was out of breath and shaky. This was a dumb idea. What would I possibly learn?

I surveyed the boxes, trying to remember which one had the papers in it. Foolishly, in my haste to get out of New York, I had done a poor job of labeling them. The first one I opened had photo albums. The top one was from the last summer we'd spent here. I eased myself down to the bare floor and opened it. Mostly they were bad photos of flowers and trees with no people. Mom must have taken them. She was an artist, but with her brain deteriorating, who knew what she saw through the lens of the camera. On the last page, though, someone had taken a picture of the three of us standing by the cabin porch.

Mother stood next to me, with her hand on my shoulder, gazing off in the distance, slightly away from the camera. Something about her look was familiar, but I couldn't put my finger on it. Her hair was still dark and thick and, at that angle, the Native American high cheekbones and rounded face stood out. My features were more like Dad's.

I put the album away. I was looking for papers—maybe a deed or something. Two more boxes yielded mostly stuff from my Queens apartment, including a bound copy of my master's thesis. Who knew the poetry of the nineteenth century would be so useless to me now?

The air in the loft was warm, and still and I broke out in a sweat. My side hurt, and when I lifted my T-shirt to look at the bandage, a little pinkish fluid had seeped through. I needed to stop this, change the dressing, and wait for Willow.

I closed the last box and pushed it into the corner. It hit something. A smaller box must have fallen behind it. Groaning, I crawled on my hands and knees over to it. Behind the box I'd just closed was a shoebox. After Dad died and I was cleaning out his apartment, I'd found the box in his closet. I hadn't even looked in it, simply swept it up and took it home with me.

Pulling it out, I flipped the cover off. Inside were letters, some opened and some sealed. I dumped them out under the overhead light. Many of them were from the real estate company that managed the cabin rental after we stopped coming. Dad hadn't opened all of them. I slit one open to find a statement of rental income and expenses. Mostly it was a wash. It looked like two years ago, when the last statement had been sent, the net to Dad was less than $500.

I set the real estate letters aside and picked up one that had a Killdeer date stamp indicating it had been sent forty years ago—from Clarence Engstrom, Attorney-at-Law.

Exhaustion overcame me as I read the letter. It was about the litigation between my mother and her sister, Patty, for ownership of the property. I now had the concrete proof of what I already knew. Patty, being the eldest, contested her mother's will that split the forty acres between the two daughters. Patty felt the entire property belonged to her because her father was full-blooded Ojibwe and my mother's father was not.

Sighing, I slipped it back into the shoebox and pulled out several letters bundled together by a rubber band. They were all from the real estate company with offers for the land and the cabin. To me, the offering prices seemed low. The last one had been sent just before Dad died. He hadn't opened it. I opened it, expecting another polite offer. Instead, the letter had more of a threatening tone. If he didn't agree to sell, the state might be forced to annex the land at a price that would, no doubt, be lower than the current buyers were offering.

"Annex the land? Was that an empty threat?"

If there were more letters, they'd probably gotten lost in the move when I cleared out Dad's apartment. The friendly real estate agent who contacted me weekly about the cabin hadn't mentioned anything about annexation—whatever that meant.

In the heat and dust of the loft, I had no ability to piece it all together.

"I can't handle this right now," I said as if Bronte could hear me. My side ached and my limbs felt waterlogged. I climbed back down the ladder. When my feet touched the floor, the floorboards seemed to rise up as dizziness and nausea overtook me. With a stumbling step, I made it to the couch, wrapped myself in the afghan, and fell asleep.

***

I woke up to the sound of a small plane overhead. I'd slept for almost an hour. It was four and, for the first time all day, I felt a few hunger pains. "Bless you, Blaine. You might be a liar, but I'm grateful for the chicken soup."

The soup was filled with vegetables and, after a few spoonfuls, a little energy returned. The bandage needed changing, and I needed to figure out how to take a shower before Willow got here and saw how pathetic I looked.

It took some doing, but I was able to cobble together a couple of plastic bags to protect the new dressing. With effort, I took a shower and washed my hair. I found it difficult to raise my arms to my head without feeling like I would pull the stitches out. The effort was worth it not to smell like dead fish.

I remembered the stinking bucket in the back and decided it would have to wait. Maybe some critters would come in the night and eat the fish. I had no energy to bury them now.

Somewhat refreshed, I sat with my computer and the thumb drive Jilly had made for me. Maybe it contained more information. It opened to more files and folders. I studied the screen long enough, trying to decide what to look at, that the words began to float around.

"This is no good."

Clicking on "Sewing Patterns," I opened the Jamie file once again and read the few words. Who did Joe overhear talking about the development? This was key to finding out what Nancy wanted to tell me before her death.

I called Clarence.

He answered on the fourth ring. His voice was gruff. "Engstrom, what is it?"

"It's Jamie. I have something I think you need to hear."

The line was silent for a moment as if he'd forgotten who I was. "Oh, Jamie. Sorry, you caught the old geezer napping. What do you need?"

Without telling him how I got Nancy's files, I filled him in on what I'd found. "She kept detailed notes about her interviews. It's quite compelling."

"Good. Good. What else?"

"Well, here's the curious part. She had a file with my name on it. It said Joe had overheard some people talking and thought it might be a threat." I read the sentence to him. "It stopped abruptly after that, like she'd been interrupted."

I could almost hear Clarence thinking as he wheezed into the phone. "Might make a good case for an alternative scenario."

"There's more. Nancy left me a voicemail the night she died. I still have it on my phone, and I also have it transcribed."

"What!" He interrupted. "Why didn't you disclose this?"

Suddenly, I felt like a little kid caught in a fib. "I…I played it for the sheriff and he wasn't interested so I dropped it."

"That's troubling."

All things considered, he was absolutely right. I sat up a little straighter. "My question, Clarence, is whether you can talk to Joe and find out who he overheard talking."

Clarence cleared his throat. "Might be worth something. I'll call over to the jail and see if I can get him on the phone. I'll let you know." He paused. "By the way, are you safe in that cabin?"

"As long as they disarm LeRoy Pruitt, I think I am."

He chuckled. "I feel a lawsuit coming on."

I groaned. I didn't see the humor just now. The growing pain in my side and chest told me I'd overdone it today. "Let's talk about that later. I have to take a pain pill and lie down right now."

A cooling breeze wafted through the window, carrying with it the smell of dead fish. It reminded me of the year the garbage workers went on strike in New York. They picked the middle of summer. The garbage stewed in plastic bags on the sidewalk until the whole city smelled like potpourri of sewage, dead meat, and rotten tomatoes. Would I want to move back to that?

Once again, I wrapped myself in the afghan and drifted off to sleep.

Chapter Forty-Four: Through the Bathroom Window

The pieces of the jigsaw puzzle came together in fragments that didn't make sense. I tried forcing them to fit and they flew from my hands, all over the forest floor. When I scrabbled around in the dirt and the debris, Bronte barked in the distance as if she was warning me to hurry.

I'm coming. But the words stuck behind my tongue. Someone had tied a rope around my throat and was pulling it tight.

"Jamie?"

I woke with a start to Willow's voice.

"Jamie, are you all right?"

The afghan lay crumpled on the floor. I shivered, even though the cabin still held the heat from the day. "I'm okay." I groaned as I sat up.

"Well, you look like shit."

I'd fallen asleep with wet hair that was now a mess of damp spikes.

Willow sat beside me, handing over a hot cup of tea. "Here, this should help. And by the way, you should be locking your door."

With no dog to alert me to strangers, she was right. I nodded, taking the tea. "Thanks." I knew I needed to ask her something about the lodge and the development, but my brain was like a wet log, too soggy to be of use. Instead, I asked the most burning question. "Did you check on Bronte?"

Willow's tone changed from friend to veterinarian. "She's comfortable, Jamie. We should know which way it will go in the next twenty-four hours."

I stared at the steam coming off the tea. "I know you'll do your best." And

I meant it. Whatever weirdness was going on, I trusted Willow would take care of Bronte.

The tea had a bitter medicinal taste. I winced as I drank it. "Did you brew this with Drano? It's awful."

Willow smiled. "Special blend. Drink it down."

Cupping the mug in my hands, I studied her. The native roundness to her face was offset by hazel eyes that had little flecks of yellow in them. She wasn't classically pretty, but the eyes gave her a distinctive look.

"What?" She readjusted herself on the couch, her hands picking nervously at her khaki jeans. "You're looking at me funny."

"Strange that I never noticed it before. Maybe because the last time I saw my mother healthy was the summer we met."

"Excuse me?" Willow looked from me to the mug of tea I held in my hand and back to me.

I cleared my throat. If I was wrong, this would be one of life's most embarrassing moments. But I wasn't wrong. Even as I spoke, though, my head felt a little woozy. My words slurred slightly. "You look a lot like my mother, except for your eyes."

Willow waited a little too long in replying. "Why would you say that?"

"I saw a photo today."

"What photo?" Her voice rose.

"One of my family at the cabin."

"Well, I'm Ojibwe like your mother. We all resemble each other because we're from the same tribe."

Slow down. "It's a compliment." I smiled. My lips were growing numb.

Willow relaxed. "Finish your tea, and I'll tell you what I know about the Lake Larissa Resort and Casino. I hear lots of things, you know."

Willow's face began to pulsate, getting larger and smaller. When it was large, I thought she was my mother. When it was small, she was Willow—and someone else familiar. But, who? I didn't understand what was happening to my vision. A little voice, the voice of survival said, *stop drinking the tea.*

Oh my God, she'd drugged the tea. Could that be right? I brought the tea to my lips and the medicinal smell grew and surrounded me. My hands shook as I set the mug on the table.

"Jamie, the resort was a pipe dream of Blaine's family. They've always wanted to expand. Blaine is on our side—trying to protect the lake. I heard his father talked with developers a couple of years ago—before he had his heart attack. Nothing came of it."

I had to do something about the poison that was making its way through my system. If not, would my cabin, the legacy from my mother, end up in a heap of ashes with me inside? Wasn't that what happened to Patty Clark? Or was I simply paranoid from too many pain pills?

In my addled state, those puzzle pieces from my dream fit together to form a picture I didn't want to look at. Was Willow, my only true friend in Killdeer, my cousin? Patty had a baby and Willow was adopted. Patty worked at the lodge her whole life. Was it to stay near her daughter? Did Willow know this? Willow, the holder of many secrets. Did she know Dorothea Grey? As the aroma of the tea lingered, I no longer felt safe with her. Would she hurt me or worse, Bronte? I shivered as the lights sparkled on the periphery of my vision. A sane part of my brain said, *stop, you're being paranoid—it's the pain pills*. Another said, *get away*.

I needed to think. "Willow? I have to use the bathroom." When I stood, the floor rolled under my feet. *Steady*, the voice coached. *Steady. Get to the bathroom.*

"I'll help you. You do look kind of wobbly."

The ground rolled like the waves on the lake. "I'm fine. Really. Just a little lightheaded from the pain pills. I won't lock the door, and I'll call if I need you." I worked hard to keep myself upright as I walked to the bathroom. In my mind, the photograph from the loft flashed over and over. Mother and Willow—the same profile.

When I got to the bathroom, I closed the door and slipped the lock. I had my cell phone in my pocket. I could call someone—but who? Blaine? Clarence? Jilly? Or Jim? Who did I trust? But no time to think about it. I put the cover down and flushed the toilet. The face of the cell phone blurred as I held it. I couldn't read numbers. If I called 911, I might get LeRoy.

Willow called from the living room. "Jamie, are you okay in there?"

246

The little room tilted, and I worked hard to get the words out through my thickened tongue. "Fine. Back in a minute." Except, it came out, "Phine. Bash in min."

If I didn't do something quickly, Willow would break down the door. I hated my brain for fogging up. Reaching over, I turned on the faucet, cupped cold water in my hands, and splashed it on my face. It dripped onto the phone.

In desperation, I sent a text to the last person I'd texted. I couldn't see who it was and prayed it wasn't Willow. **Help me help me help me.**

The cold water on my face gave me a few moments of clarity. I bought a little more time. "Out in a sec. Washing my face. Kind of woozy." I'm not sure if that's what actually came out of my mouth.

Footsteps approached the door. "Jamie. You sure you're okay? Did you take more pain pills than you should have?"

"Yuck taste in my mouth. Brushing teeth. Out in a sec." I kept the water running. I surveyed the room for some kind of weapon. I had a razor. Would that help me? Even in my altered state, I knew that was a stupid idea. A cool breeze caressed my panicked face as I looked for something, anything to help me.

That was it. Out the window. I lurched over to the shower and turned it on.

"Jamie, are you taking a shower? That's not a good idea."

"Quick one. Quick one. Stinky and sweaty."

Sharp pain shot up my injured side as I slid the window open. It was a new one that Rob had installed and was designed so the screen could be taken off from the inside.

"Jamie!" Willow pounded on the door. "Damn it! I told you not to lock it."

"Sorry. Almost done."

I scrambled up onto the toilet seat and launched myself at the window. It was an act of desperation. On the other side of the door, I heard pounding and another voice—Blaine's. It was the same voice I'd heard in the chaos after Bronte was shot. "I told you just to scare her."

Well, I was scared now.

Chapter Forty-Five: Into the Woods

I was weak and drugged and shaking as I wiggled through the open window. I wasn't a big person—definitely more willowy than Willow. Still, my sides scraped against the frame of the window, and it was all I could do not to cry out in pain from the wound just below my ribcage. It felt like I was rubbing the stitches out.

Deep breath. Deep breath. I can get out.

The pounding on the bathroom door grew louder, followed by the sound of kicking. They would have it open in seconds. With one last thrust, scrambling over the sill, I was through.

In the movies, the heroine propels herself through the window and lands in a perfect somersault that launches her into a standing position. I landed head down with my hands outstretched to break the fall. For a moment, I lay stunned on the ground, dusky clouds swirling overhead. Pain ripped at my side, and my right wrist felt like I'd either broken it or sprained it.

Inside voices yelled out, "Jamie! Jamie! Are you all right?" The doorframe splintered. I had no more than a few seconds to pick myself up and run. But run where? On my feet, my body reeled, and nausea rose up. The world tilted, but I stayed upright.

The road. Head to the road. But that little voice said, *no, that's what they'll expect.*

I turned and stumbled toward the path into the woods. If I could get deep enough, I could stop and think. My legs felt like I was trying to run through water. My body didn't want to move. It wanted to sit down, relax, and let the fog roll in. *Keep moving.*

As I passed the shed, my foot caught on the bucket of dead fish, sending the contents flying. Even breathing through my mouth, the stink filled me with their rot and an overwhelming sense of doom. I gagged but kept on running as fast as my wounded side would allow.

In the woods, I cursed the sound of my feet on the underbrush. Why couldn't I be quiet, like the stag when he leapt through the forest? Behind me, I heard voices. I stopped to catch my breath.

"My God. She crawled out the window. How could she do that?"

"We have to find her."

The voices sounded so benign. Was I wrong? Maybe Willow hadn't spiked the tea. Maybe in my injury and, with the pain pills, I'd made it all up in my head. No. Dorothea Grey, Willow Grey—same person? Daughter of Patty and...? Could I have been so naïve?

Long shadows descended into the woods. Pretty soon it would be too dark to see the trail. I could get lost and wander in circles. If I came out now and surrendered, I could apologize, play dumb, and say the pain pills and lack of sleep made me a little crazy.

It was Willow who propelled me farther into the woods when I overheard her. "She knows too much. She knows who I am."

As quietly as I could, I moved north, away from my cabin and deeper into the forest. I lurched ahead, hugging my hurt wrist against my side. The ache from the wrist crept up to my shoulder. My mouth was dry, but I felt strangely calm. Maybe whatever she'd put in the tea was working its way out of my system. Or worse, maybe it was working its way in—giving me a false sense of safety.

The voices had stopped, and I heard the sound of a car starting. If they were looking for me down the driveway, I could sneak back to my cabin and...and what? If they didn't find me running down the driveway, they'd come back. And maybe they'd come back with LeRoy or LeRoy's cousin Donald.

I needed to find the Lady Slipper Trail and follow it back to town.

Something buzzed against my hip, like a bee had gotten in my pocket. I slapped at it, but it buzzed again. My phone. It was my phone.

Oh, thank God. I had my phone. I'd forgotten.

I took it out and positioned myself behind a large, first-growth pine. Leaning against the rough bark, I stared at the phone. It was a text from Jim. My panicked text in the bathroom had gone to him.

You okay? CALL ME!

I knew I had to trust someone. I didn't dare call in case my voice carried and one of them was still searching around the cabin.

Hdng in woods

My fingers felt like I was wearing workman's gloves as I tried to add to the message.

Want me ded

I panted, mashing at the screen to hit send. Before I could find the right spot, my phone rang. The sound pierced the woods like a fire alarm. I stared at it, my brain still groggy as Willow's face came up. Willow was calling me to see if she could locate me.

The voice in my head screamed at me, *shut it off!*

I shut the ringer off, but it was too late. I heard Willow calling to me. She must have been standing near the shed. "Jamie. It's okay. It's the pain meds. They make you think funny."

I wanted to believe her. I wanted to go back to the warmth of my cabin and crawl under the afghan, like I had when I was a kid and was worn out from a day of swimming and playing at the beach.

But that voice inside me urged, *run!*

Willow continued to call out. She used the same tone she used with injured cows. "Jamie, you're hallucinating. It's okay. You know me. I wouldn't hurt you—ever. We're like sisters."

I might have been soothed by her words. It might have worked until she said the word sisters. Her mother and my mother were sisters, and her mother tried to take my mother's legacy. Sisters sometimes hurt each other.

Veering off the path, I followed the waning light that slipped its way through the thick woods. Willow knew the path from my house to the Lady Slipper Trail. We'd walked it together. She knew I'd go in that direction. I needed to go toward the lake instead.

The phone buzzed again with a text. Could she hear that?

CALL ME!!!

I stumbled through the underbrush as the land sloped down to the lake. If I could get to the lake, I could follow the shoreline back to my cabin. Maybe I could make it to a safe place if I followed the shoreline. Maybe Mavis would be at the desk in the lodge and would help me.

My foot caught on a root, and I pitched forward. The phone flew into the darkness. A stabbing pain shot through my chest. *Please,* I begged, *please don't break the stitches. Please let me breathe.*

Grabbing my side with my injured hand, I groped around on the dark floor of the forest for the phone. My fingers scraped through pine needles and underbrush. I grasped at something hard, but it turned out to be a fallen branch. Between the wrist and my side, I was enveloped in pain. My vision dimmed as spots formed in front of me.

Willow called out again. "Jamie, it's okay. Come back and we'll talk. You're safe with me." She sounded like she was closer. She had figured out I would go for the Lady Slipper Trail.

Her voice pulled me out of my stupor. I needed to keep moving. The stitches remained intact, even though the ache in my side grew. I didn't care at this point. I could still breathe.

I righted myself and slowed down. A little irrational thought nipped through my head. What if some animal found the phone and took it to his den? Would he try to eat it? The drugs in the tea still had a hold on me.

Willow would be closing in. I needed to be very quiet as I made my way to the water.

"Jamie? You'll get lost out there." She was moving away from me, toward the trail.

Another voice, Blaine's voice, rose behind her. "You go that way. I'll try the road again. She might circle back."

The voices faded as I staggered toward the lake. The sun was now behind the trees of Bear Island and cast pinkish streaks across the skies. Soon it would be pitch dark.

I heard the lake before I saw it as the waves scraped against the rocks.

This part of the shoreline, except for the small piece of beach in front of my cabin, was rocky and weed infested. The rocks were slippery, and I nearly fell crashing into the shallow water. I wobbled over the wet rocks for about twenty feet before I decided it was too hard to stay on shore. I waded into the waters of Lake Larissa. At about knee level, the rocks turned to sand. My sneakers were waterlogged, and it would be slow going, but smoother, with less splashing.

The water soothed me as if the lake had a spirit of its own. I heard the plop of a fish jumping in the twilight. My heart beat slowed as I pushed my way along. Water crept up my shorts and soaked into them. A slight breeze blowing in from the lake immediately chilled me. I was shivering and sweating at the same time. At this rate, I could collapse of exhaustion and cold. It must have been the drugs, but I felt safe as if I was in my parents' arms.

I had no idea how much time had passed. I silently counted my steps as I followed the shoreline toward my cabin. The little voice coached me, *keep going, almost there.* My toe hit a rock, and I tottered, nearly falling completely into the water. As I struggled to keep my balance, another voice, a different one in my head said, *quit running, you little fool! End this!*

"What?" I said out loud. "What do you mean?" Was part of my brain telling me to kill myself? Or was it telling me to resolve it?

I dragged myself out of the water and looked around. Ahead, I saw the outline of my beach. With effort, I slogged to my rock. Exhausted and on the verge of passing out, I sat on the rock and put my head between my knees. Maybe Willow or Blaine could see me from the cabin, but I didn't care.

Lulled by the gentle back and forth of the water, I thought about all the running I'd done in my life. In all honesty, I ran from Andrew. I knew something was wrong in our marriage and, instead of confronting it, I buried myself in work. Maybe, if I hadn't been such a coward, he would never have chosen the makeup artist. And the big run—from New York to here. Instead of dealing with my fear, I'd packed up and left.

Done running away.

Still dripping, I made my way up the slope to the cabin. I no longer cared that Willow or Blaine or even LeRoy might be waiting.

Walking in the door of the cabin, I called, "Hello? I'm done running. I can't do this anymore."

Jim stood in the living room tapping his phone. His jaw dropped as he stared at me. And suddenly the floor swept up and took me.

Chapter Forty-Six: The Reckoning

I was cushioned in a warm glow, the pain in my wrist and side gone, replaced by a sense of peace and grace. Maybe this was heaven, except, I breathed in something smelling musty and old. When I opened my eyes, instead of seeing a glorious bright light, I saw the ceiling of my cabin and was reminded I hadn't finished putting in the insulation. Some heaven this turned out to be.

Instead of the ever after, I was on my couch wrapped in the old afghan. Jim sat beside me with a worried expression. "Jamie, what the hell is going on?"

I opened my mouth, but the words stuck in my throat. What *was* going on?

"You came in the door and collapsed. Scared the shit out of me."

Constance's Sir Eddard would never have used the word "shit."

I tried again. My voice was a mere croak, "Willow. It was Willow—tried to drug me. Where is she?"

"Willow's van is here but I haven't seen her—or anyone else." Jim touched my cheek.

I closed my eyes and pictured my drugged, hasty texts. "But you got my texts?"

"No. You didn't text, and you didn't call."

Did I dream all of this? I blinked hard to wash away the fog that had taken over my brain. "Could I have a glass of water?"

When he brought it, I pushed myself up with a groan and a gasp. The dressing on my side was soaked and my right wrist ached. I held my hand out for the water and realized it hurt too much to take the glass.

Jim set the water down and took my wrist, gently examining it. Both my wrist and hand were puffed out. It looked like someone had substituted the Michelin Man's wrist for mine. "Geez, Jamie. What the hell is going on?"

I pointed to the prescription bottle with my pain pills. I was down to three. "Pain pill first. Then I'll tell you everything I know." The mists in my brain were clearing, replaced by intense aching from my head down to my toes. I took all three at once.

"I'm not running anymore." I relaxed onto the couch. "It's too hard. I want my cabin in the woods, and I want Bronte, and I want a life."

Jim continued to watch me as if I was an alien who had just landed on Earth. He leaned forward so his forehead nearly touched mine. He smelled of apples and cinnamon—a nice change from the dead fish odor that had overtaken the air outside the cabin. "Okay, Jamie. Talk."

I told him about the resort and casino and about Nancy's discovery and about Willow's relationship to me. "She's my cousin. How could I have missed that?"

Jim simply nodded. "What else?"

I hesitated when I pictured LeRoy with his gun pointed at Bronte but decided I wasn't going to run anymore. If Jim was the enemy, so be it. "I think Blaine sent LeRoy to harass me and LeRoy panicked when Bronte barked at him. They wanted me out, Jim. They wanted me to leave, and they shot my dog."

Thinking about Bronte struggling to breathe in Willow's clinic caused me to stop. I cleared my throat and the tears came. "I...can't let her suffer. I need to let her go."

Jim said nothing. He took my good hand and held it until the tears stopped.

"They want my land. This was the only thing my mother left to me. I can't give it up." I pointed to the loft, where the shoebox held all the letters from the real estate company.

"They tried to get Dad to sell. I don't think he ever responded to them. He wanted me to have the property."

A car drove up and voices neared the cabin. Doors slammed and Willow and Blaine walked in, followed by LeRoy and his cousin Donald. LeRoy wasn't in uniform.

Willow rushed over to me. "There you are! You had us so worried." She fixed her gaze on Jim. "I don't know what she's told you, but I think the combination of trauma and drugs has made her see things that aren't there."

I forced myself to sit up. "Willow, maybe you should finish my tea." The mug sat on the coffee table, where I'd set it down. "It tasted a little too much like medicine for me."

Jim picked it up. "This?"

I nodded as he smelled it. "Hmmm...smells like antibiotic soap."

Willow didn't smile.

LeRoy and his cousin stood with their arms folded, as if guarding the door. I wondered what would happen next.

In a calm voice, Jim addressed Blaine. "I understand you'd like Jamie to sell her property so you can develop the resort and casino."

Blaine put on his best political smile. "Well, it would help. But we can go ahead without it."

"You have all the land usage permits? Okays from the Department of Natural Resources? Everything in order?"

As he asked the question, I realized how much power Blaine wielded, both as a businessman and a politician. How much had he weaseled out of Racine Mining to help them with their permits? I was shocked that I felt a certain amount of sympathy for the evil mining company.

As I watched this scenario, it became clear to me I'd taken one too many pain pills. My poor body, shot at, scraped, and drugged. I was surprised my toes wiggled when I asked them to.

"Okay, I really don't get it, Willow. What does all of this have to do with you?" I asked.

Willow, who could look stoic and tough when she was dealing with sick animals, smiled in a mean way. "You got the land that belonged to my mother. She was the firstborn, and it was hers."

My brain was fading again as I tried to puzzle it out. Blaine said the lodge owned the property.

A sudden light went on in my muddled brain. "You're Dorothea Grey, aren't you?"

Willow smiled. "Terrible name to give a baby."

The puzzle pieces still weren't falling in place. "But Patty didn't want the McConnells to get the land. How did you get it?"

"Her only gift to me besides life. She willed it to me before her accident."

What had Clarence said? Patty consulted him about changing her will shortly before she died. Did she have her "accident" before she could change it? Too many questions for me as my brain cells refused to connect the way they should.

Her lips still held that menacing smile. "Blaine and I are partners now. What's his is mine. What's mine is his."

As Florice LeMay said so blatantly in her book, "All crime is either for love, money, or power." Constance, with the flaming red hair, stole for love. Was that what Willow did? Or was it for money. Or power?

I studied her and then Blaine. It was there. It had been there all the time—an expression, a way that their lips curled down when they were amused. The goddam hazel eyes. Patty's mysterious baby and Blaine's father Mickey. That was the "M" in the letter to my mother. The unholiness that Patty uttered to Mavis.

"Oh my God. You two are siblings." I turned to Jim. "Did you know that?"

"Wondered about it."

"Did one of you kill Nancy because she discovered the incest and the resort scheme?" My tone sounded like I'd just asked if one of them had gone to the grocery store recently.

No one moved. No one changed their expression. The cabin was suddenly silent, except for the fluttering of moths throwing themselves at the light over the back door.

"Enough!" Blaine's face darkened. "This is unimportant. Jamie, you can sell or not. I don't care. But no one here murdered Nancy. That vagrant Indian did it for an iPad and some jewelry."

How would he know what Joe took from Nancy's house? I sat up as straight as I could, without crying out in agony. "LeRoy is the only one here

257

DEATH OF AN EDITOR

who should know what they found in Joe's truck." I wanted to throw him a look that would pierce his brain and take that smug smile off his face.

However, his smugness disappeared with my words. "Hey, I didn't tell anyone about what we found."

The temperature in the room suddenly dropped as Blaine stared in confusion at Willow. "But you said…"

Willow turned to me and the stoic expression melted as the heat rose up on her cheeks. She pointed at me. "You. You did all this. Why didn't you stay in New York like I said you should!"

She ripped her phone out of her back pocket. "But I'm still in control, and I will have it all." She punched the phone. When it was answered, she said in her usual controlled, clinical voice, "Rob, it's Willow. I'm with Jamie. Yes, she says go ahead and put Bronte down. She doesn't want her to suffer."

I was up in an instant, pain stabbing my side. I don't know how I got to her so quickly, but I grabbed at the phone. "No, Rob, no!"

Her eyes narrowed as she clicked the phone off and pulled it away. "Too late, honey. You're too late."

"Please, someone, call him back. Tell him no! Call him back!" If I could have, I would have taken a knife and stabbed Willow through the heart.

She smiled at me with a crazy, mean glint in her eyes. "I don't like to be crossed."

And that said it all.

Chapter Forty-Seven: A New Beginning

A wailing siren neared. Everyone in the room turned as the rotating blue and reds of the sheriff's cherry top flashed through the screen door.

Jim muttered, "About goddamn time."

The rage drained from my body as something broke inside Willow. It was as if her roaring engine coughed, sputtered, and quit. "Oh, God! What have I done?" Her voice was a mix of confusion and anger. Or, was it remorse?

I watched openmouthed as she collapsed, wafting to the floor like a swaying willow branch. Before Sheriff Rick could step across the threshold, Blaine was kneeling at her side, holding her head on his lap.

A deep nausea and disgust took hold of me. As the scene unfolded, I staggered off the couch and into the bathroom. The tea, the water, and the pills all came up at once. I didn't want to hear any more of the drama in the living room. I picked myself up and stumbled off to my bed, still wearing the wet shorts.

I woke up to the early morning mist and the sound of birds twittering outside the window. I remembered only snatches of what happened after I crawled into bed. Someone rousing me to change into a dry sleep shirt. Someone redressing my wound. Someone wrapping my wrist with an ace bandage. Someone tucking me in like a little child.

While I debated whether to pull the covers over my face and stay in bed forever, Jim knocked on the bedroom door. "You awake?"

"No."

He walked in, his T-shirt dark with sweat. "You need to get up. Statements to make, crimes to sort out."

I looked at the empty spot where Bronte greeted me every morning. "Can't face it."

He sat on the edge of the bed and took my hand. "Sorry. It's not a choice."

I closed my eyes and took a deep breath. "Ugh. You smell like dead fish."

"They're all buried. Mind if I use your shower?"

"I think the door is broken."

Once I was up and had coffee and several ibuprofen in my system, I sat at the kitchen table with Jim. He filled me in on what he knew about last night's drama.

"They took Willow to the hospital and, because of her bizarre behavior, sent her to a psychiatric bed in Duluth. I expect that when the investigation is finished, she'll be charged with Nancy's murder."

"And Blaine?"

Jim shook his head. "His first phone call after Rick arrived was to his lawyer. It will take a while to figure out what to charge him with. He's got friends in high places."

The warmth of the coffee couldn't take away the chill I felt as I looked at Bronte's empty dog dish. I would have to put it away somewhere.

"What about LeRoy and his dumbass cousin?"

"I checked this morning with Rick. They're going between denying everything and pointing a finger at Blaine. The good news is that LeRoy won't be working as a deputy any longer. What happens next is up to the county attorney."

I thought about Joe, stuck in jail for something he didn't do. "Will they let Joe out?"

"If they don't, they'll face the wrath of Clarence."

I almost laughed. I wanted to laugh, but the empty dog dish was still in its spot.

A van pulled up as I was drinking my second cup of coffee and trying to choke down a piece of dry toast. "Now what?"

I heard Rob's voice after the van door closed. "Hey, Jim, can you help me?"

Wow. What a friend. Here already to fix the smashed bathroom door.

Jim joined him, and I heard the sounds of the van door sliding open and the words, "Careful now."

Jim opened the door and Rob walked through, carrying something wrapped in a blanket. I stared as he gently placed the bundle in the living room on Bronte's cushion.

When he took the blanket off, Bronte lay on her side, eyes closed, as if she was in a peaceful sleep.

I rose slowly as if in a trance and walked over to her. "Is she?"

Rob knelt by me. "She's sedated, but she'll be fine. Just needs to be home with some tender loving care."

Bronte opened her eyes to my voice and lifted her head. Jim hunkered down next to me and put his arms around me. Maybe we'd both be fine.

Chapter Forty-Eight: Knight of Lust

I woke up to the sound of light rain pattering on the roof. For a moment, I thought I was back in Queens, surrounded by buildings and people in motion, but it was too quiet outside. No trucks beeping as they backed up, no blowers moving the leaves around in the park. Just the gentle rhythm of the rain. Jim stirred beside me, his raven hair contrasting with the light blue pillowcase. I slipped out of bed, the soles of my feet tingling against the cold floor of the cabin.

Bronte, settled on her rug at the foot of the bed, lifted her head and, with a little effort, stood up. She was better, not her old robust self, but Rob assured me she was on the mend.

"It takes time, Jamie. She'll find her spirit again."

Thank God Rob had balked at following through with Willow's orders. He told me the next day that he couldn't see me giving the go ahead to put her down without saying goodbye. Rob would forever be my hero.

Through the kitchen window, the leaves on the aspens shimmered a golden yellow in the light rain. I loved the brilliance of the fall colors as the trees readied themselves for winter.

I made coffee and toasted a day-old bagel. By then the rain had stopped and the sun peeked out over the canopy of trees. Wrapped in the old afghan, I walked with my coffee down to the lake. Bronte followed, limping slightly from the healing wound in her shoulder. My side ached in the damp morning air.

"We're just a couple of pathetic old ladies, aren't we, girl?"

Bronte sat beside me, her eyes alive as she watched a loon swimming soundlessly in the lake. I had a long to-do list today and was going over it when Bronte's tail began to wag. She stood up and barked a "hello" as Jim walked up behind me and put his arms around me.

"Stealing the last bagel, huh?"

I offered him a piece. He smelled fresh from the shower, and it sent a tingling sensation down my belly. I leaned against him.

"I'm thinking about Willow."

He slid beside me on the rock. "Oh?"

I knew it wasn't rational, but I wanted to know why she worked so hard to befriend me and why she urged me to be involved with the Lady Slipper Trail. "It doesn't make sense to me. If she wanted my property, why didn't she make an offer when I was in New York?"

He pulled me close. God, he felt so good. In the past few weeks, I'd learned what Constance of the red hair understood. Lust and love were a great combination.

"Maybe underneath it all, she wanted family."

That was part of what I loved about Jim—his uncomplicated way of looking at things. Andrew used to analyze things to death. Why didn't I get the part? Maybe because they wanted someone who looked more Jewish. Maybe I reminded the director of his weird uncle. Maybe I played the role too seriously.

Whatever the case, Willow was in the criminal justice system now, charged with Nancy's murder, assault, attempted poisoning, and several other crimes. The sheriff was reopening the accidental death ruling on her mother, based on some things she'd said to one of her cellmates. Rumor had it that her attorney was looking into a defense involving impairment. Willow showed signs of the same brain disease that took my mother.

"You might have something there. I'd like to ask her, but she's refusing to see me." I shivered against Jim's warmth.

"What are you up to today?"

"Fun and not so much fun stuff."

He waited, feeding Bronte a few crumbs from the bagel.

"I'm talking with Nancy's sister to see if she will allow me to use the interviews Nancy did with the victims of the shooting for the article I'm writing on it. She sounded skeptical on the phone."

"Jamie, you're so honest and sincere. She'll come through."

Maybe. The story needed to be told and using Nancy's interviews would be a shortcut. But I'd see this afternoon.

"What's new in law enforcement?" I asked.

Jim had worked the late shift last night. I was in bed by the time he came home. "LeRoy is cooperating with the criminal and fraud case against Blaine, in hopes he won't have to do jail time for shooting you."

Several days after that fateful night in the cabin when Willow called Rob to euthanize Bronte and the ensuing chaos, Jim had finally told me why he was involved with LeRoy. "I rented a place near the casino, so I ate there a lot. I got to know some of the staff, and they told me about LeRoy showing up at the bar and bragging about the 'huge deal' that was going down and how he was going to get a big pay-out. I figured it had something to do with Racine Mining, and I was no fan of the destruction they could wreak on the land I love. I kept close to him to see if I could figure out what was going on."

"You got a clue about how they were trying to harass me off my land?"

"M&G was running low on funds. They needed to buy you out at a rock bottom price, if the casino deal was going to go through."

"Just like what the McConnells did to the natives—lowball offers to desperate people."

He nodded. "It turned out to be a great excuse to hang around you—even if you weren't very nice to me."

He was right. I wasn't very nice because I didn't trust him. When I finally confessed to my fear of law officers, he laughed. "I thought you would swoon at the sight of a man in uniform."

"Humph. It's a new century, boy. Women don't swoon."

I slipped off the rock, noting the loon had taken a dive into the water. She left behind a pattern of concentric circles on the lake. "Let's go in and finish breakfast and..." I left the words hanging.

While Jim fixed eggs and bacon, I checked my email. To my surprise, I found a note from Florice LeMay. "Jamie, wonderful news. I sold the book! It's coming out next year, and I'm halfway through another. I hope you'll be my editor again!"

I laughed when I read it, and I laughed as I ate my eggs. After finishing, I said, "I wonder if you'd be interested in honor of *Knight of Lust* that we have a 'Day of Lust'?"

Jim grinned as we both nearly tripped over each other scrambling to the bedroom. Bronte joyfully followed until I shooed her away. "This is not for your tender ears, girl." I found the rawhide bone I kept for these occasions and settled her on her rug in the living room." If there was going to be howling, it was coming from the bedroom, not the dog.

Acknowledgements

A big thank you to the following for support, encouragement and wisdom. To my agent Dawn Dowdle at Blue Ridge Agency and my editor Shawn Reilly Simmons at Level Best Books for believing in this project. To my writers group who kept me grounded: Jan Kerman, Carol Williams and Randy Kasten. To my readers: John Mathiason, Jan Clausen and Jerry Mathiason. A special thanks to Kirsten Faurie of the *Kanabec County Times* for answering my questions about newspaper publishing. And most importantly, a big thank you to Jerome Norlander who has supported me throughout my years of writing. He's an amazing manuscript advisor and he knows where the commas go.

About the Author

Linda Norlander has published short fiction and humor in a number of regional and national magazines. Additionally, she has written several award-winning books on end-of-life care including, *To Comfort Always, A Nurse's Guide to End of Life Care. Death of an Editor* is the first book in A Cabin by the Lake Mystery series. She lives in Tacoma, Washington.

Twitter: @LindaNorlander

Facebook @ Linda Norlander

Author Photo Credit: Jerry Mathiason

CPSIA information can be obtained
at www.ICGtesting.com
Printed in the USA
BVHW031938290620
582610BV00001B/41